ASSASSIN'S MARK

ASSASSINS 1

Ella Sheridan

Take the risk!

Ella Sheridan

Also by Ella Sheridan

Assassins
The Assassin
Assassin's Mark
Assassin's Prey
Assassin's Heart
Assassin's Game

Southern Nights
Teach Me
Trust Me
Take Me

Southern Nights: Enigma
Come For Me
Deceive Me
Destroy Me
Deny Me

If Only
Only for the Weekend
Only for the Night
Only for the Moment

Secrets
Unavailable
Undisclosed
Unshakable

Want exciting extras from the ASSASSINS series? How about free book opportunities and bonus scenes? They're available only through my newsletter.
Sign up at www.ellasheridanauthor.com to get exclusive access!

Copyright

Assassins: Assassin's Mark
Copyright © 2018 Ella Sheridan

Cover Artist: Mayhem Cover Creations
Published in the United States.

Dedication

This book was written at a time when writing was one of my biggest fears. When just sitting down at the computer could make me sweat. And then my twin sister, Dani Wade, convinced me to take a chance on something fun.

So I did. And it changed my writing life.

Thank you, Sis. You are my best friend. You're the only hand I trusted to hold on my way out of the wilderness. I love you!

Acknowledgments

No book is written in a vacuum. This book in particular was written for the serial reading app, Radish Fiction, who pushed the story and gave me the perfect opportunity to explore a new side of my writing psyche. Thank you to Radish and, in particular, my curator Katherine Pelz, for your support of my badass boys. We wouldn't have gotten here without you.

To my rock star beta reader, Erika, who fangirled on Levi and his brothers so hard I knew I had to finish their story. You waited months for new installments. I hope it was ultimately worth it! Thank you for your enthusiasm and your generous heart!

Chapter One

I'm not sure what I expected. I'd been to bars, but not the kind of bars with pool tables and smoke haze and men on the prowl for a one-night stand. The bars I'd been to specialized in cocktail hours and old men in business suits. The Full Moon wasn't refined or elegant or quiet.

It was everything I was not. Exactly where I needed to be tonight.

"What'll you have?" the bartender asked. He was staring at Candy's breasts, but she didn't seem to mind, just flashed him a sexier version of her friendly smile. Had she slept with him before?

It was Renee who answered. "Pitcher of strawberry margaritas, Dave."

"Make that two," Candy tacked on.

Dave the Bartender nodded at her cleavage. "I'll send 'em right over."

I followed my friends through the crowd toward a table Sarah had snagged while we ordered. The three women obviously had a routine. I'd known they were close, and the fact that they'd extended their little circle to include me from the first day we met in Nursing 101 class had touched me in ways they couldn't possibly understand. They were normal girls with normal lives and normal homes. I wasn't, but if they'd noticed, they didn't mention it. No flicker of recognition at my name, no questions about where I lived or why I never went out when they invited me. Just basic friendship, no strings attached.

They had no idea how rare that was.

"So, Abby, see anything interesting?"

Too much, actually. Heat flushed my cheeks. "Um…"

Sarah giggled. "Wait till she's got at least one margarita in her, Renee. Then ask." She bumped my shoulder with hers. "The selection always looks better the later it gets."

The selection already looked pretty good to me. Most of the men were our age—early twenties—and not a suit and tie to be found. Jeans and half-buttoned shirts and messily styled hair were the go-to. A tattooed forearm or the wink of an earring wasn't rare. Beers in hand, the men joshed each other while prowling the room, hungry gazes assessing each woman they came to. One by one they'd peel off with their choice, either to the dance floor or a table or the front door.

What was it like to be the women they chose? In the circles my family required me to frequent, the barrier of my father's name and status kept men away from me. Here, there were no barriers except my friends and my own insecurities. The idea that I could choose to ignore both and do whatever I wanted quickened my breath. Either I was excited or about to hyperventilate; I wasn't certain which.

I refused to let the terror win anymore.

The margaritas arrived and we each poured ourselves one. The fruity yet tart liquid set my tongue alight like a sparkler on the Fourth of July, a pleasure I hadn't experienced before. I savored it as I listened to the girls' giggling commentary about each man who walked by. It wasn't long before the room went hazy with something other than smoke and I found myself joining in the conversation without reservation.

I was pouring my second margarita when my phone vibrated in my back pocket. Two shorts, one long: my father. A healthy gulp helped bolster my confidence before I pulled the cell out for a look.

I shouldn't respond, shouldn't care, but I clicked on the message anyway, just to see. Maybe he'd changed his mind. Maybe he was worried about me. Maybe he wanted to apologize, tell me he loved me for once in twenty-one years.

Where the hell are you?

Or maybe not. I returned the phone to my pocket.

Sarah leaned close, her voice low. "Everything okay?"

Renee and Candy were focused on the table of men to their right. I gave Sarah a wry smile. "My dad." I took another drink. "It'll blow over, I'm sure."

Sarah laid her hand over mine on the table and squeezed. The gesture mesmerized me. I couldn't remember the last time someone had touched me because they cared. How sad was that?

My phone buzzed again. I ignored it.

"Holy shit."

Sarah's hand left mine to grasp her drink. She took a gulp, her gaze trained somewhere over Candy's head. I followed it.

Holy shit is right.

The man was tall, dark, and dangerous with a capital *D*. I'd never seen anyone like him, anyone who made my insides clench just looking at him. Thick dark hair, long on top and shaved close on the sides, highlighted perfect ears and a jaw chiseled from granite. His eyes seemed too light for that hair and his olive skin, shining like spotlights beneath dark brows, almost too intense to bear. And those lips. *God.* They hinted at sensual pleasures I could only guess at.

He prowled across the room, a lean, muscular panther intent on prey—every woman's fantasy, including mine.

And he was headed straight for us.

My gaze dropped to my drink. The tables around us held either men or couples, so I wasn't mistaken about his focus. Which girl was he interested in? Sarah with her sweet smile? Or maybe Candy, with her unabashed sensuality?

An empty glass stared back at me. I reached for the pitcher.

"Hello, ladies."

My hand froze on the handle as the words quivered through my body. *Look up! Look at him!* But I couldn't; I could only sit there like a dumbass holding the pitcher in my shaking grip and praying I didn't make a fool of myself.

No fear, remember?

No fear. I tightened my grip, lifted. So far, so good. Somehow I managed to pour a fresh drink without spilling, replace the pitcher on the table. Despite the sick pounding of my heart in my throat, I made myself glance up.

Gray eyes locked with mine.

Lord, he's beautiful.

I expected him to look away, to focus on one of the other women. He didn't. He stared—at me. Until the urge to squirm crawled up my spine and my cheeks burst into flames.

"Hello."

Was that my voice, all breathy and…suggestive? It must've been; the other girls were staring, silent, their round eyes just as awed as I'm sure mine were. I looked back to the man looming over our table.

He reached a hand out to me. "I'm Levi."

My fingers settled into his grip like they had been created to fit him. "Abby."

My voice cracked. I cleared my throat.

"Hi, Abby." He didn't let go of my hand, didn't glance around. Just held me captive with those intense eyes. "Would you dance with me?"

Me?

I barely managed not to say it aloud. Instead I looked to Sarah, who was frantically nodding. "Uh, okay. Sure."

Could I be any more awkward if I tried? Where was the vaunted hostess who demurely handled every crisis that arose?

Maybe she'd died along with the dream that someday, somehow, my father would see me as his daughter and not his pawn.

Levi tugged on my hand, urging me to my feet. My body responded to his command automatically, breaking through the nerves that had held me frozen. I didn't want to be frozen, not anymore. And I didn't want to miss this, not a minute of it.

Chapter Two

He kept ahold of me, merely lifting our joined hands over Candy's and Renee's heads. Was he afraid to let go, afraid I might run away? But no, a man like this wouldn't feel fear. Could he sense my own? Was my palm clammy? God, please don't let me make the biggest fool of myself ever.

An actual smile tugged at my lips.

"What?" he asked.

Had he been watching me that closely then? "Just…" I clamped my lips shut over the words. No one needed access to my insecurities but me. "Thank you for asking me to dance."

Surprise softened his smile. "My pleasure."

The music changed as we reached the dance floor, from the latest pop single to a slow, sultry song. Levi raised his arm and twirled me beneath it. On the second spin his body blocked mine, plastering me against the hard muscles beneath his black shirt and jeans. Hard and hot—his body seared mine, as if I'd carry the impression of him on my skin for the rest of my life. And maybe I would. I certainly wanted to. Everything feminine in me flared to painful life, urging me to rub against him like a cat, roll myself in his scent, his heat. The rough, tanned skin of his throat was right in front of me, a delicious sprinkle of dark stubble guiding my eyes down to the collar of his button-down where a hint of a tattoo peeked out. This man was nothing like any other I'd known—

hard-edged, powerful. Dangerous. And yet his arms surrounding my body made me feel utterly safe.

He ducked his head beside mine and inhaled, taking in my scent. Like an animal.

Don't faint, Abby. Just don't.

I didn't, but I did tighten my grip. My heeled boots brought me high enough that my head settled in the hollow vee beside his collarbone. I did my own inhaling. At my shiver, a hint of a smile tugged at the corner of Levi's mouth. That smile fascinated me, made me want to forget the whole world and just focus right there, right now, shutting out everything but this moment. No worries, no pain, no *but this is only*… Just Levi and now. Just this song. Just—

"So…is this your first time here?"

I jerked my head up so fast I almost clipped his chin. "How did you know that?"

Amusement lightened his gray eyes to silver. "Because I've never seen you here before."

So he was a regular. "I don't get out much."

God, had I really said that? Before I could cover my awkwardness—with what, I didn't know—Levi threw his head back and laughed. I couldn't tell which caused more goose bumps, the throaty, rich sound of his amusement or the strong lines of his neck, begging me to explore them with tongue and teeth and lips and…

Levi's amusement darkened quickly, turning into something that left me breathless, especially when that stare settled on my mouth. "I find that a little hard to believe."

The heat in my cheeks returned. "I'm glad I decided to venture out tonight, at least," I finally said.

Levi's grip tightened the slightest bit as he turned me. One thigh slid between mine, and there was no mistaking the feel of his arousal against my belly. "I'm glad you did too."

The phone in my back pocket vibrated. My father again. I ignored the buzz against my butt cheek and burrowed deeper into the male presence surrounding me.

Levi didn't chatter—another way he was different from the men I normally met. Polite conversation was a given among the rich and socially entitled. I'd learned the art to survive, not because I enjoyed it. Here, now, without the distraction of desperately searching for the right clever thing to say, I basked in Levi's heat, the fluid way his body moved, the exciting brush of his chest against my aching nipples and his hard erection against my belly, leaving very little doubt that he was enjoying having me in his arms. I lapped up every moment, let it fill the emptiness that had opened like a black hole inside me earlier tonight.

My buzzing phone refused to respect my need, however. I didn't have to be in the room with him to know my father was becoming livid—the constant vibrations against my ass told me that well enough. This was one instance where an aide wouldn't be texting me. Dad wouldn't want anyone to know his only child had run off rather than put in an appearance at the dinner where he planned to announce his gubernatorial candidacy. Not that Derrick Roslyn's political ambitions had spooked me into running off.

No, it had been the announcement of my arranged marriage that did that.

Levi's fingers skimmed down my side to grasp my hip, fingers so close to the curves that craved his touch. "Shouldn't you answer that before someone blows a gasket?"

"What?"

I glanced up, meeting the same understanding amusement as before. Not cruel or taunting, as I'd so often encountered. Just genuine enjoyment of the moment. "Your phone." He lowered his head until his mouth brushed my ear. "I don't mind vibrators, but that's not exactly what I had in mind."

I flushed so hot even the tips of my ears burned; surely Levi could feel it against his lips. A stutter fumbled my words before I managed to push something intelligible out. "He'll give up soon."

"He?"

"My father."

Levi drew back enough to look at me. "Family can be a bitch."

Or bastard. Since my mother had died when I was a toddler, my father was all the family I had.

Vibrations lit up my pocket. Levi chuckled this time, his cool fingers gripping my chin. "Why don't you go see what the problem is?"

"Because I don't care."

"And I don't want your attention divided—I'd rather have you all to myself." Heat licked at me as his hungry gaze settled once more on my mouth. "Trust me; I'll be here when you get back."

Why would a guy this hot be waiting for a girl like me? The questions beat at my brain, demanding an answer, but I'd never screw up the courage to say the words aloud, so I slipped reluctantly from his arms instead. Rather than returning to the table, I walked down the hall to the ladies' room and hurried inside. The stalls were empty, so I pulled my phone from my pocket and scrolled through my contacts until I came to my father's number, not bothering to check the texts. Personal experience had taught me that he wouldn't stop until he heard my voice.

"What do you think you're doing, Abigail?"

"Hello to you too, Dad."

Pride filled me at the lack of fear in my voice—until the fury in my father's growl made me tremble.

The sound of people talking that filtered through the phone became muffled; Dad moving to a more secluded area. "I've had enough of your goddamn games, Abigail. I'm sending a car for you; it'll be outside in ten minutes, and I want you inside it in ten and a half. You will come to this dinner, and you will be by my side when I make my announcement—or you will regret it. Is that clear?"

"That's going to be difficult since I'm not at home."

"I know exactly where you are. Do you think I'm an idiot?"

"How—" But I was no idiot either. *Or maybe I am, because...cell phone.* I pulled the device away from my ear to stare at it, dazed, my father's rants and demands registering vaguely, like flies my mind batted away without conscious thought. Only the tone flowed over me, a trick I'd learned as a young girl—or more of a survival strategy, really. The only way to endure the hours of lectures and discipline that had filled my childhood.

"Get your ass outside right this minute and wait for Charlie to arrive. I won't have you shaming this family."

That registered. Or rather, slapped me awake. *I was bringing shame to our family? Me?* My father expected me to marry for his convenience, for the good of his political career, but I was the shameful one? I squeezed down on the cell, the sound of plastic creaking in protest satisfying something inside me that ached to burst free. Too bad I wasn't strong enough to pulverize the damn thing.

And yet, a large part of me believed him. Always had. After all, if I wasn't shameful, he would love me, right?

No. Wrong. You're not going to let that bastard poison you anymore, Abby.

I wasn't the Hulk, able to crush a cell phone with a single twitch of my fingers, but I was strong enough to drop it into the trash can full of wet paper towels and walk out of the bathroom without looking back. In the hall, the sight of Levi leaning against the wall, obviously waiting, hands stuffed into his pockets, brought me to an abrupt stop. My mouth went dry. I'd spent my life trying to please a man, and look where that had gotten me.

I was already bringing *shame* to the Roslyn name; maybe I should embrace the role instead of letting my father's words cut me to pieces.

I moved closer. One side of Levi's mouth tilted up, and he wrapped those big hands around my hips the minute I came within reach. A gravelly rumble escaped him, sinking beneath my skin and sending shivers to the deepest part of my being. Heavy-lidded eyes devoured me, shouting a desire I found hard to believe, but it was there nonetheless. Hunger. Pleasure. That look sent a surge of desperation so strong through me that I couldn't speak if I'd wanted to.

It's now or never, Abby.

I didn't stop or slow. I moved into his space until my body was pressed firmly against his, lifted my chin, and met the lips that lowered to mine.

Chapter Three

His fingers bit into my hips, holding me tight, bruising with the force of his desire—and I reveled in it. I'd gladly bear bruises if it proved that, for once, someone wanted me, Abby Roslyn, not the daughter of politician and wealthy businessman Derrick Roslyn. Levi's grip, the way he opened his mouth and let me in, the urgent push of his erection against my stomach said this was about hunger, not status. I needed that, wanted it with a desperation that probably made me pathetic, but so what? My entire life probably seemed pathetic to most people.

It was time to leave that old Abby behind. And what better way to do it than with an act that would also give me pleasure?

I retreated just enough to meet Levi's eyes. They burned with the same intensity as his touch, reassuring me, fanning the flames that already consumed me. I swallowed hard. "Would you…"

His fingers speared into my hair, tangling in the thick length, his palm big enough to cup my head. That touch steadied me, secured me. I couldn't fall with someone that strong holding me. "Would I what, Abby?"

"Would you like to go someplace more…private?"

Silence. I dug my teeth into my bottom lip, that "not a *complete* fool" prayer echoing in my mind for the umpteenth time. Maybe he expected a quick screw in the bathroom? But I didn't want quick. If I was going to do this, I wanted it to last.

Levi stroked a rough finger over my mouth, forcing me to let go of my lip. "Are you sure that's what you want? You don't really know me."

I know I want you. I know you want me. I know I don't want to be locked in a cage with no way out. "I know enough."

This time he kissed me, forcing me harder against him until my curves melded into the nooks and crannies of his powerful body. I could feel the demand, the hunger in his tight muscles as he bent me to his will. Wise or not, my body softened against him, surrendering control, yielding to the ferocious roar of desire, both from without and within.

When the kiss ended, I could only hang there, a broken reed in his hands, desperate for Levi to put me back together.

"Let's go."

My laugh trembled as much as I did. "I'm supposed to walk after that?"

Levi grinned. "Don't worry. I can carry you if necessary."

I eyed the broad stretch of his shoulders. "I bet you can."

We'd just reached the end of the hall when I caught a glimpse of the front doors, situated to our left. One side opened, and in walked Charlie, my dad's chauffeur. My ride was here.

I jerked Levi to a quick stop. "Maybe we could go out the back?"

His dark brows knotted up. "Your friends will wonder what happened to you, won't they?"

My heart thumped in my throat as Charlie surveyed the crowd, frowning. He was just as capable as Levi of hauling me out of here, willing or not. He'd never had to do more than threaten before. "I'll text them."

Suspicion tinted his gray eyes. He scanned the bar, his hand tightening around mine. Whether he noticed Charlie or not, the tension in him rose, and he turned back to the hall, his arm coming around me. Without a word, without question, he protected me in a way my father never had. Stranger or not, he'd just given me something I'd never had before, and the fear of the unknown, of leaving this building with a man I'd met a mere hour ago, with the intent of making myself as vulnerable as a woman could get with him, disappeared.

I was going to defy my father, and I was going to have sex with the hottest, most intriguing man I'd ever met. And nothing was going to stop me.

Levi's car waited across the street, low and black and gleaming in the streetlight's faint glow. The barest glimpse of a limo parked in the no-parking zone in front of the bar entrance had me ducking my head, a low sigh of relief leaving me as I settled into the passenger seat of Levi's vehicle. The door closed with a solid *click*, and then he was rounding the back to take his place behind the wheel. The growl of the engine rumbled through me, beneath me, vibrating things already sensitive to sensation. I fought the urge to squirm in my seat, barely managing to stay still despite years of practice at controlling myself in public, never moving the wrong way or saying the wrong thing. I couldn't control the need to reach out, though, and lay my hand on Levi's thigh, absorbing his heat and strength through the denim, feeling the play of his heavy muscles beneath my touch. What would they feel like when he was pushing inside me?

My fingers clenched against him.

Levi shifted the car into the next gear, then settled his hand over mine, threaded his fingers between mine. I focused there as he navigated through the dark city streets, trusting him to take us where we needed to go. I'd never had a hook-up before. What did I know about places to have sex? But Levi knew; in too few minutes he pulled the car into a crowded hotel parking lot.

Levi parked. I couldn't decide where to look—at those looming glass doors leading to the lobby, the man taking up so much space next to me that I could barely breathe, the dark street that offered anonymous escape. I deliberately turned away from that last option. I didn't want escape, no matter how nervous I was. And yet…

"Hey."

Levi cupped my chin, tilting my head until his gaze trapped mine. "Okay?"

"Yeah." Hopefully the darkness hid the shakiness of my smile. "It's just…umm…"

A glint of amusement lit his eyes. My cheeks heated. "Not used to the walk of shame?"

"Something like that."

"Don't worry." He stroked my flushed skin, his gaze following the movement as if fascinated. "I'll take care of you."

The deep timbre of his voice shivered through me, his words wrapping me in silken threads as unbreakable as the thickest, strongest rope. "I know. I trust you."

Did I? Maybe the words were automatic, what you were supposed to say when you were planning to sleep with the man you said them to. Tomorrow they wouldn't matter, but I didn't want to think about tomorrow, so I reached for the door latch.

"Wait, let me." He was out of the car and around to my side before I could draw a full breath.

Inside, the clerk barely glanced up while he assigned us a room, sparing me the embarrassment of having to meet his eyes. Levi guided me to the elevator with a hand at my back. His heat both steadied me and made something deep in my core clench with excitement. I stepped through the sliding doors and turned at the back of the elevator, but he stopped just inside, reached for the button to our floor, and pushed, all without taking his heavy-lidded gaze from my face.

How could a glance make me feel so vulnerable? I wanted to cross my arms over my chest and squeeze down, protect myself—from what, I didn't know, because I also wanted to spread my arms wide and let Levi crawl inside me.

"Abby."

Two syllables. So little, just my name, but that was all it took for my nipples to throb and a warm melting to suffuse my most feminine parts. And then he surged toward me, his big body pinning me to the back of the elevator, his mouth hard and demanding on mine.

The *ding* of our arrival barely registered through the roaring in my ears.

I chased his lips as they left mine. Levi was all electric heat and searing pleasure, and I wanted more, as much as I could get. Everything he had to give. I wouldn't deny myself anything, not tonight. I didn't hesitate as he gripped my hand tight and dragged me from the elevator. I caught a desperate glance at the key card, the door numbers, and then we were at the end of the hall, last door on the right. He fumbled the entry, a fact that told me he was just as anxious as I was. We'd started stripping each other before the door clicked shut.

"Abby, Jesus." He frowned down at the lace corselet I wore under my silk shirt. The lingerie made me feel pretty, but Levi was focused on the intricate lacing holding the front together.

I laughed. "It zips."

"Well turn around, for fuck's sake."

Another laugh as I obeyed. Cool air rushed over my skin when the sides of the corselet opened over my spine. Goose bumps rose. I held the front against me for a moment, struggling with that last little shred of timidity, and then I dropped the cloth. Levi swore as he stepped close, his heat covering my back.

"Look up."

I did—and wow. The wall I faced wasn't a wall at all, but a mirror. I zeroed in on Levi immediately. His hungry eyes devoured the sight of my bare breasts as he crowded closer. My hands came up automatically to rest on the cool surface; my nipples slid against the mirror, tingled at the chill until Levi cupped them from behind.

My head fell back. "Levi!"

The scruff on his chin abraded the sensitive skin of my neck. He bit down lightly, forcing me to acquiesce as he fondled my breasts, pinching the tips, rolling them, pulling. Cries escaped me, the begging and screaming and squirming out of my control as he pleasured me, pleased himself. And that made it all the hotter, the fact that I couldn't escape, could only accept what he chose to give me, his shadowed gaze taking it all in as the mirror reflected back my torment and titillation.

If this was what foreplay was like with him, how the hell would I survive sex?

When his fingers left them, my nipples were hot enough that the cool surface of the mirror felt like ice, but I wasn't shivering from cold. No, it was pleasure that shook me as I watched him watch me, felt the trace of his hands down my stomach, my hips, around to the clasp of my skirt. He bared my body while I examined his behind me, the sight of gleaming olive skin decorated with a wash of vibrant tattoos turning me on almost as much as his touch. The ink began just below his collarbone, a sea of blacks and blues and reds that highlighted the masculine hills and valleys of his torso and shoulders. My fingers itched to trace every line, although maybe I'd use my tongue. Or maybe both.

Levi was beautiful in a brutal way, and the darkness of his gray eyes in the midst of his passion gave him a deadly edge that only added to his appeal. I wanted him inside me, wanted him to take me now, immediately. The damp heat between my legs said I was ready even if I had no actual experience with the physical act—preliminary contractions rocked my pelvis just from his look as my skirt drifted down my legs, leaving my lace garter belt and thigh highs bare to his view. What he zeroed in on, though, was the sight of my soft auburn curls framed by the delicate lace and garters. An animal growl escaped him, rumbling along my spine.

I don't mind vibrators, but that's not exactly what I had in mind.

I slammed the door shut on the reminder of my father's demands and moaned my dismay as Levi stepped back. "No. What—"

One thick arm wrapped around my belly, the other beneath my knees, and then I was in the air. Levi carried me across to the bed, proving he hadn't lied earlier. He dropped me onto the mattress with a little grunt, tugged my boots off and tossed them one at a time over his shoulder, then dropped his hands to his belt buckle. "I can't wait, Abby."

"I don't want you to."

Chapter Four

His chuckle was strained; so was his erection when he stripped his pants down his legs. I caught a brief glimpse of an angry red head before he bent to push off his shoes and shed his clothes. The size made me hesitate, but I wouldn't stop, not now. Not ever if it meant Levi would be the one over me, inside me. I wanted him more than I was afraid of my first penetration, more than the worry about what might come after. When he stood and began to roll a condom onto his hard length, I opened my arms and beckoned him to me.

He planted one knee on the bed. "Let me see all of you, Abby. Let me in." His hands felt too big on my knees, too demanding as they pushed outward, but my hunger for him overcame any hesitation. Levi crawled up between my spread legs, his gaze on the most intimate part of my body. Searing. Hungry. Still making me squirm. And then he was on top of me, all solid-steel muscles and smooth skin and glorious heat.

I hadn't known the weight of a man could feel so good. Levi was heavy, his body pinning me in place, making me feel small and protected. I slid my hands down his wide shoulders, the muscles straining with the effort to keep his full weight from smothering me, down to hard pecs and ribs layered with a dense pad of muscle. His back too—the thick ropes lining his spine were the perfect handhold as he arched above me. His hot breath stroked one nipple. The other.

When his tongue traced the aching nub, my nails dug in, my own back arching as I waited, waited…

"Levi!"

The cry escaped without permission, his name my touchstone against the overwhelming pleasure that hit with the sucking pressure of his mouth on my breast. I'd read about it, imagined it, had Levi's fingers on my nipples, but this…oh God. Every tug, every swallow, the wet push of his tongue locking my nub against the roof of his mouth—they shattered me. All I could do was squeeze my eyes tight and try to breathe as the pressure built in my breast, in my core. Drawing my knees back tilted my hips, and then Levi was there, poised at my body's entrance, a sensual threat I could do nothing but surrender to.

I tightened my knees on his hips, urging him inside.

Levi grunted around my nipple. His back curved under my hands; his shaft pressed forward, stretching me farther than I'd known I could be stretched. A sharp pain pierced my core.

His head jerked back, and a curse escaped his clenched teeth. Wide, wild eyes stared down at me, but he didn't stop his advance, and I didn't stop wanting it, despite the pain, despite the protest of my body as he hilted inside me. Only then did I realize I was biting down on my lip, tasted the blood on my tongue, heard the tiny mewling sound that escaped despite my best attempt to hold it back.

Levi heard it too. A quiver shot through him. "Breathe, Abby. Breathe."

He took his own advice, held himself still as he drew in a deep breath that mashed my breasts beneath him. When he exhaled, I inhaled. I exhaled;

he inhaled. We followed the pattern until his body stopped shaking and my hands relaxed enough to extract my nails from his skin.

I expected him to apologize, get angry that I hadn't told him I was a virgin, pull out maybe. Not Levi. He did pull back, but only so he could enter me again. The glide this time was smooth and much less painful. I moaned.

The sound sent a charge through his body, seeming to break the restraint he'd put on himself. The next thrust was hard and fast, the absorbed look in his eyes telling me the pleasure was taking over any conscious decisions he could make. A shiver of fear went through me, but then he thrust again, this time brushing something inside me that changed my moans to guttural groans. I pulled my knees higher, trying to climb him, to get closer to the source of that searing pleasure. "More. God, more, Levi, please!"

His chuckle was strained, muffled against my shoulder where his teeth clamped down once more, pinning me beneath him. He set up a rough, heavy rhythm that rocked my body hard, nothing I had expected and definitely nothing I could have imagined—a place where pain became pleasure and the hunger for completion took over every thought, every moment until I thought I would scream with the need to climax. The scent of sweat and sex, the weight of Levi's body above me, the rough rub of coarse hair against my thighs and vagina and nipples, the push of his penis inside me—all of it was too much, yet not nearly enough. And then it was there, that pinnacle I'd so often wondered about and longed for, the feeling of coming outside myself and being bathed in complete sensation. In pleasure. In peace. It went on and on, even through the sudden strained groan Levi released as he climaxed.

By the time the spasms eased, he was staring down at me, his gaze stealing every intimate detail for his own.

My mind was blank, unable to cough up a response. In lieu of words, I raised my hand to stroke his stubble-roughened cheek.

Levi gave me a quick jerk of a smile before rolling slowly to one side. "Let me take care of the condom."

"Of course." Uncertainty tried to rise, but I pushed it down in favor of watching his graceful trek across the room—or, really, watching the beauty of his hard rear as he walked. Only when that sight disappeared into the bathroom did I lay my head back and close my eyes. My body felt…different, foreign. Aches and throbbing abounded. There was no doubt I'd been thoroughly and completely taken. A tired smile tugged at my lips.

Would he take me again before we slept? I desperately hoped so.

"Here you go."

I opened my eyes to Levi standing above me, an open water bottle in one hand. Scooting up until the headboard met my back, I smiled. "Thank you."

He sipped from his own bottle as I took mine. "I figured you'd be thirsty."

I was; I drank a good quarter of the bottle in one go. Slipping into the bed beside me, Levi snagged the sheet and pulled it up till it covered our legs, leaving my breasts bare to his gaze. I wanted his body bare too, all of it, so I could trace every inch of his skin with my gaze and my fingers and my tongue.

Especially his cock. The memory of it inside me, how big it had felt, made me curious about how much I could take in my mouth, what it would feel like. What his mouth might feel like on me. My body tingled, and above the sheet, my breasts ached, my nipples hardening. I shifted onto my hip, hoping to hide the reaction with my bent arms and the water bottle in my grip.

Levi's expression said he hadn't missed the move or the reason behind it. I blushed.

A final sip emptied his water. Levi set it on the nightstand, then mimicked my position. "Drink up, Abby. I can't have you dehydrated, not with all I've got planned."

Hmm, promising. I hid my relief with a few more swallows.

A yawn surprised me.

Levi chuckled. My mostly empty bottle was removed from my hand, his strong fingers replacing it. Levi laced them with mine as he kissed me, his lips softer now, his tongue more curious than demanding. The husky moan that escaped him when I captured his tongue between my lips and sucked hesitantly assured me he enjoyed the gentle foreplay despite the lack of urgency.

Another yawn forced its way forward.

I found my head tucked against his broad chest without realizing how it got there, but I didn't argue. I couldn't seem to do much but blink sleepily. Maybe my first sexual encounter—or the events leading up to it—had taken more out of me than I'd thought.

The sprinkle of dark hair on his pecs beckoned; I traced it lazily. Gentle fingers pushed my hair back from my face. "Why don't you doze off for a few minutes?"

I shook my head. "I'm okay."

He tipped my chin up. "I think you're tired, and no wonder." He slid us down in the bed until our bodies were prone, touching, faces close together. "I don't want you tired; I want you fully awake. I'm not going anywhere. Close your eyes and rest; you'll need it."

In this, just like in everything else, I couldn't resist him. My eyes closed, and the last thing I remembered was the sound of his steady heartbeat beneath my hand, his arms tight around me.

Chapter Five

The sheets were soft, a second skin wrapping around my body. I'd expected arms holding me when I woke, but I must've slept longer than I meant to. Levi had probably gone to shower or something.

Opening my eyes confirmed that the sun sat higher in the sky than I'd anticipated, just peeking over the lip of the high windows I faced. Unfamiliar windows, about twelve feet up, sans curtains. The sunlight spilled in unfettered, gracing smooth walls painted a cool gray, not the generic tan of the hotel room last night.

Because this wasn't the hotel room from last night.

What the—

I shot up a little too fast. The room, right or not, spun sickeningly around me, and I clenched my hands in the sheets, trying to anchor myself to something solid. A minute, maybe two passed before I could open my eyes and not feel like I would throw up, and a thousand questions whirled in my brain in that time. First and foremost, why did I feel like this?

Every story I'd ever heard through high school and college about girls partying and being drugged ran through my head, and my heartbeat surged to a gallop. No, I didn't feel right, but surely Levi…he wouldn't. He'd been too good to me last night, even tender afterward. I remembered that; I remembered everything. I wouldn't have those memories if I'd been drugged, would I?

As if I needed more questions. This room definitely wasn't the hotel—it was bare of anything but a bed, a chest of drawers in one corner, and two doors in the wall opposite. No lamps, no nightstand, no pictures, nothing. Where the hell was I?

And where was Levi?

Gingerly placing my feet on the floor, I discovered that I could, in fact, stand, if shakily. I was dressed in the clothes I'd worn last night, but I'd been naked when I fell asleep. Had Levi dressed me? How had I slept through that? The last thing I remembered was drinking the water he'd given me, then drifting off wrapped in his arms—at the hotel, not here, wherever "here" was. The metallic taste in my mouth wasn't morning-after breath; it was fear, and before it got the better of me, I needed answers.

The first door I opened was a bathroom, pristine white, the shower and toilet only accompanied by toilet paper, a packaged toothbrush, and a tube of toothpaste. While I was there, I made use of all three. My body ached in places I didn't want to acknowledge, not now, not with a lot of crazy things running through my head. I tried to blank it all out, but one look in the mirror made that impossible. The fact that I'd had sex last night stared back at me—wild hair, swollen lips, stubble burn around my mouth and on my neck. I didn't want to think what my breasts must look like, the aching spots on my hips where Levi's fingers had dug in as he held me and—

No, don't think about that now. There has to be an explanation. After that, then you can think about sex.

Maybe.

I ran my fingers through my dark auburn hair, taming it as best I could, made sure my clothes were on straight, then returned to the bedroom. My fingers shook as I reached for the doorknob, but I forced them to function anyway. To grasp, twist, pull.

And look, damn it! You can't meet this head-on if your eyes are closed.

"I know very well where I'm at, Eli. I don't need you to tell me."

The voice checked my step into the room. Levi's voice, but…not. Last night it had been a low, sexy rumble. Now? The words were all steel and ice. And who was Eli?

I forced my legs to move. My bare feet chilled, the concrete cold beneath them. The room looked like a warehouse, or what used to be one—the inside had been finished, at least until about twelve feet up, just as it had in the bedroom. Clean gray walls. Long rows of windows up too high to see anything but the sky. A metal roof towered above me, giving a sense of vast openness that made me want to wrap my arms around myself and squeeze down tight. Instead I focused on Levi's back where he sat at a desk halfway across the space. The sight of his bare skin drew me forward.

"You've always been a bastard, Levi." The voice sounded small, tinny—was mystery man Eli on speakerphone? "Not this time. Remi needs you, so get your ass down to the hospital. I can't leave him long enough to force you."

"Remi doesn't need me; he needs you."

"Levi, he could've died—"

"I know that!"

33

The barked words jerked me to a stop nearly halfway to the desk. A squeak escaped. Levi swung around, his gaze narrowing on me. The lack of emotion there chilled more than my feet; it froze my heart. My foot slid back without conscious thought, driven by a sudden instinctive need to flee.

Levi stood. My mouth went desert dry.

"Look, you don't have to worry, little brother," Levi said, his tone absent, attention never wavering from me. "You take care of Remi your way. Rest assured I'm taking care of him mine."

A long pause. My anxious breath roared in and out, a white-water rush in my ears.

"What have you done?" Eli finally asked. Levi's brother, he'd said. Somehow I couldn't imagine the man standing in front of me, watching me like a panther stalking its prey, having a brother. The Levi from last night, yes, but...

But the Levi from last night had disappeared, obviously. Or had he? Was I misreading that expression? Surely this was all a misunderstanding. Maybe he was simply upset about whatever had happened to this Remi. Hadn't Eli mentioned a hospital?

I needed to know. "Levi?"

My voice came out as hesitant as my steps forward, too shaky in the massive space, but it was the best I could manage. Loud enough for Eli to hear it over the speaker, though.

"Who is that? Answer me, Levi!"

Levi leaned back against the edge of the desk, thick arms crossed over his ink-decorated chest. A smirk that didn't match his eyes tugged at his lips.

Lips I'd kissed. Lips that had caressed and kissed and sucked—

"That, Eli, is Derrick Roslyn's daughter."

My father's name rang in my ears, setting off another wave of confusion. Shock. Resignation began a slow crawl up my soul at the satisfaction saturating the words. Levi had targeted me? Because I was my father's daughter. I shouldn't be surprised, but that's exactly what I was.

This hadn't been about me at all. So what was it about?

Eli's curses filled the air. Levi chuckled. "I told you, I'll take care of our problem. Abby here is going to help me, one way or another."

"No!" Eli's voice hardened, becoming as frigid as Levi's had been mere moments ago. "You know the code, brother. We've never broken it, and neither have you. Don't hurt the innocent."

What code? What innocent? Why would they hurt anyone, either of them?

"Oh, she's not innocent. Not anymore."

Tears stung the backs of my eyes at Levi's tone, at the dismissive way his gaze traveled over my body. I looked down, seeing what he saw—my crossed arms had plumped my breasts above my corselet in a display I'd never intended to put on, but I couldn't seem to let go, couldn't relax the only thing holding me together right now.

"Don't you hurt her; you hear me?" Eli yelled this time, and I swore I heard a hint of something close to panic in the words. "Don't do anything you'll regret later."

"I don't feel regret. I don't feel anything, not anymore." Levi reached back toward the phone without looking, his finger hovering over the Off button. "Take care of Remi."

Click.

The sound hit my body like a lash.

"Good morning."

Levi's words should have been friendly, but no matter which way I turned them in my head, I couldn't find even a hint. And I didn't know where to start.

With the obvious, of course.

"You know who I am?"

"Of course I do. I knew before I ever laid eyes on you."

I swallowed hard, determined not to give in to the sick churning in my stomach. "And when was that?"

"Long before you walked into a club and set yourself up as bait."

So he'd been following me. Why?

Does it matter? Only one thing mattered, and that was where I needed to focus. "I want to go home now."

Levi shook his head. The sick feeling got stronger. "You're not going home. You'll be here a long time, in fact. Until your father gives me exactly what I want, though I plan to drag him through hell first. And rest assured, Abby"—he leaned toward me, one brow raised—"I know hell much, much better than he does. But not for long."

It was like a line from a movie, something you'd see on a screen and think, wow, that's cheesy villain dialogue. Only the villain was standing in front of me, big and terrifying and *real*, and the dialogue was anything but cheesy. "And—" I had to stop and clear my throat. "What...what is it you want?"

One dark eyebrow arched. "Him, dead. After he loses everything he ever cared about. Every last thing."

"Why? What has my father done to you?" I'd never so much as heard of Levi before; how could he be that closely connected to my father?

"He put out an order to kill me."

I laughed; I couldn't help it. I was afraid, confused, ashamed—though why I should be ashamed of having sex with someone, I wasn't sure. But come on, did Levi really expect me to believe my dad was trying to have him killed? "My father isn't a killer; he's a politician." Not a nice one, but that was a far cry from what Levi was accusing him of. My father, a killer. Right.

Right?

"Why would Derrick Roslyn, city councilman and future governor, want you dead, Levi?"

"Because he asked me to do a job for him. A very messy job, and he wants all the evidence of that job to disappear, including me."

That was even more ludicrous than believing my father was trying to have someone killed. "What kind of job?"

"Murder."

Chapter Six

"That's ridiculous. My father wouldn't—"

Levi's laugh cut me off, dark amusement and knowledge far beyond anything I could comprehend. I was looking at the man in front of me, being told he'd murdered someone, and despite that, I couldn't imagine him as—what? A hit man?

This had to be a dream. Any minute I'd wake up and this would all be gone and I would be wrapped in Levi's arms in the hotel bed, feeling his arousal and seeing wickedly hungry eyes looking down at me with zero malice.

Yes, I was delusional even considering that. Apparently I was delusional about a lot of things.

"You're not…an assassin."

"No?"

I eyed him warily. "Who did you kill, then?"

His snort hit me like a shot, proving my nerves weren't taking this as calmly as my mind. Which wasn't truly calm either, so… "More people than I can count, but I could narrow that down for you. I won't, though—that would be telling." His gaze strayed to the computer screen half-obscured by his body. "The point is, your father tried to make sure I was next."

Probably a good objective if you looked at it without bias.

What was I thinking? Dad wouldn't do this. He wouldn't.

The deadly gleam in Levi's eyes said differently.

Play along. "So my father hired a hit man—you. That's between you and him. What does it have to do with me? How do I fit into this?" I wasn't sure I wanted the answer, though I desperately needed it if I was going to figure my way out of this hell. "You said I can't go home. Are you kidnapping me? Do you plan to kill me?"

"You're just the start, but a good one. An enjoyable one." Remembered pleasure softened his expression. A shudder jerked through me. "I don't plan to kill you, Abby." A pause. The tension in my muscles eased. "Not yet, anyway."

"Why? What have I ever done to you?"

"Nothing. It's not about you."

"Then what?"

"It's about destroying your father's life." He stalked forward, stopping far too close for me to be comfortable. "Do you know how you destroy a man's life? Start with his reputation—or in this case, the reputation of those closest to him."

"How?"

Levi stared me down for a long time. I couldn't read the look, but then, I couldn't have trusted anything I read, anyway. He'd proved that far too effectively. And then he stepped aside, allowing me access to the desk behind him. A wave of his hand invited me forward. "See for yourself."

Ignoring the warnings screaming through my head, I walked toward the desk. He seemed amused at my wariness, but right now I couldn't bring myself to care. My head was too full, too confused, my heartbeat too fast, my breath too shallow. I was going to pass out if something didn't give. And then I reached the desk and moved my gaze from Levi to the computer, and the possibility of fainting grew exponentially.

Pictures. Of me. There were a dozen open on the screen, a sea of naked skin—*my* naked skin. I was asleep, my hands and feet tied in leather restraints I'd only seen associated with the little bit of BDSM culture that had leaked into mainstream with the release of *Fifty Shades of Grey*. My hair was after-sex wild, my skin bearing the faint darkening of raspberries and beard burn and bruises in intimate places.

That can't be me. But it was. Staged, maybe, but me nonetheless. I glanced down at my wrists. In the clear light of day, they bore no signs of the cuffs in the picture. And Levi hadn't tied me while we were at the hotel.

Levi seemed to follow the path my own thoughts had taken. "Don't worry. I made sure you were asleep for that part."

His amusement stung, sharp enough to spark a reaction in the fog of disbelief smothering me. "Am I supposed to thank you for that?"

"You should."

I met his eyes and agreed. I wouldn't have enjoyed the experience, even as role-play; the look on his face promised that.

He hadn't enjoyed last night at all, had he? Or at least not the way I'd thought he had. He got off, but that look… I turned away, letting my hair fall forward to hide my face, my tears as I stared down at the computer screen. I'd fallen asleep content, filled with a quiet joy that my first time had been so good. I hadn't been imagining diamond rings and wedding dates—that was an impossibility for me, even if I did manage to avoid the marriage my father wanted—but I hadn't felt cheap either, not like I did now. And naive for imagining that last night was anything but cheap sex. I hadn't even suspected, not for a second.

Was that what made me prey instead of predator, that inability to see, to protect myself from men like Levi and my father? I stared at the red marks on my breasts, glaring in the light of the computer screen. Accusations, every one of them.

Stupid, stupid, stupid.

I'd believed a man as hot as Levi would want an inexperienced girl like me. What a fool. Funny that the first time I'd taken my fate into my own hands, stepped out of the cage that was my life, I'd ended up here, at the mercy of a…of him. A killer? A lunatic? Definitely a kidnapper.

My fingernails dug into the tender skin of my palms. Maybe all these years my father really had been protecting me, from myself if nothing else. I obviously wasn't smart enough to be let out on my own.

Except…Levi must have had plenty of practice fooling people. There hadn't been even a hint of this hard, emotionless man last night, even in the throes of climax. And all my father's control had gotten me was misery and an arranged marriage with someone I'd never even met.

Levi's hands came into view, settling on the mouse and keyboard. He pulled up a Gmail account.

"What are you doing?"

A click to open a new e-mail. Panic squeezed my chest.

"Levi?"

My father's personal and work e-mail addresses appeared in the *To* line. In the Subject line...my name.

My vision grayed out as he attached photo after photo.

"You can't send those."

"Why not?"

"Because—"

He turned his head, the threat in his stare cutting off my words. I closed my eyes, desperate to protect some small part of me from that look, and yet the backs of my eyelids blazed with the images Levi had taken.

Could someone die from humiliation?

"Please...just don't."

No response except the clicking of keys. I could not let that e-mail go out. I wouldn't.

I opened my eyes.

I have your daughter. Be ready. I'm coming for you next, motherfucker.

The cursor settled over the Send button on the e-mail.

"You didn't ask him for anything." Didn't kidnappers make demands, tell their victim's family what they needed to let them go?

"He doesn't have anything to give that would stop me, Abby. Ever. He signed his death warrant the minute he decided to come after me."

"And what about me?"

He shrugged without looking my way. "Maybe we'll make sure you're awake for the next session."

His fingernail paled as he pressed the mouse, and a white-hot blast of panic threw me forward.

Too late. A distinct *click* echoed in my ears even as my body hit his.

I went a little crazy after that. The fight was a blur, and then my back hit the desk, Levi forcing me down. Pain shot through my hips, my shoulders, the wrists he slammed onto the hard surface, locked in his hard grip.

He wasn't even breathing heavy. I could barely suck in air as tears streamed from the corners of my eyes to wet my hair.

"Want to move up our timeline a bit?" Levi asked, his face right in front of mine, his stare unavoidable. "There wasn't time for a second go-round last night before I drugged your water, was there? At least, not for you."

He'd drugged me? And jerked off while taking those pictures? Or was he talking about something else? My stomach knotted suddenly, the urge to gag surging up my throat. I jerked beneath him, rolled, did everything I could, but there was no escape, not when his full weight settled on me.

I knew that weight. I knew the breath that brushed my cheek, my hair, the wet trails on my skin, and then his mouth was at my ear, tracing the sensitive edge, my trembling jaw, the pounding beat of my pulse in my throat. Wet heat stroked my skin. I quivered, eyes squeezed tight against a reality I could do nothing to escape.

Some small part of me didn't want to.

Levi knew too. His grip bit into my wrists. "I think you might like being tied up," he whispered against my skin. "Maybe those pictures weren't a lie after all."

Chapter Seven

I shut down then. It was a survival mechanism I used with my father, presenting the perfect emotionless doll to please him, to escape the pain and frustration I couldn't seem to avoid. A small protection in this world gone mad.

Levi seemed to sense the withdrawal. His growl—of frustration or anger; I wasn't sure which—signaled my victory, but it wouldn't last long.

It did win me a reprieve, however. Levi spun away, left me lying there on the desk, alone and aching. I stayed still through his retreat, only moving when I heard heavy footsteps coming my way.

He carried a duffel bag. Where it came from, I had no idea. Levi dropped it at my feet, his intimidating expression denying my instinct to pick it up, open it, see what he'd brought me.

More rope? Sex toys? I shuddered, half in fear and half... I wasn't ready to admit that half. The crazy half.

"I'll get us some breakfast. Clean up while I'm gone."

He was leaving? *Yes!*

I obviously didn't hide that well enough, because Levi smirked. He knew exactly what I was thinking, and that I'd never succeed.

Everything in me ached to somehow, in some way, prove him wrong.

Without another word he stalked toward the door. A pause while his broad back blocked whatever he was doing at the key pad, and then he was outside, the *click* of the latch loud as it locked firmly in place. I tried it anyway, to no avail.

The duffel beckoned, and I investigated. Soap and shampoo and clean clothes—nothing I could use as a weapon. I left the bag where it lay. If the bastard didn't want to look at me dirty, he could lock me in the bedroom. This might be the only chance I got to escape. I had to do it fast. Just imagining him catching me in the act, going against his commands made my mouth dry up and my heart race. He didn't need rope to restrain me; his mere presence was paralyzing. Too bad he hadn't had that effect on me last night too, or I wouldn't be in this mess. Levi was the consummate actor. I had to remember that, protect myself no matter what happened. Of course, if the Levi that just left was the real Levi, I'd have no trouble remembering.

That wasn't what you were thinking when his hands were on your body.

I flipped off my conscience, then set about exploring. There wasn't a lot to search. The warehouse was mostly empty, as if Levi hadn't wanted to clutter up the openness. Or maybe like he didn't spend much time here.

Or maybe he captive-proofed the place before you arrived.

That too.

This main room was open, sections divided by furniture defining each space—living room, kitchen, office. Not a lot of necessities—the living area held a couch and TV on a stand, a remote, and a rug. I could smash the TV, use the broken shards or the cord, maybe?

Right. Who was I kidding? I knew absolutely nothing about defending myself. That's what bodyguards were for, according to my dad. Still, I couldn't give up hope. The kitchen seemed the most likely place to find a weapon, but a search found no silverware, plastic dishes, definitely no knives. Pretty much no food either. I hoped takeout was a possibility, because cooking here would be a challenge.

Only if you don't get out.

And I couldn't count on my father to rescue me—not that Levi had offered him that option. No ransom demand, no *if this, then that.* Dad wouldn't want that anyway. Hard as it was to imagine my father hiring an assassin, I had no illusions when it came to Derrick Roslyn's mercenary outlook. Having your daughter kidnapped could play well on the public's sympathies, and he would do anything to advance his political career, including selling his daughter to the candidate with the highest pedigree. I shuddered, memories of his anger last night playing through my head.

The office area was the last to be searched. Basic desktop setup, again with the cords... I squeezed out a sigh. Not even drawers to hide pens. I'd seen that in a movie once. The antihero had killed an attacker with an uncapped pen. My stomach churned, imagining doing the same to Levi, but I couldn't fool myself; it might come to that.

Unfortunately, no pen. What else?

I went into the bedroom.

An empty vista greeted me under the bed, free even of dust bunnies, so I tried the dresser. The top drawer held boxer briefs—*why couldn't he be an old-fashioned, less attractive tighty-whities guy?*—socks, and plastic zip ties. Like those weren't suspicious at all. Second drawer: T-shirts. Black and white. Levi obviously wasn't a fan of variety, except when it came to his ink. Those had surged with almost painful color beneath my hands last night.

I shook the memory away and moved to the third drawer. Fatigues. No shorts, sweatpants, nothing comfortable. I guess assassins didn't curl up on the couch in comfy clothes and watch a movie. He probably never got the flu either.

The last drawer wouldn't open. A surge of excitement hit me, almost painful after a half hour of worry and hopelessness. But how to get it open? This wasn't some discount-store particleboard dresser; it was solid wood, and the lock would be strong—Levi had been meticulous so far, and that wouldn't change now. Maybe the third drawer…

But no matter how much I pulled and jiggled, I couldn't get the pants drawer to come out. Some kind of catch in the runner refused to release it at its full extension. I tried lifting and even yanking, pounding the base of the drawer with my fists, but…nothing.

And there was no more time to waste. Levi had gone to get food; he could be back any moment. I swallowed my sigh of defeat and began moving each neat pile of clothing from the floor back to the drawer. If I couldn't find a weapon—and if I wanted a chance to try again later—it was better that Levi never know I'd looked.

The last stack was farther away than the others. I reached, wavered, only to knock the fatigues out of their tidy pile. With a curse I gathered the stack back into its original neat column, but when I lifted the pants into my arms to transfer to the drawer, a small frame fell from the folds of the bottom pair.

It was one of those old-fashioned frames, the metal kind that weighed a few ounces despite only being big enough for a wallet-sized photo. Three boys stared out at me, young ones with stair-stacked heights, sitting on white-painted steps situated before a gray studio backdrop. The oldest child looked like Levi around the eyes and had his black hair. The other two were dark blond, resembling him in every other way so closely they could've been twins if not for the hair and heights. His brother, Eli? Did Levi have two brothers? Where was the third?

I refused to care. Levi didn't give a shit about me; that much was obvious. Why should I care about him and his family? He wasn't the small boy in that picture anymore.

I weighed the frame in my hand a moment longer. It was old enough that the front was glass, not plastic like most frames now. I turned the picture over and removed the backing, the photo, and finally the glass, replacing everything else and carefully tucking the frame back where it had been hidden. The pants went into the drawer, but I couldn't stop glancing at that glass lying on the rug. A weapon. A way to protect myself. Now I just had to use it.

By the time I heard the lock click on the door Levi had left through, I was ready. A shard of the glass I'd found, one end wrapped with a thigh-high, was clutched in my fist. I'd hidden the other in the water tank of the toilet, praying Levi wouldn't look there if I failed the first time. Of course, if I failed, there might not be a second time, but I had to try. I couldn't trust that my father would get me out of this; it was up to me, just like always. So I huddled behind the door, barely breathing, and waited as the doorknob turned and the door opened.

The scuffed sound of Levi's boot on the concrete sounded like a gunshot in the quiet. I tightened the muscles in my belly, forcing myself to be still, to wait. To think like the predator instead of the prey.

Levi stepped into the room, allowing the door to slide closed behind him. I grabbed it before the latch could connect.

He must've heard me moving, caught something from the corner of his eye, maybe, because I didn't make it around the door and out. A solid arm blocked my path, effectively clotheslining me before I'd even gone three steps. Choking, sputtering, I raised the glass shard.

Levi cursed. He grabbed my arm and twisted me around, sending a sharp stab of pain through my shoulder, and then I was hauled hard against him, my back to his stomach. "What the fuck?"

One arm jammed against my ribs, squeezing every ounce of air from my lungs. His free hand gripped my wrist tight and twisted, forcing my hand to bend backward until I cried out and leaned in that direction, trying desperately to give myself some relief from the pain.

"Now where did you find that, little bird?"

I was disarmed just that quickly. After a too thorough search of my body for any other hidden weapons, Levi picked me up off the floor and carried me into the living area. I kicked and hit, struggling for release—and, okay, maybe going a little bit crazy with panic. This guy could kill me, after all. I no longer had doubts about that.

He didn't, though. He didn't even seem bothered; instead he chuckled like I was some child trying to entertain him. Which only made me want to hurt him even more.

When I turned my head and bit down, teeth cutting into the bicep of the arm crushing my ribs, Levi stopped laughing.

Chapter Eight

"Damn it!"

He dropped me. My belly did that funny flip thing it does when a sudden drop comes out of nowhere, and then my head slammed into the coffee table. Pain radiated through my temple and eye socket, staggering me. I vaguely heard some cursing and muttering, and then I was on the floor, blinking and wondering how the hell I'd ended up there.

Levi knelt in front of me, his fingers digging into my upper arm the only thing keeping me upright.

"Don't do that again," he barked. "There's a reason you're not tied up. Keep attacking and you might not leave me any choice."

"Asshole."

Levi grinned. Actually grinned. "Did you call me a name?"

I'd call him another one if I could get my brain to spit one out. Granted, in a hit man's world, calling people names probably had zero impact, but words were the only weapons I had as I wobbled in his grip.

His hand rose, aimed for my face, and I flinched back.

"Be still." He probed the bruise I could already feel rising along my cheekbone. "Nothing's broken. Get up."

Like I had any choice with him pulling on me. "Do you do anything but bark orders and manhandle women?"

"I also deliver breakfast, but it doesn't look like you followed orders to clean up." His gaze dropped to the fast-food bags on the ground near the front door. "Maybe the prisoner doesn't deserve to be fed."

The word *prisoner* made this all too real. "How do I know it's not drugged? Maybe that's your way of keeping me in line; then you wouldn't need ropes."

All amusement drained from his face, leaving behind the cold, dead eyes that scared the living daylights out of me. A quick yank up brought me nose to nose with him. "I have plenty of ways, little bird, and you really don't want to explore them."

I hauled back and smacked my forehead into Levi's face.

Ow.

The excruciating pain in my head blocked out everything else until Levi's fingers clamped onto my jaw. I opened my eyes to face a deadly glare that had me all but cowering. God, I wanted to be strong, but…

"So that's how you want to play it, then?" Dropping his hand, Levi turned, hauling me across the room by my elbow like I was a naughty child. "This cage is going to get a lot smaller if this keeps up, I promise you that, Abby. But in the meantime"—he stooped to grab the duffel bag on the run—"let me show you exactly how much control you have in this situation."

My heartbeat went quick and light, fluttering like the little bird he'd called me. I didn't think that was a good sign since it only made the feeling that I was about to faint stronger. Maybe my brain had taken all the hits it could handle. Or maybe the dread growing in my chest as we barged through the bedroom door had something to do with it. I hadn't thought Levi would rape me despite the photos—a rapist wouldn't put me to sleep for those, would he?—but when he forced me into the bathroom...

Jesus, don't pass out, Abby!

I might not have a choice. Being unaware could even be a good thing, but I needed to know what was happening to my body. Every time I thought about what might have occurred last night while I was unconscious, I wanted to gag. I couldn't leave it to chance—I had to know.

Not that I wanted to go through this either, but Levi wasn't giving me a choice. He dropped the duffel and started stripping me almost in the same breath. Fighting him did nothing—he had me naked in seconds, my clothes from last night littering the floor around us in shreds, my chilled skin breaking out in goose bumps as he pulled me closer to the shower and reached to turn on the water.

"No. No!"

I struggled, yelled, tried to kick and scream, but nothing affected him, it seemed. He adjusted the water and shoved me into the shower as efficiently as if I was a passive doll in his hands—and I began to get the picture he'd painted all along. I could fight him, but I was only hurting myself. There really was no control in this situation. The only saving grace was that he hadn't hurt me on purpose, no matter how angry he got. Every injury had been an accident or my own fault.

Don't hurt the innocent, Eli had said. Maybe he'd been telling the truth? God, please let him be telling the truth.

I finally did the only thing I knew to do. I turned as far away from him as I could and huddled into the corner of the shower, back to Levi, one arm crossed over my breasts—a futile attempt to protect myself. Levi kept his grip on me for a minute, maybe to test my compliance, and then he let go. My second arm joined the first.

It was pointless, I knew, to try to hide. He'd seen every inch of me last night, places I'd never even seen. He knew my body more intimately than I did, but I couldn't deny the instinct, no matter how ridiculous. I pushed into the walls as if they could absorb me. The only thing I could control was my voice, and I kept silent, denying him the reaction he probably wanted, denying him at least one small part of me.

A metallic scraping sound startled me, but I didn't look. Told myself it didn't matter. Until hot water hit my head and poured down over my trembling body.

Only then did the tears come.

"Please...don't..." I couldn't let him take care of me, couldn't let those lines blur while I was vulnerable. They were all I had to protect myself.

But Levi didn't speak—and he didn't stop. The water blasted my aching head and muscles, easing knots, calming me against my will. It stayed in place until my shuddering stopped; then came warms hands and soap in my hair. Levi massaged my head, building up suds and lowering my resistance even more. He took his time rinsing, then conditioning. The scent of vanilla and flowers filled my nose, soothing me even more—a scent I'd always loved, which was why I used this same soap every day. Yet even that realization couldn't startle me out of the web he was weaving, using my body and my senses against me as if they were ropes and chains, hands and bars caging me in. When he started to soap my skin, I didn't even protest.

He was playing my body like a violin, and I knew with sudden clarity that this, above anything else he could do to me, was what could destroy me.

His fingers moved gently over my aching arms, down to my wrists, into the hollows between each individual finger. My palms tingled as he washed them, and then he placed them on the shower wall in front of me before moving back up to my neck and shoulders, my back. My underarms didn't escape his notice. Neither did my breasts—he palmed them from behind just like he had last night in front of the mirror, taking their weight, rolling my nipples, tapping the too-sensitive tips until my breath sped up against my will. He smoothed his soapy way down my stomach, dipped lower. A strangled protest left my throat.

"Shh…"

His hands were so big they covered both rear cheeks easily, squeezing and rubbing, gentling me to his touch. But when one pushed between my legs, it felt too big, too overwhelming, forcing my legs apart to accommodate his size. Slick, blunt fingers traced my nether lips, circled my clit, and I realized I was leaning into the wall, my butt pushed toward him, panting with arousal. He'd introduced me to the pleasures of sex just last night, and lesson or not, my body couldn't seem to ignore them now—I wanted release, if for no other reason than to return to a mindless state where everything I'd seen and heard and endured in the past few hours disappeared.

When Levi slid a thick finger inside me, I knew I'd get what I wanted.

"You're wet, Abby," he whispered huskily. I could feel the soaked clothes still on his body where he brushed against me. Did that mean he wouldn't take me? Did I seriously want him to? A finger was safe; a penis? No.

I shook my head silently—at him or me, I wasn't certain.

That invading finger pulled back, then slid smoothly inside once more. "Yes, you are. Feel how easy it is to get inside you?" Another retreat, and then a second finger joined in. The pressure sent me up on my toes, my head falling back as a groan escaped me. "You're so tight, but you take me anyway. You let me in, and your body welcomes me with slick heat."

"No." But I didn't try to escape the rhythmic invasion of his fingers.

"Yes."

Yes.

I couldn't admit it aloud though. The admission was in the widening of my stance, the pressing back of my hips, the moans and cries that escaped me as he thrust those hard fingers into my needy body. I chased the pleasure like a drug addict desperate for a fix, because that's exactly what I needed: oblivion; anything to make me feel good, and this did. It felt good, wrong or not.

When he shifted his hand so a knuckle bumped my clit on every thrust, a high whine rose from my throat in unison with my rising climax. Everything finally, *finally* fell away—it was just my core, those fingers, and the tidal wave of pleasure rising, rising, rising.

Until at last the fear and hurt and hunger coalesced into a hard crest that washed me clean.

Chapter Nine

He left me alone in the shower, as if now that he'd proven his point, he had no further use for me. I'd have believed it if I hadn't felt his erection against the small of my back, hadn't heard his moan of frustration mingle with my cries of release—cries I'd give anything to take back now that sanity had returned. But that was no more possible than fairy tales coming true, so I simply closed my eyes and let the water soothe me until it began to cool. Only then did I step out and dry my hypersensitive skin.

The contents of the duffel bag brought me fully out of my fog. I'd noticed the shampoo, the soap, the familiar scent registering in a vague way. Too vague against the demands of my body. The clothes, though...

They were mine. Or, at least, they looked like mine. Tags still graced each item, even the underwear, but there was no doubt about it, no denying it: Levi had been watching me, and even more, he'd been inside my house, in my private spaces.

How had he managed that?

My hands shook as I selected panties, bra, jeans, and a button-down shirt that would cover more than the tees in the bag. I'd never been so grateful for the protection of clothing in my life, as if each piece bandaged a gaping hole inside me until the scattered pieces finally came into some semblance of a whole, however temporary. Finger combing was the best I could do for my hair without a brush, but the moisturizer I used every day sat at the bottom of the bag, a reminder of just how deep Levi had delved into my life. I shuddered as I lathered it on.

After dumping my clothes from last night into the tiny trash can beside the sink, I took a pair of socks with me into the bedroom. No sign of Levi. How long would he let me lick my wounds? Would he touch me again then? Did I want him to?

I knew better than to hope we'd hear something from my father this soon. He would decide which approach was most advantageous for him first. At least, I was pretty sure that was what he would do. I wasn't a love child any more than the marriage he'd arranged for me had anything to do with love. He and my mother, a Hollywood starlet who'd died when I was a toddler, had formed an alliance more than a marriage, according to the rumors. She'd needed the money my father possessed, and the prestige of being his wife. He had needed an heir, preferably one with my mother's good looks. That I'd been both female and too short and curvy to be a classic beauty were major disappointments, but even then, Derrick Roslyn's daughter had a purpose. The same purpose as his short-lived marriage: to enhance his status.

Despite the tiny part of me that prayed he cared enough to come get me, to give in to Levi so his daughter could return home, I wasn't holding out hope for it happening. The reality of the past twenty-one years had taught me that.

My feet had barely lost their chill in the soft confines of their socks when raised voices in the living area caught my attention. Voices, plural. Someone else was here.

Dad?

I scrambled for the door. It wasn't my father waiting in the living room, though. Amber eyes turned quickly to narrow on me as I slid to a stop just outside the bedroom. Late twenties, tall, powerful build, intimidating. He had to be Levi's brother, Eli. Aside from the eyes and dark blond hair, he was practically Levi's twin, just like in the photo.

Levi raked my body with detached coldness. "Eli, meet Abby."

Eli let loose a string of profanity, half of which I didn't understand. I did understand his, "What the fuck have you done, Levi?"

Levi's expression gave nothing away. "What I had to, Elijah."

It was telling that Eli didn't budge from his position near the couch—no running to my aid, no checking for injuries or evidence of being tied up. Had he seen the pictures too? A flush of heat hit my cheeks despite the knowledge that they'd been staged.

And Levi drugged you to stage them. Don't forget that, Abby.

Eli turned away from me, stalking his brother instead. "You didn't have to do this and we both know it. You should stop playing with that bastard and just kill him. Get it over with."

Was he talking about Dad?

I'd thought Levi's eyes were cold before; now the arctic chill seemed to invade my bones. I'd never seen a man so stone-cold angry.

"I'm not playing, Eli. You know that better than anyone. I want Roslyn to suffer before he dies."

"You're starting a war is what you're doing. Having her here is just your opening salvo."

Levi moved behind the kitchen island. I could see the bags from earlier sitting there, beside plates, on the counter. My stomach growled.

"He started the war when he set his sights on me, and you know it," Levi said, calmly placing food on the plates. "When he missed me and hurt Remi, he guaranteed that I'd finish it."

My father was the reason Remi was in the hospital. No wonder Levi had launched a counterattack. I could almost understand if I wasn't the fraying rope connecting the two.

"Tell me you haven't hurt her."

Levi didn't answer, turning instead to put one of the plates in the microwave. Was that a yes or no? Maybe he thought drugging a woman so she didn't have to endure being tied up and photographed naked was mercy. Maybe holding me against my will wasn't harm if I wasn't in handcuffs. My father might even agree with him. So why did it feel like Levi had ripped me apart and barely left me with enough pieces to put myself back together?

Because he ripped your control away when you'd only just dared to find it.

Eli rushed his brother. "Tell me, Levi."

Levi shrugged. "Ask her."

Eli stalked toward me then. I found myself backing up until my shoulders hit the wall—Eli might be younger and arguing for my safety, but that didn't make him any less intimidating. I stood, trembling, as he pushed up my sleeves, tipped my head from side to side, ran his hands over me. Those amber eyes seemed to see everything: the darkened spots on my arms from Levi's grip, the redness from Levi's stubble around my mouth and neck, the way I cringed at his touch. The swelling on my cheekbone and temple got the most attention. I couldn't read his expression, but the way his gaze narrowed on Levi, I figured the message was *not happy but reserving judgment.*

Great.

I held my breath until he returned to his brother, now carrying two plates toward the table. The rich sent of chicken and biscuits wafted across the room. The growling of my stomach resumed as if given permission.

"If you want to eat, Abby, I suggest you get your sweet little ass over here."

The *sweet little ass* made me cringe once more, a reminder of what I'd allowed him to do in the shower, the memory of his big hands cupping me, kneading me. My steps were slow as I approached the table. "How do I know it's safe?"

"Why wouldn't it be?" Eli's affront would almost be cute if it weren't for the whole your-brother-is-a-hit-man thing. I mean, really? "You dead puts us in a helluva sitch."

Levi shot his brother a sharp look, one that transferred to me as he picked up a chicken biscuit and took a huge bite. The biscuit went back on the plate, and Levi exchanged it for the second dish. That biscuit got a bite taken out of it too. "There, happy?"

I sat a couple of seats away without answering. When I gripped the rim of the plate closest to me to slide it over, Levi arrested the motion with two fingers. An arched brow told me exactly what he wanted.

Bastard. "How can I be happy? I've been kidnapped, drugged, photographed naked—"

"What?"

I ignored Eli. "And taken advantage of. I'm hungry. My head hurts—"

"Whose fault is that?" Levi asked.

I noticed he didn't deny any of the other charges. "Partly yours." He had dropped me, after all. I paused, struggling with words I didn't want to speak. "No, I'm not happy—I'm pissed off and frustrated and scared shitless—but I do appreciate that you aren't starving me. I think." I raised my own brow.

Levi released the plate.

Eli cursed, turning to pace away from the table. I watched the two men from under my eyelashes as I ate. Levi watched his brother, his smoky eyes filled with resolve—Eli wouldn't sway him from the course he'd set.

Eli at least had a sympathetic edge. Maybe he could give me some insight. "What happened to Remi?"

Eli thrust a hand through his hair, looking suddenly tired. "He was shot."

"Not her business," Levi growled.

All of this affected me; how could it not be my business?

"So what do you plan to do with her, huh?" Eli asked. "Just keep her locked up here until, what, Roslyn calls a cease fire? You know he's not going to do that. He wants all evidence of that job to disappear, and that includes you."

"What job?" I asked.

Levi kept his attention on Eli. "I'm sure we can find plenty to occupy ourselves while we wait. After this morning, he knows I mean business."

Eli planted his hands on the end of the table opposite Levi, leaning forward. "And then what?"

Levi didn't answer with more than an arched brow. Some communication passed between them that I didn't understand, couldn't read, and then Eli pounded a fist into the thick tabletop. "Fucking Christ, Levi!"

His brother ate the last bite of his biscuit, unfazed. Maybe I had finally hit overload on the whole situation, because I barely flinched.

"Remi can't be moved, you know that." Eli shoved a hand through his thick blond hair. "What do you want me to do?"

"Stay with him." Levi stood and picked up his plate. "Roslyn found me last time through a fake buy. Since I'm off the market right now, that won't happen again. We've altered the records as best we can, but we can't ignore the possibility that he may connect Remi to me through the gunshot wound."

A faint trill had Eli reaching for his pocket. He pulled out a phone, tapped the screen, and stared. After a moment he gave a halfhearted chuckle. "What was that you said about not starting a war?"

Levi crossed the kitchen. "What about it?"

"Roslyn took your opening salvo and fired back his return shot." He turned his phone around to face Levi. "He just began a press conference. It seems his daughter has been kidnapped—and they have a suspect. Look familiar?"

Chapter Ten

"I think blurry's a good look on you, brother."

Of course the image was blurry—my father only hired the best, and I assumed that went for hit men too. Levi would've known where the cameras were and how to avoid them.

Too bad I hadn't known to avoid *him*.

The surveillance photo showed us in the hall of the club. Even with the grainy quality, it was enough to draw up the memory, to feel the visceral reaction to that moment in my muscles all over again. I'd wanted Levi so much, and the emotion was plain on my face, right there for everyone to see. A stupid girl fascinated with the man looming over her.

I should be used to it, the humiliation. I guess I should be thankful they hadn't released the nude photos I knew my father had received, but I wasn't. I couldn't be, not when everything inside me screamed that the man in that press conference, the man who was supposed to protect and love me, didn't. He hadn't reached out to my kidnapper, asked for demands. No, he'd gone straight to the media, a preemptive attack, with me still in the line of fire.

I existed only for two powerful, dangerous men to argue over, apparently. My fingers itched with the urge to strike out—at Levi, the TV, Eli. It didn't matter what the target was as long as I could be the one to choose it.

"We believe this individual lured Ms. Roslyn out of the establishment and took her to a secondary location," the man standing to the left of my father at the podium was saying. A suit and tie and the badge dangling from a thin chain around his neck proclaimed him either an investigator or someone from the PR office at the local PD. "Anyone downtown last night, in the area between First Street and Colonnade, might have spotted something. Call the number at the bottom of your screen should you have any information. We are considering the suspect armed and dangerous, however, and ask that anyone with a lead keep their distance. Do not try to interfere with this man under any circumstances."

The angle of the camera looked over Levi's shoulder, revealing no more than his jawline and cheekbone. Dark hair, broad shoulders. Pretty generic. I didn't think they'd be getting any reports of sightings based on it. How many tall, dark-haired, broad-shouldered men had been at the Full Moon last night?

My guess? At least a hundred.

Onscreen, a hand went up in the audience. "Other than the photo, do you have any further leads at this time?"

The officer frowned. Was he really looking for me, or was he another pawn for my father to use? "We cannot comment on that directly."

Another hand. "Councilman Roslyn, do you believe this kidnapping is related to your gubernatorial candidacy?"

My father adopted an appropriately contrite expression. I had to hand it to him—it even reached his eyes.

"Yes, we do. The timing is not a coincidence. But make no mistake." He stared directly into the camera, wearing the same sincere, intense mask that always made an appearance when he was in public. I shuddered. "My daughter's safety is my first priority. She should be returned to her family, not used as a pawn."

"Does that mean you will withdraw from the race, Councilman?"

"Of course not. We don't give in to terrorist threats."

So much for me being first priority. Of course, it hadn't escaped my notice that a murdered daughter would do more for my father's campaign than a kidnapped daughter. The sympathy vote was a powerful element in any election.

Eli crossed his arms over his chest. "Tell me you covered your ass, Levi."

"I'm the one who taught you, remember?"

I tucked that bit of info away to think about later. "But you said he hired you, right? So he knows who you are."

Levi shook his head, his eyes still intent on the screen. "No such luck, little bird. He knows what I look like and how to contact me. Not the same thing."

"And he has all the resources money can buy. How long before he figures the rest out about you?"

"Long enough."

"Do you intend to kill me?"

I hadn't meant to ask. I mean, who really wanted to know ahead of time that they would die when their captor finished toying with them? But my tightly strung nerves couldn't wait any longer.

"We don't kill the innocent," Eli barked. "That's what got us in hot water in the first place."

Levi slashed a hand at his brother. "Shut the fuck up."

Eli didn't, though. "We're not the ones you need to worry about, Abby. Just consider this a vacation from your life. You'll get back to the real thing soon enough."

"A vacation where I'm drugged and humiliated?" A strangled laugh escaped. "It'll take more than words to reassure me of my safety, Eli."

He shrugged, the lack of emotion in his eyes giving me little hope. "Considering the bastard you have for a father, we're probably doing you a favor, sweetheart."

"Eli!"

Levi's shout startled me; a jerk of my hand set my glass wobbling. I focused on grabbing it, on gathering my dishes in shaking hands, on hiding my emotions by turning my back to the men as I walked to the sink. I wouldn't get any help from Eli any more than I would from Levi; I knew that. Still, despite his cool, calm, deadly air, Eli had argued against kidnapping me. That had to count for something, didn't it?

His brother lured you into bed, took your virginity, and is now holding you against your will. Counting on anything—or anyone—connected to Levi is even more foolish than going to bed with him.

I growled at my conscience to shut the hell up and reached for the dish towel to dry my hands, keeping the brothers at the edge of my sight.

"Remi's the one we have to worry about," Eli said, almost too soft for me to catch across the room.

"They can't track you, but they might connect a recent gunshot wound to your successful getaway."

"That why I need you at the hospital."

"Levi—"

He turned on Eli, menace in every line of his body. It was like watching two bulls face off, neither willing to back down. My breath caught in my throat.

"The only way to keep you both safe is to eliminate the threat," Levi grated out. "I'll do that or die trying. No more discussion! Now get back to the hospital and stay aware. I'll keep you updated."

Eli snapped his mouth shut, not looking my way as he stalked to the door. His body blocked my view of the keypad as he entered the code, unfortunately. I stuffed my disappointment down deep, but Levi's smirk when I turned his way said he knew it was there all the same. Bastard.

And speaking of bastards… My father once more took the mic. As I watched, he motioned a younger man forward—a tall model-worthy blond. Perfectly groomed and perfectly stoic. The perfect right-hand man for the governor of Georgia. The sight of him sent ice through my veins. There was only one reason for him to be at the press conference—to play the victimized fiancé and cement his position in the would-be governor's new cabinet.

No, Dad wouldn't do that. He wouldn't.

"Mr. Pellen, how do you feel about your fiancée's disappearance?"

"No!"

The denial left me without thought. Only when the word echoed in my ears did I realize the ammunition it could become. I closed my eyes, scrubbing them hard at the sound of Levi's footsteps growing closer.

"What do you mean, no?"

I dropped my hands to stare blankly at the screen. "No, I'm not engaged."

Levi scoffed. "Of course you are. Your father announced the news last night."

What?

My swollen tongue refused to utter the question, but my brain sped forward, working overtime to sort the threads, reveal the truth. When it hit me, I gasped, choked.

"You knew, didn't you?" My resignation came through loud and clear, answering my own question without Levi's help. "Last night, when you came to the Full Moon, you already knew what he'd planned."

Levi's heat reached me first, that familiar warmth that filled me with despair. When his breath brushed my ear, I gave in to the instinct to hide and closed my eyes.

"Of course I knew, little bird. I know what brand and size panties you wear. I know exactly how the silk looks when it cups the curves of your ass. You bet I caught that conversation about your father's arrangement." A nip of my earlobe sent a zing of shock through my body. "Kyle Pellen is a cold prick, by the way. You could do better."

Arguing was pointless, but I couldn't help myself. "I didn't agree to any engagement."

Levi shrugged. "What Daddy wants, Daddy gets."

"Except when it comes to you, I guess."

The words were bitter. I hated that, hated revealing even the tiniest bit of myself to the man at my side, but there was no holding back. He'd bared my body against my will; why not my emotions too?

A broad, hot palm settled on my stomach, easing the roiling tension there, gentling me like a mare to her stallion. The too tight confines of my throat didn't quite strangle my bark of protest.

"Shh…"

The sexy rumble of his voice broke my threadbare restraint. I bolted.

Levi didn't follow me.

I ignored the disappointment swirling in my gut, right where he'd touched me, and instead watched him cross to the computer desk. It took two tries to get my question out. "What are you doing?"

He jerked the mouse. The screen came alive. I'd never seen the program he opened, couldn't follow what he proceeded to do. I needed to know, though. My life could depend on it.

"Levi?"

He growled at the interruption. Head tilted barely to the side, he directed his words at the desktop. "What?"

"What are you doing?"

A sarcastic grin played around his mouth. "I'm upping the pressure, little bird. Time to watch Daddy lose his cool for once."

Chapter Eleven

Levi went to work—on what, I had no idea. Columns of numbers lined his computer screen, though they didn't look like dollar amounts. We settled into a companionable impasse, if that made any sense, Levi at his computer and me on the couch, watching. I might not understand what I was looking at, but I wanted to stay aware, to see any surprises coming.

That didn't mean I could stay silent.

"If you don't need me anymore, why am I still here?"

I caught half of the smirk that took over Levi's lips as he continued to type. "You've seen too much, Abby. I could never let you go now."

"That sounds like a line from a really bad movie."

His gaze slid to me briefly before returning to the computer monitor. "It is."

The TV was still running, now back on regular programming. I grabbed the remote off the coffee table and began flipping channels. "No Netflix, huh?"

Levi snorted, gaze glued to his computer screen.

"Right. Old-school it is." A quick search showed local channels playing game shows and soap operas. I happened on something old enough to be black-and-white and settled there, remote in hand, butt on the couch. We could've been an old married couple occupying the same room in companionable silence, if not for the fact that I couldn't leave. Oh, and that my companion was a killer.

Surreal didn't even come close…

Only one thing gave me any clue as to the ongoing saga outside our eerily calm oasis: the second monitor, this one on the opposite side of Levi's desk. He turned to it periodically, the angle of his shoulders allowing me to catch a glimpse of a camera feed showing a white room occupied by a narrow hospital bed. The man in the bed looked too big to be lying there, unmoving, a tube and oxygen obscuring most of his face. But his matted hair matched Eli's, who passed occasionally in front of the camera.

So this was Remi.

I might be reluctant to draw attention to myself at the moment, but the three men wormed their way into my thoughts so insidiously I couldn't ignore them. Every time Levi returned to whatever he was working on, I caught the tension around his eyes, the frown, the clenched jaw. Had it been anyone else, I'd have said it was worry or fear, but on Levi?

I glanced at the hospital feed again. Maybe fear wasn't too far off.

Family loyalty was as foreign a concept to me as an assassin's life was. It had certainly never been a factor in my own—Dad had bought my first boyfriend, just like he'd arranged my marriage without my permission. Hell, he hadn't seemed to blink at receiving naked, drugged pictures of me, tied and helpless. What would it be like for these men, so used to violence and danger, to care enough about their brothers, to worry about their safety? To protect each other against the world instead of abandoning the people closest to them?

I couldn't wrap my head around it. I shouldn't want to, either. Levi was as bad as my father. Wasn't he?

When the light began to fade from the windows far over our heads, Levi stood and stretched. I jerked my gaze toward the TV, unwilling to indulge the impulse to drink in his taut body, unwilling to give him another weapon to use against me. I'd given him enough last night. And this morning. Why couldn't he be old? Ugly? Violent? That last was relative, of course, but I couldn't deny that he hadn't truly hurt me. I just wished I could forget the look in his eyes last night as he'd touched me before the mirror, the moment when he'd realized I was a virgin. There had been too much care then, even if he'd faked it. Knowing what he would look like if he wanted me gave him an in I knew he'd exploit if he needed to. And I doubted I'd be able to resist, even knowing it was a lie.

The scuff of Levi's boots drew my attention to where he stood beside the couch.

"I'm headed out for dinner. Any requests?"

"Does it matter?"

"Doesn't have to," Levi said. The even tone of his voice, dripping with patience, settled like scalding water on my head. I bit down hard on my tongue.

"Fratelli's it is, then."

My eyes went wide. Fratelli's was my favorite, my go-to restaurant when I came home late from class and knew Dad wouldn't be home. The Italian restaurant was too lower-class for the next governor of Georgia, but their melt-in-my-mouth pasta and authentic sauces filled the hole inside me that had always craved home-cooked meals around a family dinner table, one that wasn't covered in gold-plated china and crystal.

Levi chuckled, and the knot of anger in my stomach returned.

"If I come home with Fratelli's, are you going to find something else to bash my head in while I'm gone."

I arched a brow in his direction. "If it meant I could keep all the food for myself, I'd cut you in a heartbeat."

Wait, was I really joking with a hit man? With my kidnapper?

This isn't supposed to be fun. He's not a good guy, Abby.

But then, neither was my father, apparently.

"So we're somewhere near Fratelli's then?" I didn't remember any warehouses in that area.

Levi threw me a crooked grin over his shoulder. "That would be telling. Maybe, maybe not." Each step toward the door made his words harder to catch. I strained for each one, praying for a hint, something I could use against him. "Am I driving straight there? Does that mean you can calculate where you are based on the time it takes me to return. Did I order online somehow and arrange to meet someone somewhere along the way? Are they bringing the food to our door and I'm only pretending to leave?" He pulled the door open, paused, glanced at me. "The computer is password protected, by the way. I wouldn't try using it if I were you."

"You're not me," I snapped. Levi had likely never been kidnapped, taunted, used.

I swore sympathy lit in his eyes. "No, I'm not. But I am telling you the truth, Abby."

"Shut up, Levi."

A chuckle drifted back as he closed the door behind him. Jerk.

I did try the computer, but he was right—it was locked down tight. Same with the door, again. Since attacking Levi when he walked in the door would likely end up the same way this morning had, I decided to reserve my final shard of glass for an opportunity that had a better chance of winning. One where Levi was unaware—if that was even possible. With my luck…

I paced the confines of the room until Levi returned. The aroma of creamy alfredo, melted cheese, and warm bread accompanied him, proclaiming the freshness of the food, but I refused to try to calculate how fresh. As Levi had so patronizingly pointed out, there were any number of ways to fool with the timeline. Instead I sat at the table and dug in, feeding my hunger and stuffing the questions away for later.

One great thing about constant takeout and the lack of real dishes? No cleanup. Levi even put the leftovers in the fridge and threw away the trash. I retreated to the bathroom to go through my usual nighttime routine—with all the same supplies; how creepy was that?—and avoid a few more awkward minutes in Levi's presence. Coming back out, I jerked to a stop mere seconds before slamming into Levi's broad, bare chest.

"Time for bed."

Hell no. "I'm not tired."

"Of course not," Levi said. "It's not even eight. But I have things to do."

Did that mean he wouldn't be joining me? Please, God, let that be what he meant. I definitely wouldn't be disappointed. Really.

"What kinds of things?"

He smirked but didn't answer, gripping my wrist instead. Why did his fingers have to be so long? No matter how I twisted and turned, those overlapped digits stayed strong, clamped relentlessly onto my fragile joint. By the time he'd dragged me to the bed, I was panting hard and wishing I'd left my bra and jeans on. Granted, the tank-and-shorts pj combo covered all the important bits, but I still felt oddly naked despite the cotton obscuring my skin.

"What are you doing?" I asked, hating the whiny edge to my voice. When I caught sight of the handcuffs on my side of the bed, the whine turned into panic.

"I'm ensuring that I have a safe night's sleep. It seems you have some tricks up your sleeve." Levi nodded toward the dresser. There, lying on top, was the second shard of glass I'd hidden inside the toilet tank.

A hard bump sent me tumbling onto the bed on my back. "No! Levi, no!" I scrambled backward across the bed. "You've got everything. I don't have anything else that might hurt you, I promise."

Those fingers clamped onto my ankle and pulled. Levi wasn't even breathing hard as he leaned over me. Cold metal circled my wrist, then snicked shut. "And this will make sure of that, won't it?" He threaded the chain around a slat in the headboard.

"No!" I tugged, felt the metal bite into my wrist. "That hurts."

"Then stop pulling. I'm not going to worry about you smothering me in my sleep."

"I'd smother you while you're awake if that was an option. Why wait?"

I had my uncuffed hand outstretched as far as I could get it, trying to evade Levi's capture. I should've known he never took no for an answer. He was more like my father than he wanted to admit. Rather than fighting, he simply laid over me, his heavy weight forcing me still and preventing me from breathing all at once. Panicked instinct had me lifting my legs, kicking up, bucking, anything to get free, get air.

"Uh-uh-uh." Levi rolled, his legs covering mine—and just like that, our bodies lined up. I hadn't realized the wrestling had excited him—or me—until that moment, until his rigid erection settled against my core and a thrill of pleasure shot through me. Levi used that moment of distraction to secure my second wrist.

I let myself go limp beneath him. "Is this the only way you can get any?"

His breath washed across my throat as he nuzzled the sensitive skin there. "I don't need tricks to get pussy, little bird."

"Could've fooled me."

Levi propped himself on his elbows above me. "I didn't need them last night, now did I?"

I closed my eyes, turning my head away from what I was sure was a gloating face. "Just leave me alone, Levi."

A slight squirm settled his hips more firmly in the cradle created by my spread legs. "Believe me, I'm trying. There is nothing more risky than sleeping with a mark, but…"

I couldn't let him finish that sentence; I just couldn't. "I'm not your mark; my father is. Go sleep with him if you want risky."

Levi brought his lips close, rubbed them gently over mine until the skin tingled and I couldn't fight the instinct to open to him. A sharp nip of his teeth stung my lower lip. "Sorry, you're the one in my bed, the one tempting me every time I look at you. If you don't want me, you should stop drawing attention to yourself."

"I didn't—"

"You did." Leaning on one elbow, he drew his calloused fingers along the tender skin of my inner arms, bared by the position he'd cuffed me in. I hadn't realized my tank top had risen until he skipped down to the bare skin of my stomach, teasing higher and higher until he brushed the underside of one breast. "You breathe and I notice, Abby. Your scent, your accusing eyes…" His storm-gray gaze locked with mine. "Stop all those things, and maybe I can ignore you."

I squirmed beneath him, trying to get him off me—or get him closer; I wasn't sure. "I don't want you to touch me."

"I've got a little secret for you," he whispered against my ear. "It doesn't really matter what you want."

Wet heat enveloped my earlobe. I choked on a gasp. The position Levi had me in meant I couldn't escape, couldn't evade his mouth, his fingers, the rub of his erection against my clit every time I moved— and he used all three against me. Just a few short minutes and I was whining beneath him for a far different reason than I had earlier. The fire in my veins threatened to burn me to cinders, no matter its source. I could deny it—deny him—all I wanted, but it wouldn't make the truth disappear. Levi could play me like a violin, and with far superior technique than any musician ever conceived of.

And yet, when he had me on the very brink, when one more stroke against my mouth, my nipple, my clit would send me plunging over the edge—he pulled away.

I lay there, fighting the instinct to writhe on the bed, and glared at him through slitted eyelids.

"Easy." He gave me a somewhat pained smile. That should've made me happy, I knew, but the ache of need inside me left little room for anything else. "Maybe, if you play nice, tomorrow night will end up differently."

I sputtered at that. Levi ignored me, turning to leave instead. He didn't stop until I finally managed to spit out a coherent, "Keep wishing, asshole!"

"I will." With a wink he exited the room, leaving me cuffed and aroused, with no hope of either changing anytime soon.

Chapter Twelve

It was amazing what frustrated lust could accomplish. The longer I lay awake, tied to the bed, the harder I fanned the flames of my anger, until the need to retaliate felt like it would burst from beneath my skin.

And still I lay there.

Levi came in hours later and walked straight to the bathroom. I heard the water come on, and immediately images of him naked, water skimming that beautiful body, filled my mind. Was he just as aroused as I was? He'd been hard when he left me here. If that bastard was taking care of himself in the shower while I was stuck, helpless, cuffed and angry, I would—

Well, I would nothing, apparently. What could I do but lie here and fume? Damn the man.

He didn't speak when he came to bed. Moonlight kissed the naked skin of his torso, skirting the edges of his tattoos and the black outline of his boxers. Ignoring my glare, he leaned over, and I felt the tug on the cuffs as he tested them, the skim of his fingers along the insides as he checked my wrists. His chest was right there above me, the sight and scent drowning my senses, and I had to fight the impulses warring inside—to kiss that delectable expanse of skin or bite hard, sharing my anger and frustration with the man who'd sparked them both.

I counted it a victory that I did neither.

Long minutes later I was rewarded by the sound of Levi's breathing going heavy and deep. Time passed at a snail's pace. My arms began to ache as the night wore on, and sleep slipped farther and farther away. Rolling from one side to the other did little to settle me, nor did my wandering thoughts or the unfamiliar heat in the bed beside me. Eyes closed, eyes open—it didn't matter, so I took advantage of the lack of surveillance and used the time to memorize Levi's features in the faint light descending from the windows.

Most people's faces softened when they slept. Some looked silly, all slack-jawed and smushed into the pillow. Not Levi. If anything his face took on a sharper edge, as if he was working hard to hurry through the night. The full lips, so soft against mine, were thin and tight, a deep vee creasing the skin between his eyebrows. My fingers itched to trace those lines, to soothe the determination into relaxation. My body curved toward him without my consent, seeking out his warmth, his strength, the solid presence I needed to anchor me in the endless night.

If only he could anchor me when I was awake as well.

Levi shifted, the faintest rumble coming from his throat. A dream?

"No!"

The sharp bark startled the lassitude from my body. Definitely a dream, and about nothing pleasant if his growing agitation was any indication. But then, he was an assassin. He'd done plenty to cause nightmares, hadn't he?

The tossing and turning grew worse, and more than once Levi called out in his sleep—nothing I could understand, but the tone… I shivered, the movement clanking my cuffs against the headboard.

Levi's head jerked around. His eyes were open, staring, their expression chillingly blank. I shrank back toward the edge of the bed.

"Levi, wake up. It's okay; it's just me. Wake up."

A feral growl left his lips.

"Levi?" His name wavered as I tipped back, praying I wouldn't fall. "You need to wake up now, okay?"

His eyes narrowed. I blinked, and that quick his hands were around my throat. Long fingers squeezed down, cutting off my air, sending me into a spiral of panic. No matter which way I turned, how I bucked, how hard I tried, I couldn't get air, couldn't speak, could do nothing but stare into those blank eyes and pray Levi woke up before he killed me. My cuffed hands burned from the scrape of the metal on delicate skin, the screaming pain in my lungs echoing in the joints as I instinctively fought to free myself, to escape—but I didn't have my hands. The only free part of my body was my legs, lying like dead weights on the damn mattress.

Instinct flared awake. I lifted, trying to get my knee between us, trying to shove Levi off. His body stiffened, his head turning toward the attack.

My shin hit him square in the face.

With a bellow he fell back. I sucked in air, frantic to fill my vacuum-sealed lungs, to cry and scream and fight, all the things I'd been denied with his hands strangling me. When Levi reared over me, blood dripping from his swollen nose, instinct threw me backward, away from the threat. Away from the fury raging in his eyes.

Air met my back as I fell off the bed. Most of me, anyway. The cuffs trapped my wrists still, sending sudden agony shooting up my arms and finally drawing out the scream I'd held inside too long.

"Fuck! Abby—"

Levi disappeared from view. Moments later a *snick* signaled the release of my handcuffs. Relief howled through my muscles, stealing all my attention as I huddled against the wall, face mashed into the side of the mattress to muffle my crying.

I don't know how long I hid there, making myself as small as possible. Long enough that the fear and pain trickled out with the tears. Long enough that Levi's absence finally registered. And yet I couldn't keep from tensing when the whisper of his footsteps approached.

He didn't touch me, not at first. Instead his breath coasted over my face as he leaned close, his forehead almost against mine, turning the hot trails of my tears to cool paths of relief. Fingertips, rough and yet oh so gentle, followed. His touch, a weapon mere moments ago, now brought the shattered pieces of me back together. I ignored the warning that thought triggered at the back of my mind and shifted closer to the strength surrounding me.

Hard hands pushed behind my back, beneath my legs. A cry escaped when he lifted me, but I had no more than a moment to absorb the heat of his body before he settled me on the bed.

"Wha—"

But Levi was gone before I could get the question out. Probably best. I doubted I could do anything but croak, my throat thick and swollen and still gridlocked with fear.

He returned moments later with a wet washcloth. Ignoring my flinch, he wiped the blood from one wrist, then the other, threw the rag over his shoulder without looking to see where it landed, and turned his attention to my neck. I couldn't hold back a whimper of pain when he tipped my chin up.

"You need some ice for that."

"No, I—"

Levi was already gone. I snarled my frustration, though it came out more like a squeak. "Would you stop walking out on me every time I speak?" I croaked when he got back.

His answer was a dark look. Not promising. The ice pack he settled gently against my throat felt good, at least.

"I take it you've never strangled a woman before."

The dim room couldn't hide the way he paled. "I'm a killer, Abby, not a monster."

Guilt sharpened my voice. "What's the difference?"

Levi's fist tightened, but he didn't drop his stare. I did. "I'm sorry."

My breath caught as the mattress dipped, rolling me toward the middle, toward Levi's big body bathed in the faint moonlight. He stretched his length out against me, tangled his long legs with mine. Hard hands forced my chest to his, wrapped around my back without apology, leaving zero space between us.

I raised the hand not holding the ice pack and let my fingers drift along the midnight shadow roughening his cheeks. Sandpaper scraping me, giving way to the tough skin of his neck, the thin stretch along his collarbone. Every part of the spectrum—that was Levi. Not that he'd admit it.

"You didn't consciously hurt me, Levi." I knew that, even if my anger had used the lie like a lash.

His dark head shook once, denying my words despite their truth. My heart squeezed.

When the massage began, all I could get out was a moan. Muscles rigid from hours spent over my head cried in relief. Was Levi mentally cursing himself? With my face mashed into his chest, I couldn't tell. And if he was, what was I supposed to say? *It's okay, Levi. I know you tried to kill me, but you didn't really mean it.* He'd been the one to cuff me to the bed, render me helpless. Now he was the one taking care of me. The whiplash of emotions only added to the headache pushing to the forefront of my brain.

I pressed harder against him, willing the pain away. As if reading my mind, Levi moved his kneading fingers up the relaxed muscles of my neck and across the back of my aching head. Long moments passed, the only sound the soft rustle of my hair through his hands and the rough thud of his heart beneath my lips. *Thud, thud, thud.*

Tha-thud, tha-thud, tha-thud.

His palm slid along the curve of my cheek. My heart picked up speed too.

"Levi, I—"

A rough tug on my jaw and then his mouth met mine, cutting me off before I could figure out what to say. It didn't matter. Everything inside me stilled at the pressure of his soft lips. His warm, insistent tongue. The unique scent of clean masculine sweat surrounding me. Bit by bit the lingering fear inside me dissipated. My eyes fluttered closed. I'd been dropped into a vat of safety, of peace, and I never wanted to leave.

Levi drowned me, and I let him.

Chapter Thirteen

Levi rolled me onto my back. He followed me over, his weight blanketing my body just as it had last night. Deep in my bones, I recognized the visceral pleasure of it—his heaviness constricting my ribs, my lungs, the hard press of his pelvis against mine. It was as if my entire being surged up, reaching for him, longing for his body to overpower my own. When he licked into my mouth, I caught his tongue, sucking lightly, desperate to keep some small part of him inside me.

Levi jolted as if he'd touched a live wire. A growl burst from his throat as he curled around me, crawling deeper. The pleasure in that sound did something to me, something I didn't want to acknowledge but couldn't ignore—it melted me. So wrong. This was the man who'd kidnapped me, who'd humiliated me, who'd just had his hands around my throat, squeezing the life out of me while remembering someone he'd probably finished the job with in the past, and all I could think about was the ache between my legs and how I wanted him to fill it. It was sick. Twisted. Inexcusable.

Undeniable.

I jerked away from him.

"No, you don't—"

Steely arms and legs caged me in, preventing my escape. The bastard was solid rock, immovable, pinning me tighter than a butterfly on a board, but that's all he did. Just held me beneath him, panting raggedly in my ear, his hand fisted in the neck of my sleep shirt, denying me escape. Like that was anything new. And yet, as he crouched over me, his heavy thighs more effective than any bars or handcuffs, something inside me stilled. As if this was where I was meant to be. What I'd needed all along.

Definitely sick.

Levi bent onto his elbows, planted now on either side of my head, and stared into my eyes. Looking for what? I didn't want to know and certainly hoped he didn't find it. I focused on his chin, that powerful jawline covered in prickly soft stubble. I knew how that stubble felt on my neck, my breasts. My inner thighs. I couldn't stop thinking about it. When Levi bent to run that stubble-roughened chin along the sensitive skin at the top of my breasts, it felt inevitable—and sizzlingly sexy.

I wanted more. And I wanted to run. The story of my life.

Warm lips trailed along the barest hint of cleavage revealed by my tank, my shoulder, the aching skin of my neck. Levi nudged my chin up with his nose, nuzzled into the space I made for him there, his warm breath and tender lips soothing my pain and ripping away any armor I hoped to have against him. At some point that wonderful weight was on me again, grounding me, covering me like a blanket. I was safe. Secure. And it was all an illusion, whether or not I wanted to admit it. Lust didn't change who he was, didn't erase what he'd done to me, either yesterday or mere minutes past. How could I forget that even for a second?

Because of this, something whispered as his mouth slid across my cheek, his breath caressing my skin, his scent filling up the air I breathed. When firm fingers forced my head to turn, to meet his smoke-gray eyes, the inevitability hit me like a blow.

My swallow hurt.

Voice dropped to a mere rough whisper, he asked, "Do you want me, Abby?"

My nipples tightened against his solid chest, begging where my mouth would not, where it was safe to beg—where he wouldn't see. But he could feel; I knew because his back arched, rubbing his firm muscles against my hard tips. A moan escaped against my will.

He didn't gloat; he kissed me. The surge of his tongue between my lips became the perfect echo for the roll of his body, the thrust of his arousal against my belly. Want couldn't describe what I felt then—it paled in comparison to the fire Levi ignited inside me, the hunger that roared out of control, begging to be sated. Only one man had ever been able to do this to me, snatch me away from right and wrong, expectations and propriety. Only Levi stripped away the proper veneer to reveal the woman inside. I hadn't known she existed until now. And maybe she shouldn't, but God help me, I couldn't escape her any more than I could escape him.

"Tell me, Abby, right now. Do you want me?" The sweet stroke of his fingers along my throat, across my lips, coaxed me to answer.

"Yes." The word was ragged, barely audible, but there nonetheless.

"Then let me have you. Be the brave little bird you've been all along."

I snorted. "You've got me confused with some other girl, Levi." I'd never been brave. Reckless, maybe, but look where that had gotten me—in bed with a killer.

A killer whose irises darkened at my words. He took me in for long moments, displeasure narrowing his eyes. I held my breath until a faint smile curved one corner of his mouth, the tiny tilt completely transforming his expression. "I'm definitely not confused."

He abandoned words for action then. Caressed my bare skin with ruthless hands and lips. Nipped the shuddering flesh. Laved it with the lingering trace of his tongue. I watched, unable to look away, as he dipped his head, his teeth catching a fold of flesh between shoulder and breast, and sucked lightly. And I knew. God help me, but I knew right then I'd give in. He was killing me not with a knife or gun, but with kindness. I couldn't resist it, didn't want to. My soul soaked it up like poisoned nectar, sweet and deadly, and all I wanted was more.

My rigid muscles relaxed. Levi eased a hand under the hem of my shirt and pushed up, even as his body moved lower. Tiny bites teased the underside of my breast, then trailed toward the other. "You were built to pleasure." His lips brushed shivering skin on his relentless journey up to one hard nub. "Let me give you pleasure." Harsh breath hit my nipple.

With a whimper, I arched my back.

"That's it, Abby; that's so it." A hot lick. A soft bite. "Relax for me. Let me have you. Please."

The last word was no more than a breath, but it shot through me like an arrow. I wasn't the only one needing here; Levi did too. I wasn't alone, not in this.

When his warm mouth surrounded my nipple, I stopped caring about right and wrong, need and domination. The rhythmic suction took over my world, but I wanted more than my own pleasure. I wanted his. My palm trailed shyly along the thick ridge of muscle protecting his rib cage, the curve of his hip, that small hollow between belly and groin. Levi lifted his lower body as if I'd requested entry, and I eased farther down, brought my fingers to the curls at his pelvis, arrowing down to the base of that thick stalk. A grunt escaped him as I gripped, tugged, explored.

He switched breasts, but when my thumb slid along the narrow slit at the end of his cock, he released me to choke back a curse. I didn't catch the whole thing; I was too busy holding my breath as he slid down, down, out of my reach, his shoulders making a place for him between my thighs. And then his mouth was on my clit and I couldn't concentrate on anything but panting and clutching the sheets, praying I didn't pass out—I didn't want to miss a single second of this. Without permission my hips tilted, pulsing in time to the rhythm of his licks, urging him on, begging for him to come closer, deeper.

When his tongue speared inside me, I saw stars. When he did it again, the stars exploded behind my eyelids.

The sharp edge of teeth surrounding my most sensitive spot greeted me when I returned to awareness. "That was way too fast," Levi gritted out.

My chuckle was hoarse. "Not my fault."

A hard suck jerked my hips off the bed. Levi shook his head, sending pre-orgasmic tingles from my clit to my core to my nipples. Even my lips tingled. I recognized the sensation now, welcomed it and the oblivion it brought with it.

Levi eased back. "That was the fault of your innocence. You'll learn."

I highly doubted it.

My eyes slid closed as I listened to Levi shift. His knees pushed beneath mine, kneeling between my spread legs. One moment I was flat on my back; the next Levi jerked me up his legs, planting my rear on his bent thighs and positioning me perfectly for his heavy surge inside my body. A scream ripped through my lungs.

I was wet, but I was also not that far from a virgin. The tight fit had sweat breaking out on my forehead. Thank God Levi simply settled as deep as he could possibly go, then stopped. No thrusting, no withdrawal, just long minutes where my body adjusted to the thick width of his invading erection. The hard flick of his fingers against my softening nipples reminded me to breathe. When I sucked in air, he rewarded me by rolling the tender tips between thumb and forefinger, one at a time, bringing them back to rigid awareness.

Hunger flickered back to life inside me.

It was the palm on my lower belly that held my attention, though. Levi pressed, the weight forcing any space inside me to disappear, making the tight fit of my body around his even tighter. I was full—overfull. Overwhelmed.

My hunger surged higher, strangling me.

I arched into his touch, the move pressing my clit against the thatch of hair above his cock. Tingles shot through me once more. "Levi?"

As if that was the signal he needed, he pulled back—so, so slowly, the bastard. A quick surge inside, hard enough to mash my clit against his pelvis and draw out a whimper of need, and then he was retreating again, torturously slow. His rhythm took over my world, every bit of awareness centered on the wet glide of his cock and the aching press of his pelvic bone and the hard tugs and rolls and pinches on my nipples. Nothing else mattered; nothing else existed. All that I was and all I would ever be was wrapped up in this man's body, his actions, his heat. I lost myself in him just like I'd feared, the anticipation building and building and building until I couldn't stop begging for relief, until my words became screams of frustration and desperation and overwhelming desire…

Until he leaned over to kiss me, ground so tight and hard into my body that we truly became one, and my world detonated into oblivion.

Chapter Fourteen

The bed was empty when I woke the next morning. The sheet next to me was cold—Levi had been up for a while already. Last night's climax could be felt in the unfamiliar soreness of my body, but no matter how hard I tried, I couldn't remember going to sleep. Maybe I hadn't; maybe I'd simply passed out after that mind-blowing peak, and that had been that.

Loss dragged at me as I slid from the bed. Would I ever get to experience the afterglow part of sex with Levi? Find out if he was the cuddling type or the roll-over-and-snore type? I'd probably never know if all the sex was like the last two times.

And really, did I want to know any more about him than I already did? That would just be one more memory to haunt me after all this was over, and there were already more than enough.

I trudged into the bathroom and showered. Turning my face up to the water helped blast away the cobwebs of sleep, but it couldn't erase the questions, couldn't quiet my overactive mind. I could add armor, though—clothes, makeup. Anything to patch up the holes last night had torn in my defenses. Levi wasn't a good guy any more than my father was, and I was asking to be screwed over if I didn't remember that. What was between Levi and me wasn't love or even affection, just sex.

Damn good sex, but still…

When I left the bedroom, Levi was standing at the stove, his back to me. The smell of bacon and pancakes filled the air. So did curses. Despite the growling of my traitorous stomach, I approached the source of both with caution, but the closer I went, the more I struggled to hold back a laugh.

"Did we finally find something you aren't perfect at?"

Levi swung around, a plastic spatula gripped in his fist like a sword. The kitchen certainly looked as if he'd gone to battle. Flour and pancake batter coated the counter, bacon grease splattered the backsplash, and both were smeared over Levi's T-shirt in liberal amounts.

Laughter bubbled out before I could stop it. "Need help, or have you vanquished your foe?"

Levi growled. "Don't push your luck, little bird."

Maybe a push or two was exactly what this demigod of the criminal underworld needed, just to help him remember he was part human. I smiled my sweetest smile.

Levi narrowed his eyes at me, but I didn't miss how they dropped to trace my body as I moved the rest of the way into the kitchen. I ignored the flame that look sparked in my belly and waved a hand at the mess. "So…what's the occasion?"

Levi turned back to the stove to flip pancakes. "We're celebrating."

If he was this grim when he celebrated, I'd hate to see him at a funeral. "Celebrating what?"

Starting at one end of the skillet, he began turning the bacon. "Your father's campaign fund made a generous donation last night."

I blinked, the spark of happiness inside me flickering out. What had I expected? Surely not some gushing praise for screwing like bunnies after he almost killed me. Because that would be stupid. And dangerous, especially if I ignored the "he almost killed me" part. Last night had been about releasing tension and sating needs that had no other outlet at the moment. Nothing else. *Remember that, Abby. No matter what happens, for God's sake, remember that.*

This wasn't a romance and Levi wasn't a hero. Of course he was happy about some massively reckless step forward in his plan to take my father down.

Did I really want to know details?

"To whom?"

Levi finished with the bacon and turned to prop a hip against the counter, grinning at me. "So proper. 'To whom?'"

I shrugged a shoulder. Being proper was a survival skill in my world.

"To the bank account of a well-known mob boss."

I winced.

"How much?"

Levi turned back to the food. "Enough that he won't feel like celebrating with pancakes."

The amount really didn't matter in the long run—my dad came from wealth, and he was good at building his own. Whatever Levi had taken wouldn't hurt him. It was the blow to Derrick Roslyn's reputation at the start of his campaign that would hurt. But for Levi to reach his objective, someone had to know about the contribution.

"He won't let information like that leak; you know that, right?"

Levi transferred pancakes to a plate, his lips still curved into a smile. He was enjoying this, obviously. The win, not the cooking. Too bad the course he'd set us on made my stomach hurt. "Oh, it'll leak. Don't you worry."

All I could do was worry, not that the men around me, caught up in their power games, gave a thought to that or the ulcer I was likely developing, as long as they got what they wanted.

Levi had breakfast on the table in minutes. When I didn't move to the place he'd set for me, a growl escaped him. "Sit."

As I cut into the fluffy pancakes with a plastic knife and fork, Levi set a steaming cup of coffee on the table next to my plate.

"Cream and sugar?" As if I really needed to ask—the man knew my most intimate secrets. But something in my aching chest wouldn't allow me to simply accept the kind gesture of providing food. Maybe the same ridiculously high-school part of me that had wanted him happy over us, not getting something else over on my father.

There is no us.

"Cream and sugar and a splash of coffee," he agreed, confirming the stupidity of my question.

I stuffed a bite of pancake in my mouth and ignored my mocking conscience.

We ate in silence, Levi seeming totally relaxed, me pressing down my resentment and frustration until I thought I'd choke. Unwilling to let the pancakes go to waste, I grasped around for a distraction. "How is Remi this morning?"

Levi forked up several pieces of pancake. "The same."

"What happened to him?" Maybe if I knew that, I could make sense of the rest.

"Your father sent someone after me. They missed."

No wonder he wanted my father dead. I didn't think that was the whole picture, though. Levi had been the one to accept the job. He'd also been the target when Remi was almost killed. Guilt at bringing danger too close to his brother would be just as powerful a motivator as my father's actions, whether Levi would admit it or not.

I twirled a piece of bacon between my fingers. "Why was my father trying to have you killed? You worked for him, right? That would make you an asset, not a target."

"If I'd taken the job, yes."

The bacon clattered onto my plate. "You refused him?"

Levi chewed his bite for long enough that I thought he wasn't going to answer. Finally he swallowed, took a sip of coffee. Then, "Not at first."

Not a good guy, remember?

"How did he hire you?"

"If you ever need an assassin, I'll tell you."

I snorted. "Oh, I need one now, thanks. There's this guy that needs taking out. He has a thing for kidnapping women, so…you know…he's not an innocent. I've heard you have rules about that." Not that I fully bought the principled hit-man bit, but…

Levi grinned at my sass, but the humor turned serious as he glanced toward the computer. "Wait till

Remi's better; then one of my brothers might do the job for free."

It might be too late by then.

"So he hired you. And?"

Levi threw me an impatient look. "Why do you want to know, Abby?"

"Maybe because whatever happened between the two of you has totally fucked up my life."

"Was it really that good to begin with?"

No. But maybe that was the sex talking.

I thought back over the hours of my life since Levi had walked into it. *Definitely the sex talking.*

Not that I'd be sharing that. But the gnawing need to understand what had led us to this moment, here, at his table, eating pancakes and waiting for the next bomb to drop, refused to let me go. "What happened, Levi? Just tell me."

He picked up his empty plate and crossed to the sink, and I thought that was the end of the discussion. Then, his back still to me, he spoke.

"A couple of months ago I was offered a contract. I never take a contract without knowing everything there is to know about both the client and the mark."

How had he gotten information on my father? I couldn't imagine career politician Derrick Roslyn making the contact directly; it would be far too risky. "Were you surprised that a potential governor contacted you?"

Levi turned around but didn't rejoin me at the table. "No."

Considering what he did and the fact that powerful people invariably had enemies—or obstacles in their way—that was probably the truth.

"What surprised me was the mark."

"Why?"

"He was a nobody." Levi leaned against the counter, his hands braced on the edges at his hips. What the position did for his broad, heavy chest threatened to derail my train of thought. "A trucker with no connections to organized crime, no connections to Roslyn…no connections to anything. Clean record. Liked by his employers. Just a hard-working, middle-class, struggling trucker. He had no family, nothing."

"He could have hidden a crime."

"Sure he could've"—Levi shook his head—"but he hadn't. The man was squeaky clean. If someone is dirty, there's always a hint somewhere, and I'm very good at finding it. Very good."

"So this man wasn't dirty. Why did my father want him dead, then?"

Another head shake. Levi stared across the room, his gray eyes unseeing. "I didn't know. Didn't want to know. But I refused the contract."

"Why?"

Levi shot me an expectant look.

Right. Never harm the innocent. A killer with a conscience. If it was true, Levi had more honor than my father had displayed in a lifetime.

"We both know how much Derrick Roslyn likes the word no." A wry grin tilted Levi's full mouth. "He set up a separate contract under a false name. Every first meet, we always have backup. Remi was my backup."

"And he was hit when my father tried to kill you."

Christ. If I'd had any hope that Levi might change his mind, drop this crazy plan to ruin my father's life, it shattered in that moment. Levi might not care about much, but his brothers? He'd die defending them—or avenging them.

My father didn't stand a chance.

A sudden alarm blaring from the computer jerked Levi's attention in that direction. Heart leaping into my throat, I stumbled out of my chair. "What? What's that?"

Levi was already rounding the island on a run. "Fucking trouble."

Chapter Fifteen

Levi had his phone out and dialing before he reached the computer. I followed, the sound of my heart thumping in my throat blocking out his curses. The screen I'd spent so much time watching yesterday lit up just as Eli answered his cell.

"Yeah."

"They've hacked the records."

Eli cursed under his breath.

I stepped up behind Levi. "What does that mean?"

"I set a program to watch, make sure no one accessed Remi's hospital records who wasn't supposed to," Levi said grimly, taking a seat at the computer and beginning to type something faster than I could even track.

"And they did?"

"They did."

But… "How do you know it's… How do you know it's Derrick?" Not *my father*. If all of this was true and he really was the bastard Levi said he was—and I was running out of excuses not to believe him—I no longer owed the man my loyalty. I never had, really. I'd just been too afraid of the consequences of saying no.

Could those consequences really be any worse than being kidnapped? Used? But then, my father had used me all my life, if for nothing else than to further his career. At least Levi gave me something in return.

Or maybe I was justifying all of this so I didn't go insane.

Levi growled—at the computer or me, I wasn't sure. "I know it's Derrick because it is."

I didn't think a man like Levi had only one enemy, but right now wasn't the time to argue. And if my father had discovered Levi's little trick this morning, he'd likely put the pressure on to get some answers. From what I'd gathered the past couple of days, Remi was his only access to those answers.

Onscreen, Eli rubbed a hand across his spiky hair, his gaze on Remi lying in the bed. "Any idea on timeline?"

"I'm not gonna risk projecting—I want him out of there now."

Eli's eyes went wide, frantic. "Fuck no!"

"We don't have a choice," Levi barked. "They could already be on their way, probably are. We have to get him out of there."

Eli waved a hand over his brother's still form. "How the hell am I supposed to do that? He's still in a coma, Levi. He can barely breathe on his own."

"Then find someone who can keep him stable, and bring them with you."

Kidnap someone else? A protest lodged itself on my tongue, but I looked at that screen and bit it back. Remi was lying there, so still and pale, with wires and tubes and monitors surrounding him, invading him. Completely helpless. At the mercy of anyone who came into that room. Someone could be on their way to torture or kill him right now, and he had no defenses, nothing and no one to save him except his brothers.

I looked at him, and something inside me crystallized in that instant. Could I choose between these men and my father?

At that moment, I not only could; I did.

On his central monitor, Levi brought up a series of camera feeds like Remi's, only these showed corridors and entries around the hospital. One centered on the nurses' station, presumably outside Remi's room. Levi zoomed in on the desk.

"The blonde," he said into his phone. "Prep him first."

Onscreen, Eli nodded.

I turned away. I might understand what they were doing, but I'd been on the receiving end. I knew how scared that nurse would be. Deep, slow breaths did nothing to calm the churning in my stomach. "Can't you just ask for her help?"

Levi grunted. I guessed that was my answer.

This was real. Really real. Pain in my hands alerted me to the fact that, without conscious thought, they had fisted tight, the nails digging into my palms. I pressed them in harder, desperate to ground myself against the panic surging inside me.

When I turned back to the monitors, Eli was shoving his belongings into a backpack. "Where to?"

Levi switched screens. "Here for now. If they've blown you, they'll likely find this place eventually, but we should have a few days to stabilize Remi first. I don't want to risk an unprepared location in his state. We'll get things ready here."

We? Why had Levi said *we?* Did he mean him and me, as if the two of us were a team working together to take care of his brother? Last night he couldn't trust me to sleep beside him without handcuffs, and now we were a *we*?

If Levi realized what he'd said—or the sheer ridiculousness of the words—he didn't show it. He seemed oblivious to everything but Eli and his computer, his frantic clicking providing a staccato counterpoint to my footsteps as I paced behind him. "Call the nurse in when you're ready," he said. "I'll make sure she's the only one at the station. You drive, and she can take care of Remi."

"How do you know?" Eli asked with a worried glance at his brother.

"I know. Don't worry about her; just steal an ambulance and go, damn it. I'll take care of erasing your tracks. No one will know where you end up."

Eli quit arguing. Finished with his own things, he circled Remi's bed, gathering what equipment he could put on the narrow spaces on either side of his brother, avoiding the major stuff. No more than a minute passed before he lifted the call button, glanced into the camera, then pressed down firmly.

Levi switched back to his view of the nurse's station. Though I had no idea how he'd accomplished it, the blonde was the only one at the desk now. She glanced to her right, presumably at the signal from Remi's room, then stood.

She was tall. It was an incongruous thought, but it hit me all the same. Tall and curvy; her scrubs couldn't hide that fact. Her hair was pulled back in a ponytail that allowed me to see her face, all pale skin and innocent eyes. Had my eyes looked like that when Levi found me? They didn't now.

I pushed the thought away and held my breath, the heavy beat of my heart loud in my ears.

Levi clicked off the nurses' station, splitting the screen between Remi's room and the view of the hallway just as the nurse came into view. Behind her, at the bend of the corridor, a door opened and a tall, dark man stepped out. Black clothes, black shoes, light skin, but it could barely be seen because the black ball cap he wore obscured his downturned face. Something about his body language, the way he held himself reminded me of someone, something…

A whimper escaped before I could clamp my lips shut. He reminded me of Levi.

I wasn't the only one to pick up on the threat. Levi's shoulders went tight, just like my lungs. "Eli, target approaching. She's got a tagalong."

Eli had been intimidating standing here in the room with me, almost as intimidating as Levi, but the knowledge that they were killers, dangerous men, had remained in the surreal part of my brain, known but not truly understood. Even on the grainy camera feed, though, I could see the mask drop down, see him go into warrior mode. His expression hardened, his body seeming to expand as tension built. Walking to stand behind the door, he reached for his belt, removed a knife, and flicked it open, the silver catching the bright hospital lights as he waited.

My lungs burned, protesting my held breath.

The door to Remi's hospital room opened, its solid surface blocking Eli from view. The nurse entered.

Without warning, Eli's hand snaked out to grab her wrist. A hard jerk pulled the woman out of the way as her shadow followed her into the room. Eli's knife flashed as the blade struck the man in the chest.

Eli's opponent grunted, bowing around the knife, but the penetration was off—the blade didn't go in like it should. Levi cursed, but I wasn't sure why. My gaze was glued to the screen as Eli pivoted his blade and slashed across the man's neck, just missing as his opponent flung himself backward. Eli followed, and the fight was on, not just for Eli's life, but his brother's. The two men wrestled for the knife, their hands both fisted around the handle, their legs and elbows and heads becoming weapons. I'd never seen a no-holds-barred fight for survival; the brutality shocked me. The fact that both of them managed to avoid the knife? Even more unbelievable.

The nurse didn't appear to have the same issue. Even as the men toppled onto Remi's legs, she was rounding the corner of his bed, bending at first one end, then the other. Eli shoved his opponent into the opposite wall, and the woman used the opportunity to shift Remi's bed into the far corner of the small hospital room. It wasn't much of a buffer, but she gave him what she could, then climbed up to crouch over her patient's legs, drawing something from her pocket.

Eli's head jerked in her direction, taking in the changes in a single glance. His eyes went dark and dangerous as he gripped his opponent's arms, shifted to one side, then threw a leg behind the other man's. Off-balance, the attacker fell back, his head and shoulders landing once more on Remi's bed. Like a snake striking, the nurse stabbed down quickly, revealing the needle in her hand. Whatever she injected the man with worked immediately—he slid down to the floor next to the bed, not making a sound as Eli kicked him hard in the ribs.

Levi released a pleased grunt. "Get him out of there, brother."

Eli dragged the now unconscious attacker out of the path of the bed. His mouth formed the words *I'm trying, asshole*, readable despite the lack of sound. Levi chuckled.

The sound was cut off when a red warning box appeared on the computer screen in front of him.

Chapter Sixteen

"Daddy's on the ball."

Levi's tone held a note of admiration, a warrior seeing the brilliance of their enemy's move in battle. I really didn't want to know what my father had done to earn the admiration of an assassin, but I did want to know what would fuck up my life next, so I asked.

"What now?"

"Derrick has scheduled a press conference. Apparently your situation needs an update."

Sure it did. Or Derrick needed to keep his face—and his "concern" for his daughter—in the news.

The fact that he was holding another press conference didn't surprise me. What did was that I could care less. It would all be lies anyway—about me, certainly about him and how he "cared" about his daughter. It wasn't worth listening when you couldn't trust anything that was said. But apparently Levi felt the need to listen, because he clicked the on button for a blank monitor to his right and, moments later, what looked like a live feed from the same press room the last conference had occurred in appeared on the screen. The grainy texture and forty-five degree angle told me this was likely a security feed Levi had tapped into. The faint murmur of voices and a few moving figures in the seats came through, but no one stood onstage—the meeting hadn't begun. Yet.

I turned away from the screen. The desk. Levi. Nothing made sense anymore, and that fact didn't change no matter how much I paced. My father had always been a liar, but not about me. Or so I thought. Bad men were always bad, but Levi and his brother were trying to save their sibling from someone who'd…what? Wanted to torture a man in a coma? Use him as bait? Simply question him? Would he have hurt the nurse? He'd followed her into the room; surely he couldn't have left her as a witness to criminal activity. Which was worse, that their mystery man might've hurt her or that Eli had kidnapped her?

I didn't know, and the lack of answers was pounding against the inside of my skull so hard a gallon of Tylenol probably couldn't ease the pain of it.

"Be still," Levi snapped.

The command startled me out of my churning thoughts, igniting the anger that lay in wait just beneath the surface of my control. "Fuck off."

I realized my mistake immediately. My muscles went tight, my chest squeezing with fear. But the blow my instincts screamed was coming, didn't. Levi turned in his seat, so so slowly, to pin me with that silver gaze. Molten silver now—he was as angry, or angrier, than I could ever be.

"Sit. The fuck. Down. We don't want to get the handcuffs out again, do we?"

A chill shivered down my spine. Hadn't we learned our lesson about the handcuffs last night?

I stared at Levi's stone-hard expression. No, apparently not.

One dark eyebrow arched. I scurried toward a chair, shame eating at my insides.

He didn't wait for my butt to hit the cushion. He didn't have to; my obedience was expected, therefore it would happen. He turned back to the screen and his brothers with a quiet grunt of satisfaction that made me wish I had something hard to throw at his head, like a brick.

Levi probably had a steel plate for a skull anyway, knowing my luck. Asshole.

While I simmered in irritation—and admittedly, a little fear—Levi went back to work. He focused on his computer screens and Eli's occasional comments through his cell with narrow eyes and a clenched jaw. I got it, even if I didn't want to: he needed to keep his attention on his brothers, and I was a distraction. That didn't mean I liked being afraid.

But I focused on the computer screens too, watching the trio's progress on the video feeds over his shoulder. Eli and the nurse seemed to race through the bowels of the hospital, one at each end of Remi's bed. Levi typed rapid-fire on the keyboard, clicking the mouse faster than a striking snake, and though I couldn't tell definitively what he was doing to help his brother, I assumed he was in some way clearing their path just as he'd made certain the nurse he wanted for Remi had answered Eli's call. Halls miraculously cleared. Locked doors opened. And in the half-empty garage, an ambulance stood parked in a dark corner. I couldn't help noticing that Eli now wore a hat very similar to the man he'd fought, his face hidden, only the nurse identifiable. He knew what he was doing, just as Levi did. A professional.

My headache resurged with a vengeance, tightening around my skull like a vise.

Remi's eyes never opened as they loaded him into the ambulance. I waited, breathless and conflicted, for the nurse to argue, to run, but she kept her focus and her steady hands on her patient the entire time. Only when Eli went to close up the back doors did she speak.

Levi growled at the minute delay. "Get her secured and get out of there, E. You've got sixty seconds."

If Eli responded, I couldn't see it. I didn't see the handcuffs either, not until one was wrapped securely around the woman's wrist. Eli secured the second to the rail of Remi's bed, then shut the ambulance doors.

Relief and disgust surged like bile up the back of my throat. I turned away from the desk as I swallowed back my nausea. Only the sound of Derrick's voice brought me back to awareness.

It was anticlimactic, really. There was nothing new on the abduction—big surprise. So why was Derrick holding a press conference?

As if asking the question flipped on a light in my brain, I knew. "He's establishing an alibi, isn't he?"

Levi grunted a response. When I stood, turning toward the desk, I could see what looked like traffic camera feeds on the monitors to Levi's left. He scanned them continuously, maybe tracking Eli's progress through the city. How would they hide an ambulance with so many eyes on the roads? If Levi could follow it, surely someone—

Why the hell are you worrying about that, Abby? Worry about seeing where the ambulance is going, to your *location!*

As if I'd shouted out loud, Levi clicked a button, and one by one the feeds turned to static. I should be surprised—absolutely nothing in my life was under my control, right?—but I couldn't help the burn of tears at the backs of my eyes.

"Establishing alibis is what we do," Levi said, flicking a glance at my father on-screen. "If we're not good at covering our tracks, that is."

If you're not a pro, in other words. Hardly comforting.

"Councilman Roslyn," a female voice called. Levi's spine went tight and straight, the air around him seeming to vibrate with sudden excitement. I didn't know why, and I really didn't want to remedy my lack of knowledge, but, again, zero control…

I moved to stand behind Levi so I could see the screen on his right.

"Yes, Ms. Downing?"

Derrick was staring at a petite blonde reporter, consternation creasing his brow.

"Councilman, it seems the abduction of your daughter is not the only concern plaguing your run for governor of the state of Georgia. Our office received a tip this morning that a substantial donation was made from your account to a business we know from FBI sources is considered a front for mob activity. Care to comment?"

A mottled red flush rose up Derrick's neck, into his cheeks—not embarrassment. Rage. I held my breath and glanced at Levi. Pleased gray eyes locked with mine.

"See? You have to be good at covering your tracks," he said.

I didn't answer; I couldn't. The flood of emotion that swamped me right then was too heavy, too confusing, too…everything. Satisfaction, anger, loss, worry, fear—it crashed into me like a brick wall tumbling down, smothering me, making it impossible to breathe. I couldn't fight it, couldn't hide from those all-knowing eyes, so I did the only thing I could. I retreated. Turned around without a word and walked out of the living room. The bedroom was quiet, especially with the door closed, but even so I climbed onto the bed, curled up, and dragged the covers over my head.

Then, like a child, I closed my eyes and pretended I'd disappeared.

Chapter Seventeen

It was the shouting that woke me. Shoving the blankets off my face, I blinked hazily as the ceiling came into focus and the noises from the living room began to make some sense. When I realized exactly what they were, I shot to my feet.

Bad move.

I must've slept deeper than I'd thought, because it took a couple of minutes to gain my equilibrium, but then I was moving toward the door, my heart pounding in my throat. Instinct urged caution, but I needed to know, to see—that Levi was here, safe; that Eli had gotten his brother here all right; that the woman he'd coerced was unharmed. Of course, from the sounds of it, her lungs were performing above and beyond expectation, so…

The living room was chaos. Eli struggled to guide the bed Remi still lay on toward the back wall of the warehouse while Levi struggled with the nurse. She, apparently, had no problems fighting her way out of her captivity. Of course, she hadn't been drugged like I had, but still, I envied her her courage. If forced to lay bets on who would win, I might actually consider betting on her.

Levi lost his patience quickly, gripping her arms tight and shaking her. "Shut the fuck up and do your job before I decide you're more trouble than you're worth!"

The woman went still, glaring up at him through the tousled strands of her thick blonde hair even as she cringed away from his hold. I didn't blame her. Levi's capacity for either bullshit or distraction seemed to lower in direct proportion to his brothers' involvement and/or safety, as seen by the way he'd snapped at me earlier, the one and only time he'd lost his temper since I'd been here. That look directed at me would've had me wetting my pants, effectively wiping out the urge to interfere on my fellow captive's behalf. I circled the couple warily and went to help Eli.

Remi lay still, not even a flutter of his long blond eyelashes indicating that he knew he was being moved. Eli's mouth tightened at the sight of me, but he moved to Remi's head without a word, maneuvering his end toward the back wall as I took my place at Remi's feet. We worked together, Eli pulling and me pushing, until we reached the wall near the end of the kitchen cabinets. A mechanical whir sounded, and a section of the wall recessed, then slid to one side.

What the…

Eli continued backward as if nothing unusual had occurred. I glanced over my shoulder at Levi. He was staring down the nurse, but his left hand had lifted, pointing toward us, holding what looked like a key fob. A remote. One that opened a door I hadn't been able to find no matter how hard I'd looked—God, had it only been two days ago?

Remi's bed slid smoothly through the opening.

The nurse's footsteps echoed as she marched in directly behind me. Guess Levi won the stare down.

"We have to get him still and stabilized," she announced. Barked orders lashed the air as everything from the position of the bed to the lack of tables to hold the equipment were questioned. Apparently the stare down was the only thing she'd conceded.

Eli positioned the bed headfirst against a side wall, the light from a high window spilling onto Remi's blanket-covered feet. The nurse immediately bent over him, one hand on his chest, the other beginning to move equipment from the bed to the floor. "Tables!"

"Demanding little thing, ain't she?" Eli smirked, but I noticed he hustled for the door. I moved to the opposite side of the bed to help settle Remi in. Levi stood, a silent, intimidating presence as the three of us made short work of arranging his brother's new room.

"Eli."

Eyes still on Remi, Eli fished in his jeans pocket at Levi's demand. Only when he pulled out a set of keys did he turn for the door and rush out. The nurse, whose name tag I now noticed said *MARRONE*, ignored everything but her patient. Because he was the only thing she could control? I'd certainly felt that way, though with fewer options. I wanted to reassure her, to tell her no one would hurt her, no matter how much of a badass Levi seemed to be, but she wouldn't believe me, not right now. I knew that all too well.

"What now?" I asked, automatically adopting the hushed tone people used in hospitals and funeral homes. Levi had no such compulsion.

"We wait," he said gruffly.

Nurse Marrone's head whipped around. "I am not waiting here."

"Well, you're not going anywhere, so..." Levi shrugged.

Beneath the flush of anger, the woman's face went sheet-white. "I'm not waiting. I have a daughter. I have to go home. You've got two choices: let me go, or I'll make your life a living hell until I escape."

Levi crossed his arms over that broad chest, one eyebrow arching as if the nurse amused him. "Only two choices? I could think of a few more."

I was actually beginning to understand him. Scary thought. Our new friend didn't, and Levi's statement lit her shortened fuse like a fire-breathing dragon lighting a candle.

She charged.

Levi cursed.

The woman might be tall, but she was nowhere near strong enough to subdue a man like Levi. Short minutes later he had her trapped against his chest, thick arms caging her ribs as she kicked and screamed and bucked. Levi's jaw was clenched, anger and frustration mixing in his eyes as he fought to hold her, and I found myself wondering for the briefest moment if it turned him on, if the woman in his arms was making his body react the way it had to me.

Christ. I seriously needed to get my head on straight before I started fantasizing about Levi being Prince Charming with a freaking castle in the clouds. A Prince Charming who could snap my neck without a thought. Hers too.

"Stop!"

The nurse froze, fear shimmering like tears in her gaze as it locked onto me. Behind her, Levi glared, his lips opening, the explosion barreling down toward me. He needed a target—his world wasn't cooperating, and it was pissing him the hell off. Really he should be used to it after me. I would've laughed if I wasn't certain it would be the last straw, possibly for all of us.

I glared right back. "Just tell her."

His expression said he'd rather strangle me, but I ignored it. "Tell her why she's here and when she can go. You worry about your brothers; she's worried about her kid. You get that, I know you do."

He didn't move for long seconds. The slow release of his arms told me how very reluctant he was to cooperate, but he did it anyway, eyes narrowed on me instead of the woman in front of him. I braced myself for whatever alpha bastard bullshit he was about to spill.

"You're getting pushy," he barked.

I shrugged, fighting back a swallow of fear. Not that there was anything to swallow; my throat was as dry as a desert, my heart pounding so hard against my ribs I thought they might crack. But I had nothing to lose, right? No one had helped me, but I could help her and her daughter. No child deserved to wonder where their parent was, if they'd ever return. If they cared enough about you to try.

"What's your name?" I asked her.

The woman rubbed her hands up and down arms that I knew probably ached from Levi's grip. "Leah. Leah Marrone."

"Leah." I nodded in what I hoped was a reassuring way, then cocked a brow at Levi. "Tell her," I said again, the words rasping the sides of my throat. "Please."

He crossed his arms over his chest. "What'll you give me if I do?"

Bastard. I didn't respond aloud; I didn't have to. He knew anything he wanted was his for the taking—hell, he'd proved it more than once. And I was fooling myself if I thought I wouldn't give in.

Levi's chuckle said he knew it too.

Leah stepped away, turning to face off with her enemy once more, though I noticed she kept a healthy distance. "I have to go," she said.

Levi grunted. "I get that. And you will." He glanced at Remi, eyes haunted. "Help us stabilize him, tell us what he needs, and I'll make sure you get back to your daughter safely."

Leah looked to me as if for reassurance.

"It's okay. They won't hurt you."

The words burned in my throat, but if I believed anything anymore, I believed them.

She didn't; her snort said so. "How would you know?"

"Because they took me too."

The surprise that flashed across her face made my cheeks heat. Levi had kidnapped me, and I was vouching for him. Standing up for him.

Don't forget sleeping with him.

I ignored my bitch of a conscience and held Leah's eyes. "He'll keep his word," I assured her. "Just help us get Remi stable. He wasn't safe in the hospital; his brothers can keep him safe. And you'll see your daughter as soon as he's out of the woods."

Her gaze ricocheted between the two of us, eyes narrowed. Whatever she saw, she didn't fight, simply turned her back and went to Remi's side. Levi's focus shifted to me, his burning gaze trailing down my body, and I wished suddenly that I had something, anything that would keep me busy and far, far away from that look.

Chapter Eighteen

I tried to help, sitting beside Remi's bed for the afternoon and into the evening, but Leah refused to rest. Her lips were white, her eyes anxious. Afraid. She took turns hovering over Remi, fiddling with the tubes and wires leading in and out of his body as if getting everything just right would mean the difference between life and death for her patient—or herself—and pacing the length of the room and back, biting her nails down to the quick. I lost count of the times she would stand at the opposite end of the room, staring up at the windows that revealed a darkening sky, eyes clouded with what looked like panic. Not worried about herself, but her daughter, obviously.

"Isn't there someone who will take care of her?" I asked.

Leah snorted, the sound at once grim and amused. It was the only response I got.

A hand settled on my shoulder sometime much, much later, waking me from a light doze. I'd nodded off after dinner, I guess, but I wasn't sure when.

"Go on to bed, Abby."

I blinked up at Leah in the gloomy light. "You need sleep too."

But the woman only shook her head. "Not gonna happen tonight. Besides"—she nodded toward Remi's still form—"I'm used to long hours and late-night vigils."

I imagined that was true. Standing, I stretched my cramped muscles and glanced toward the door to the main room. "What time is it?"

Leah looked at the slim watch on her wrist. "Eleven."

Levi hadn't come to get me. Was he still awake? Would he have the cuffs waiting?

I rubbed the phantom aches from my wrists. "Can I get you anything before I go get ready for bed?"

Leah settled herself in my chair, eyes locked on Remi sleeping a few feet away. "No."

She didn't trust me. I didn't blame her.

I grabbed a plastic cup and poured myself some juice on my way through the kitchen. The warehouse was eerily still, the only sound a slight snore escaping Eli with every exhale as he lay on the couch, a pillow bunched under his head at one end, his big feet hanging off the other. Levi stared at his computer screens, the faint glow spotlighting him in the otherwise dark room, emphasizing the chiseled cheekbones and tight jaw. A god directing mere humans to carry out his whims. He didn't look up as I passed.

"Grab a shower," he said quietly, though not quiet enough to miss the thread of steel underlying the command.

I rolled my eyes, knowing my back was to him as I continued toward the bedroom. "Sure. I'll enjoy the hot water until it runs out. Thanks."

I wouldn't swear to it, but I thought I heard a sound almost like a laugh, choked off abruptly. The man was a pain in the ass, so why did my step lighten at his response?

True to my word, I stood under the hottest water I could stand until it turned tepid. When I flung the curtain back, a squeak escaped.

Levi stood, feet planted, arms crossed. The god was no longer interested in carrying out whims; or maybe he was. Maybe that look in his eyes said the whim he was interested in included me.

I cleared my throat. "What do you want?"

"You."

My laugh sounded strained, even to me. "I'm not on the menu, but there's a cold shower available." My gaze dropped to the straining crotch of his jeans. "Looks like you need it."

Levi was on me before I could do more than lift my towel to my chest. My wet back met the warm tile as he crowded me against it, his wide shoulders blocking the light, the room, everything. Sight and sound and sensation—all were overtaken by Levi's presence. He became my world. My temptation.

My rising hunger.

I clutched the towel to my naked skin and punched his shoulder with my other hand. "Back off."

What the hell has gotten into me?

"Your tongue is going to get you in trouble, little bird."

See?

And then the image of my tongue on Levi's most vulnerable places flashed across my mind's eye. In that case, would it be me or Levi in trouble?

A chuckle drew my focus. "Now what was that thought?" Levi asked, leaning in. The rough press of terry cloth against my aching nipples had me sucking in a sharp breath.

"Should I start calling you naughty bird, Abby? Is that what's got your attention? Something naughty?"

Like I'd tell him. "What? No." Modesty and the need for escape fought inside me, but all it took was the lift of a disbelieving eyebrow for escape to win. Letting go of the towel, I palmed Levi's pecs and shoved. "Get off me!"

The push barely rocked his big frame. He stared down, implacable, unmovable, amusement creeping into his gray eyes. "Frustrated?"

"Yes," I snapped. The man chuckled as I strained harder and harder, trying to push him away, to free myself from the need swirling like molten fire in my belly. I had to escape, to run, to hide, not let this, this…other…take me over. I wanted to—no, *had to*—fight him, but the desire to feel him, to have him inside me again, was equally as strong.

And so much more tempting.

The knowledge only made my anger swell out of control. Levi's sexy, self-satisfied smirk shattered the final tattered remnants of my self-restraint.

I leaned forward and bit down on the muscle along the ridge of his shoulder. He groaned, the sound guttural, rough with pain and something else, something almost like…need. One big hand cupped the back of my head and pulled me closer; the other pushed between me and the wall to splay across the vulnerable small of my back in a blatant show of possession and control.

My bite gentled without my permission, turning into a desperate kiss that glided up the rough skin of his neck until I took his mouth with my own.

My decision. My kiss. My need roaring through me like an avalanche.

I rocked back on my heels. My hands went to Levi's belt.

"That's it, Abby." Levi watched with hooded eyes as I tugged and fumbled and cursed. "That's it; take what you want. Use me however you need to."

Exactly what I planned to do.

Dropping to my knees was probably not what he'd expected, but he didn't protest as I lowered his zipper and then his jeans and underwear. In the stark fluorescent light of the bathroom, every centimeter of Levi's private skin was laid bare—the tight stretch across his stiff cock, the thick, pulsing vein underneath, the vulnerable trail of soft black hair from navel to pelvis. I leaned into that spot, nuzzled it, let my cheek rest there as I breathed in the scent of man and desire and power. My knees hurt, digging into the ceramic beneath me. My hands trembled at the enormity of what I was about to do, what I'd chosen to do. And still I forced them to grasp the thick stalk and hold it steady for the swipe of my tongue across the wet tip.

Levi sucked in a startled breath—one short, sharp sound, so seemingly insignificant, and yet it changed everything between us in a single moment. Because here, on my knees, I was the one with the power.

I opened my mouth. Levi's fingers tightened in my hair—to hold me back or force me forward, I wasn't sure. I only knew which direction I wanted.

I leaned in.

"Abby."

He was too big for my mouth, and yet, not. I opened wider, fed him in until his rigid penis fit in the hollow between my tongue and palate as if the space had been made to his exact measurements. When my lips closed around him, his erection kicked inside its moist confines.

I slid toward the tip. Back down.

Levi's knees shook. "Abby."

I sucked gently.

"Goddamn it, Abby." Pain tingled through my scalp as his fingers tightened, but he didn't stop me. Didn't force me. Didn't—

I drew back, sucking. Pushed forward. Did it again. Then again, a little faster.

Levi's breath was a harsh rasp in my ears, mingled with curses and groans and the occasional straining silence as he held the air in his lungs, anticipating my next move. I'd heard oral sex described, had listened in when Candy and Sarah and Renee discussed both the giving and receiving of it, but I could never have imagined the power of the act itself. The enormity of controlling another person with only your mouth and hands and breath. The sheer awe of reducing another human being to involuntary thrusts and groans and shaking as they pursued the pleasure only you could give them. Levi strained against me, chasing my tongue, my throat, and with every push, the power and the pleasure ballooned in my core until I thought I'd be the one climaxing in the cramped confines of the bathtub.

"Abby!"

Levi beat me to it.

My name sounded as if it had been ripped from his lungs. Levi's beautiful body bowed toward me, shoving the tip of his erection to the back of my throat, and I felt the splash of his cum as I choked. A swallow forced them both down. Tears trickled from the corners of my eyes, washing the rigid lines of Levi's tattoos and straining muscles with a watercolor brush as I watched, fascinated at the depths of the pleasure I could bring him. Even when the pulses in my mouth stopped, he held me tight against him, breathing hard, softening on my tongue for long moments.

And then his eyes opened. I'd expected, I don't know, something soft? Relaxed? Not Levi. The fire that blazed down at me tensed every muscle of my body. Even his grip in my hair couldn't keep me from lurching back, away from the threat in those steely eyes.

"Your mouth is far too talented."

The menace threading through the words made them sound like anything but a compliment. My heartbeat kicked into high gear.

"Get up."

I had little choice unless I wanted to end up bald. A bubble of hysteria tried to choke me as I rose on wobbly legs, the throbbing ache in my knees echoing the sickening thud of my heart. This was the downside of power—it only mattered until you came up against a stronger source, and Levi was the strongest source of power I'd ever met. "What—"

His hands slid from my hair. "Out. Dry off."

"But—"

"Now!"

I turned my back, grabbed a fresh towel, and dragged it roughly over my skin. What the hell had I done? Why had I decided to—

Stop it, Abby.

I took a deep breath. Worrying and wondering would get me nowhere. I'd done that with my father for years, trying to find the best avenue to please him, agonizing over every decision and every word until I thought I'd go insane. Levi might have control of my body, but I wouldn't give him control of my mind. I couldn't, not if I wanted to survive.

A final swipe of my legs for any last traces of water, and then I turned back to my captor. Levi's gray gaze bored into me.

He held his hand out for my towel. As he hung it up, I noticed that his clothes were gone. I'd been listening to my neurotic inner voice; he'd been undressing. When he faced me again, my gaze dropped immediately to the stiffness of his penis. My mouth went dry.

"Into the bedroom," he demanded.

It took a moment, but I finally gathered enough saliva to choke out, "Why?"

"Because you've been a naughty little bird, Abby." He stepped closer, and I managed not to flinch as his hand came up to cup my jaw firmly. "And naughty little birds deserve punishment."

Chapter Nineteen

He couldn't be serious. And yet, looking into that face, I found it impossible to tell. This man that I'd been able to read clearly earlier today, when his fear for his brothers had shredded his control over his temper, and minutes before, when my mouth had crumbled his control over his body, was now an enigma I couldn't decipher.

He didn't wait for me to. His big body loomed over me, crowding step by slow step into my personal space, stealing every molecule of air, every bit of choice. That was all it took to force me into the bedroom. My stomach fluttered with anticipation and cramped with intimidation at the same time, all of it mixing with a sense of inevitability I couldn't quite shake. Every step I'd taken, every move I'd made had led me here, literally and figuratively.

The only question was, now what?

The hard push of the mattress into the backs of my knees startled me out of my fixation on the enemy. Thrown off balance, I fell backward onto the bed. Levi leaned a knee on the edge. "Scoot back."

I scrambled for the feeling of control I'd had mere minutes before. "No."

"Do what I say, Abby."

"No."

But a denial couldn't keep a man like Levi away. As if he was lifting a five-year-old, he gripped my arms and shoved me farther onto the bed, his massive torso following. I tried pushing him back, only to have both hands gathered into one of his and planted firmly above my head.

Trapped. Why was I always trapped by this man?

Because you don't really want to get away?

I closed my eyes against that voice—and against the breathtaking sight of Levi above me. Whatever I imagined we'd shared in the shower, it would never be real. In the morning it would all be smoke, just like that first night.

"Don't play the coward with me now, little bird."

My eyelids snapped open. Satisfaction lit the eyes mere inches above my own. Bastard. He wanted me to be brave? Fine. "This is just another game, Levi. I'm tired of games." I wanted something mutual or nothing at all. "I'm done with other people controlling me. Just leave me alone."

Dark brows narrowed to a vee as he stared down at me. "I should. I really should." His gaze shifted to my mouth. "So why do I find it so fucking impossible?"

I opened my mouth, but he didn't give me time to reply before his lips met mine.

God, I loved how he kissed—and hated how thoroughly it ripped through my defenses. His tongue thrust inside, reminding me of his relentless invasion of my body just last night. The sensation lit me up from the inside out, destroying my resistance in an instant. Instead I strained toward him without thought, needing him deeper, needing to devour him as thoroughly as he was devouring me. If my mouth had been free, I'd beg him to take me, to fuck me—anything to make me forget the fear, the helplessness, but most of all, to forget how much he didn't care. No one cared; the sooner I accepted that, the better. The pleasure Levi gave me was a cheap imitation, but it would do for now—if he let go. The slower he went, the more time I had to think. Mindlessness was my only refuge right now.

Levi's lips left mine. He moved to my ear, my neck, my shoulder, a trail of hard, sucking kisses that sent shafts of sensation straight to my core. I held my breath, waiting, wanting, a cry of need at the back of my teeth, and then his rough lips were gliding down my skin to meet my nipple. The tip crinkled up hard beneath his breath, begging where I would not.

Levi didn't let it beg for long.

His mouth surrounding me brought tears of relief and torment to my eyes. The cry I'd held back escaped in a sharp burst of air. My hands went to his head without thought, pulling him harder against me, urging him to take more, always more. And it wasn't enough. I needed him inside me, filling me. I wrapped my legs around his narrow hips and pulled.

Levi sat up. Cold shock pierced my lust-fogged brain, jolting me back to conscious thought. "What—"

A hard palm landed on the flat plain of my stomach and pressed me firmly into the mattress. "I'll give you my cock when I'm ready, not before," he growled, the words gravel rough, dark...dangerous.

Exactly who he was. How could I forget?

I lay there, conflicted, bereft, staring at the ceiling, trying to push away the sense of loss. The need to hide swamped me, and yet I couldn't turn away, not with him between my legs, holding me down. But I could turn my head. Deny him with my words.

"I don't want to play games."

There was a pause. Weighted silence. And then Levi was leaning over me once more. "Abby, look at me."

I didn't want to—or rather, I didn't want to want to. But there was something in his command...

That was it. The words were a command, but the tone...he was asking.

I turned my head. Met his eyes. In the dark I couldn't read him well, so I waited for the words, the tone, once more.

"This isn't a game," he said. There was something almost...hesitant in the statement. Tentative. Except this was Levi we were talking about. There was nothing hesitant or tentative about the hardened assassin between my legs.

One big hand cupped my jaw, his rough thumb running over my skin. "You gave me…something…back there. Let me return the favor."

Something? I'd given him not just something; I'd given him a part of myself. And he'd taken it, enjoyed it. So what else was new?

I frowned beneath his touch.

He made this sound in his throat, almost like he was clearing it, then, "Let me give you something now."

"What kind of something?"

Instead of answering, he spread his legs in a vee, his knees pushing my legs wide. Cool air hit my overheated folds.

"Some of us were built to take control," Levi said, his voice like gravel as he stared down at the most vulnerable part of me.

I flinched. "And I was built to be controlled; is that what you're saying?"

My voice quivered, damn it. I'd spent years honing my skills until every last molecule of emotion was hidden from my father, every uncertainty and fear buried until I was the perfect hostess, the perfect daughter. And yet here, now, with Levi, I revealed far too much—and it felt far more dangerous than it ever had with Derrick.

Maybe Levi heard it, that note of vulnerability I couldn't seem to hide. His big body lowered, blocking out all light, and covered mine, his breath whispering over my skin, my breast, my nipple. Sharp teeth grazed the hardened tip.

I flinched again, this time at the zing of pain along too-sensitive skin. A punishment.

"You enjoy what I can give you," he said, his lips rasping my throbbing breast. "That's not the same thing."

It felt like it was, but I didn't want to argue. "What can you give me?"

"Escape."

My snort had a corner of his mouth curving the tiniest bit before it hardened back into a determined line. "Think about it: how hot can you go, little bird?" He ducked his head and dragged the tip of his nose down the slope of my breast, down my rib cage, my hip, across the line where thigh met torso. When he came to the crisp curls protecting my mound, he nestled deep. "How bright can you burn? How hard can you explode?"

My fists tightened in frustration, my jaw clenching against my answer. "I don't know." But I wanted to. God, I wanted to.

Levi's firm hands gripped the undersides of my thighs and lifted, up and out. "Then let me show you."

I locked eyes with his across the expanse of my own body. Fire burned like molten metal in his gaze. I don't remember choosing, but one minute I was locked in the secrets behind his eyes, and the next, my legs relaxed into his hold. Still, when his warm breath hit my naked lower lips, I instinctively tried to close my legs. The fact that I couldn't move an inch in his grip sent a wave of heat straight to my core.

You like what I do to you.

God forgive me, but I did.

And then his tongue was on me, right there on my most intimate place. Lapping, laving. He traced every inch of my vagina, a murmur of pleasure escaping him when he reached the cream spilling from my core.

He speared inside.

"Levi!" My head fell back, my body clenching on the slippery invasion. "Levi, please!"

His tongue retreated, then advanced again. My hands went automatically to my breasts, squeezing down, needing more, now. I panted his name again.

"That's it, little bird. Pinch those nipples for me."

I did. Levi replaced his tongue with his fingers in reward, his mouth moving up to surround my clit. When he sucked it inside, laving me with heat and wet and the most glorious pressure I'd ever experienced, I couldn't hold back anymore. I squirmed, writhed, cried out beneath him, my body on fire, my need so high it hurt. I knew in that instant I would give him anything, promise anything, if he would just keep touching me.

And if a part of me deep down, where I couldn't even admit it to myself, wanted more?

It would be disappointed, but my body wouldn't. That would have to be enough.

My walls tightened around Levi's fingers until pain shafted through me with every thrust, and then it was there, the pinnacle, the oblivion I so desperately needed. It shattered me from the inside out, tore me into a thousand pieces. A high wail escaped as I crested the peak, Levi's hands and mouth throwing me over. Long before I hit the bottom, everything went black.

Chapter Twenty

There was something hard underneath my head. Something moving. It took me a moment to figure out that the something was Levi's chest, and the instant I did, I froze. I was wrapped around my captor like a limpet, head on his pec, arm over him, leg across his hips. And even more weird, he was letting me. Or maybe he was simply too deep in sleep and hadn't realized what was up yet.

I could feel something up, though, and it wasn't Levi waking. At least not *all* of Levi.

I didn't dare move my thigh, but neither could I ignore the slowly firming line beneath it. How the man could want sex, asleep or not, had me baffled. He'd taken me twice more before we'd finally fallen into an exhausted sleep last night, which was probably how I'd ended up on top of him—we'd both been too worn-out to notice. And yet, even while sleep still dragged at me, I couldn't resist the temptation to scan the landscape of Levi's body beside and beneath mine. He was living, breathing, brutal power on display; even unconscious, no one would mistake Levi for weak.

The ache deep inside my body agreed.

Was this what I'd missed the morning after losing my virginity? What a normal morning-after was like? Two people, sated and sleepy, curled around each other as they came awake in the early morning light. I closed my eyes and held very, very still, absorbing the rise and fall of Levi's chest, the heat of his skin against mine, the twitch of his penis beneath my thigh. For one crazy moment I let myself imagine that the two of us were normal, that he wasn't an assassin intent on killing my father and I wasn't his captive, forced to bend to his will whether I wanted to or not. We were simply lovers, wrapped up in each other. Alone. Satisfied. In love.

Lost in the fantasy, I turned my head. My lips brushed the pebbled tip of Levi's nipple.

The muscles under me instantly went rigid. Levi's heartbeat thundered beneath my cheek. Instinctive rejection. Normal had been shattered the moment I kissed him.

The covers rustled as Levi lifted them oh so carefully, then eased sideways, out of my grip. I squeezed my eyes shut tighter, pretending—for him and for me—that I was asleep as he left the bed. I had no desire to see distaste in his expression or, even worse, pity. Nor did I want to look at what I couldn't, shouldn't have.

The door to the bathroom closed. I rolled over and pulled the blanket over my head, blocking out the sun and prying eyes.

Don't hurt the innocent, they'd said.

Right. Then why did more than my body ache? If, by some great stretch of the imagination, I managed to get out of this complicated mess of a situation, I should probably get ready for some massive therapy bills. For the next ten or fifteen years—or more.

Levi came out of the bathroom. The weight of his stare sizzled through me despite the covers separating us, but I forced myself to breathe normally, pretend I was asleep until the faint *click* of the bedroom door closing registered in my ears. I threw back the covers, huffing random strands of hair from my face, and glared up at the rectangles of bright morning sky. Only when the tingling behind my eyes finally faded did I get up and dress.

My mask was firmly in place when I walked into the living room. At first I didn't realize the broad back visible in the desk chair wasn't Levi—he and Eli might have different hair colors, but they shared the same build. Remi seemed to as well, though it was harder to tell with him lying on a bed, covered. Hopefully he'd wake soon, for his sake and for Leah's. Someone deserved to get out of here, and she had a daughter to worry about; all I had was a megalomaniac of a father.

Eli shot a glare over his shoulder as I moved closer. I'd put up with that look from Levi because a single glance from him could scare the crap out of me, but I wouldn't let his brother have that advantage.

"Who pissed in your corn flakes?" As if I couldn't guess. The brothers shared a bond, that much was obvious, but like most siblings they also seemed to rub each other the wrong way.

"Your father."

Great. "What did he do now?"

Eli turned back to his screens, ignoring my question. Figures. With a shrug, I headed toward Remi's room. A quick peek in told me the two occupants of the room were fast asleep—Remi still flat on his back as if he hadn't moved all night, Leah curled up in the chair, her neck at an angle that made me wince.

Since Levi was nowhere in sight, I assumed he was getting breakfast. I grabbed a bottle of water from the fridge and went back to bugging Eli.

"Remi's still sleeping."

Eli snorted. "He's probably the only one that got a full night's sleep last night."

Considering the way Eli's feet had hung over the edge of the couch, I figured it hadn't been the most comfortable place to rest. "I'm sorry."

"You should be," he said sourly. "All that caterwauling kept me up."

I choked on the sip of water I'd just taken. Fiery heat doused me, centering in my cheeks. I'd been lied to, lied about, photographed naked and exposed to my father, choked, and scared shitless—and yet somehow, knowing that Eli had heard us last night, had heard *me*, was more humiliating than all the rest. I stood, frozen, as the silence between us spread, took on weight, choking off my air like rough hands around my throat. Funny how, after the past few days, I knew exactly how that felt, and yet after all my years of social training, I had no idea of the appropriate response to someone's commentary on how much noise you made during sex. They didn't cover that in hostess school. My father certainly never—

I cut that thought off. As long as I didn't embarrass him, my father didn't care what people said to me. Or did to me, apparently, if his lack of progress in finding me was any indication.

The sound of the alarm beeping broke the heavy silence.

Levi entered a second later, the smell of sausage and biscuits preceding him into the room. A loud growl rumbled through my empty stomach. Ignoring the noise and the humiliation still clinging to me, I hurried to grab the bags in Levi's hands and take them to the kitchen to plate—anything to give me a few more minutes for my hot cheeks to cool. Leah's portion went into the microwave. The men grabbed theirs without a thank-you and settled at the table.

"You're welcome," I muttered. Being a hit man didn't mean you had to lack manners, for goodness' sake.

When I turned with my plate in hand, Levi's steely eyes were on me. I froze.

An abrupt nod somehow transmitted his appreciation. I ducked my head, scrambled into a seat.

"What did you find?"

At first I thought Levi was talking to me, but Eli answered around a mouthful of biscuits and gravy. "The authorities are coming up blank. Hospital security reported an attack and the abduction of one of their nurses, but surveillance couldn't identify the assailant and he was awake and ghosted out of there before Leah and Remi were reported missing."

"And nothing outside—no car, no pickup from someone else, nothing?"

"Nothing."

"Good."

What?

The brothers didn't seem to notice my confusion, their attention on the food and each other.

"Did *you* find Ray?"

The skin around Eli's eyes went tight. "No. Axe's men don't slip up often."

Who was Axe?

"Ray did," Levi said. "He underestimated his opponent—he thought Remi was alone. Big mistake."

They were talking about the man at the hospital. Ray. Who worked for someone named Axe. I looked from Levi to his brother and back again, an inappropriate bubble of laughter rising. *Just another day searching for my killer coworkers. Totally normal.*

When had my life become so bizarre?

When you slept with an assassin.

The laughter died in my throat.

"He's just lucky I didn't have time to really make him regret that mistake," Eli grated out, his fist clenching around his fork. "And a witness."

No killing in front of witnesses—was that a rule too? If Leah hadn't been in that room, Eli would've killed Ray. And yet, when I pictured the scene on the security cameras, Leah alone, unaware, Remi unconscious and vulnerable, I couldn't bring myself to condemn that decision.

I swirled my fork in the generous amount of gravy I'd dolloped onto my flaky biscuits. "Are you saying you know the men Derrick sent after you?"

Levi glanced at me, his gaze dropping to my plate. A frown curved his lips. "Eat, Abby."

"But—"

Levi's stare burned into me. "Eat," he said again.

Why did he care? Frustration coiled in my stomach, but I couldn't bring myself to spout the words—which upped the frustration tenfold.

Across the table, a dark wing of an eyebrow rose on Levi's granite-carved face. I forked up a bite and shoved it in my mouth, glaring the whole time. A useless rebellion, but a rebellion all the same.

Totally useless. Levi turned his stare back to Eli. I chewed and swallowed.

Eli ignored the byplay taking place. "You know he's not gonna stop. And neither will Axe. Ray's ass is grass, but once Axe gets a contract, it gets finished, one way or another."

Levi grunted around his final bite of breakfast.

My mind grabbed on to Eli's words and wouldn't let go. Derrick might've made a mistake in the first assassin he'd approached, but this new set wouldn't stop. Had they taken the original contract, the one Levi had rejected? Had they succeeded?

"What happened to the man?" I asked.

Two pairs of narrowed eyes zeroed in on me. "Which man?" Levi asked.

I took my time answering, trying to sort my own jumbled thoughts in the process—and, okay, also trying to make sure I didn't sound like a total idiot. "You said Derrick asked you to kill an innocent man. You researched him, knew who he was, but you couldn't find any wrongdoing. What was their connection? It was big enough to kill for, if you're telling the truth. That could be the biggest secret of all, the one that could stop all of this. Hit men expect to get paid, right?"

Eli widened his eyes dramatically. "No, we do it for the good of humanity."

Smart-ass.

"My point is, if you figured out why Derrick wanted the man dead, and his secrets came out, my...Derrick would be finished. Whatever he's hiding would be out in the open. He wouldn't be paying anyone to come after you then." And hopefully whoever this Axe guy was would accept that.

Maybe no one else had to die.

I dared to meet Levi's steel-gray gaze. "Follow the original trail, and you'll find the real ammunition against Derrick. That's what he's trying to prevent by killing you, isn't it?"

"Your girl is smart, Levi."

Between one blink and the next, a shutter slammed down on Levi's expression, his eyes hard on my face. "She's not my girl."

I absorbed the blow with all the grace I'd been taught from childhood, refusing to look away no matter how the knife twisted in my chest. Levi was the one who dismissed me when he turned to his brother. Only the risk of Eli's seeing how much it hurt kept my face blank.

"How soon before Axe trails us here?" Levi asked.

I noticed Eli kept his gaze glued to his brother's, a small act of kindness I couldn't help but be grateful for. "Let's just say we need Remi to wake up sooner than later."

"Well, you got your wish," a sleep-roughened voice said behind us. Leah stood in the door to Remi's room, rumpled and groggy, her frown a severe slash across a tired face. "He's coming out of it."

The brothers shot out of their chairs so fast they rocked backward; Levi's actually fell over. I righted it as I rounded the table, then followed them into the sickroom. The men were surrounding Remi's bed by the time I got there, peppering Leah with questions. I took up a spot at Remi's feet and surveyed the brother I hadn't truly met yet. Amber eyes clouded with sleep and pain stared back at me, a vee forming between his dark brows.

143

Levi gripped Remi's shoulder and squeezed down. "It's good to have you back, brother."

The relief in his voice couldn't be missed, but it drew Remi's attention for less than a second before he came back to me. Recognition sparked a moment later, and a guttural groan escaped. "That's Abigail Roslyn," he muttered. His grasp on the bed rails was shaky at best, but he forced himself upright nonetheless. Leah moved close, her sure hands supporting his back to keep him that way. Remi barely seemed to notice—the entire time, he stared at me, eyes wide, incredulous. And increasingly angry.

The stare jerked to his brother then. "Goddamn it, Levi, what the fuck have you done?"

Chapter Twenty-One

"What I had to," Levi said, impassive as stone, but his gaze traveled over his brother despite the blankness of his expression, seeming to catalog every sign of weakness and strength. When Remi listed to one side, he was right there, holding him up.

Remi jerked away. "Don't—" The effort it took to hold himself upright shook through his muscles, seeming ready to topple him at any moment, but these brothers shared more than their skills with weapons, apparently. I'd never seen three more stubborn men.

"You've painted a target on our backs."

Levi nodded his head toward the gunshot wound in the hollow of Remi's shoulder. "Do you really think it matters?"

We'd had this argument more than once with Levi and gotten nowhere, but one look at the brothers' faces convinced me to stay out of it. Not Leah—I swear the woman didn't know the meaning of the word *intimidated*. She ignored Levi's looming presence as she fiddled with the controls on the side of the bed. Slowly the back part rose until Remi was fully supported. He tried to hide his relief as he settled against the pillow, but I could see it in the softening lines around his mouth, the returning color in his knuckles where he gripped the railing.

His tired eyes found me again. Remi sucked in a ragged breath. "Yes, I think what we do matters."

It was what Levi had taught them to believe. *Don't harm the innocent.* But I was beginning to realize that what Levi had taught his brothers and what he lived weren't necessarily the same. There was a different rule, a higher purpose that Levi answered to, and looking at him now, watching him watch his brothers, I thought I knew what that purpose was.

Eli ran a hand through his hair, leaving the blond strands standing on end. "Do we really need to have this discussion now?"

"If not now, when?" Remi asked him.

"I don't know, maybe when you're not just waking up from being in a coma for a week and still healing from a hole in your fucking shoulder?"

Neither Remi nor Levi was going to leave it alone; one look told me that. Levi stood granite-still, impassive, thick arms crossed over his chest. The cold, dangerous assassin I'd seen for the first time the morning after Levi had taken my virginity was back, and he was immovable. Remi, though…his nostrils flared, and the glare he shot Levi glowed with amber fire. For a moment I saw not a wounded man but an avenging angel, intent on justice. A warrior fighting for a cause. He was Levi's opposite; one brother shunned emotion, and the other blazed so bright with it that I had to look away.

No, there was no stopping this head-on collision.

"There was a target on our backs the minute we took Roslyn's contract, and you know it. Getting rid of him is the only way out."

"So you kidnapped his daughter?" Remi barked. A grimace of pain crossed his lips. "That's not getting rid of him. That's heaping coals on the monster's head and hoping you can handle the fallout."

"I don't have to hope. I know."

"Remi…" Leah moved closer to the side of the bed and grasped Remi's wrist, fingertips on the pulse point. Checking his heart rate. Her frown said she didn't like what she was feeling.

Remi shot her a confused look before turning back to his brother. "You need to let her go. Now. You didn't have to do this."

"I didn't have to." Levi leaned in, satisfaction in every line of his body. "I wanted to. I want to annihilate that son of a bitch's life piece by piece until there's nothing left but his body; then I want to destroy that too. And nothing can stop me."

"Then you're no better than he is," Remi yelled.

Levi didn't flinch away from his brother's accusation. "I haven't been better than him since I was eleven years old. You know that as well as I do. You are better, you and Elijah; that's all I care about."

And there it was, Levi's entire purpose in a nutshell.

Remi was shaking his head. "That wasn't your fault."

"No." Levi's chuckle had a bitter tinge. "Maybe I inherited more from old Uncle Amos than any of us realized."

"You are nothing like him. You never were," Eli countered.

"Eli—"

Levi's voice overrode Remi's. "I wasn't? I trained and I waited, and when I knew I could take him, I bathed in his blood." Every word grew louder and louder until Levi's voice boomed through the room, through my heart. "And you know what? I enjoyed every minute of killing him. Every fucking minute."

An alarm sounded, something beside the bed.

"Remi." Leah's voice was at its most soothing, dripping with calm in the midst of the raging emotions dominating the room. She reached to turn off the annoying sound. "You need to calm down a bit."

No one but me seemed to hear her. "Remi…" I said.

"No." Remi swallowed hard. His sick-bed pallor took on a green tint. "No."

Levi flung his arms in the air. "No, what? You don't think I savored cutting that bastard into tiny little pieces? I did. He *killed* our parents! His own flesh-and-blood. And for what? Fucking money. That sick fuck wouldn't have stopped there, either. I hid you both for a reason. Amos Agozi deserved to die, as painfully and slowly as possible, and I didn't care who or what I had to mow down to make sure it happened. For you. For Eli. For our family." His steel-gray gaze glittered with ice. "I didn't regret it then, and I still don't."

"If you did it for revenge, maybe you should," Remi argued.

"No." Levi gritted his teeth on the word, spitting it out like a bullet. "I shouldn't."

A second alarm sounded, this one louder than the first. The men ignored it, staring at each other like strangers who'd never met before. And maybe they hadn't—these parts of themselves, anyway. I could see the cold rage building in Levi's expression, quivering through his big body like an eruption waiting to blow. Who would get caught in that blast? A glance at Leah's worried expression had me hoping it wasn't the brother he'd done so much to save.

"Revenge is just another word for what I do—and I do it well, thoroughly, and without emotion. I don't have the luxury of feeling anything," Levi growled, his tone belying his words. "Emotion died in me a long time ago; it had to. All that matters, all I care about, is keeping *my family* safe. And I'll do that no matter the cost."

"That's where you're wrong," Remi growled right back. "If you didn't feel anything, she wouldn't be here." He pointed my way without looking at me. "You're not doing an emotionless job—you're acting on nothing but emotion. Once you took Roslyn's child, you gave in to the need not only to kill him physically, but to tear out his heart."

Between one breath and the next, Levi was in Remi's face. "I'll tell you what I feel—a burning need to keep you alive." He shot a glance at Eli. "Both of you. Nothing and no one else matters. Period."

"Of course other people matter. She's a person. She has a life. You had no right to use her in your game against Roslyn. There's always another way. You taught me that."

"I lied."

Remi's laugh was filled with gravel. "No, what you lied about was keeping your emotions out of it. You like to play the coldhearted bastard, but the truth is, you were in a rage after I got shot, and you took it out on her instead of the real target."

"No! No." Levi's hands fisted at his sides, the palpable force of his anger thickening the muscles in his arms and neck as he tensed. "I hurt the real target by taking her."

"Did you? At what cost? You saw how he treated her when I did the surveillance. You know what that bastard is like. She's been hurt enough."

"What?"

The question escaped before I could stop it. Remi had been watching me even before the shooting? I'd thought… Levi knew intimate details—my habits, my comings and going. It had never occurred to me that he'd known the exact nature of my relationship with my father. He'd known how little I mattered, and still he'd used me as a pawn.

His opening gambit. The most insignificant pawn in his arsenal. Even the money had been more important.

"You didn't tell her, did you?" Remi asked.

Levi scoffed. "Believe me, she figured it out quick enough."

Not all of it, apparently. I wouldn't feel this way if I had.

My gaze met Remi's, and I knew he read the truth there, the revelations and wounds and pain. His eyes went dark.

"Like my methods or not, I am protecting you."

Remi huffed out a breath, and for a moment I swore I saw a sheen of tears in his eyes as he stared at his brother. "Sure. Right. That song and dance is getting pretty tired there, *brother*." He shifted in the bed, and a grimace twisted his mouth as he reached up to rub near the site of his gunshot wound. His breath sped up, the sound ragged in the quiet. Leah swore, her gaze on the machines beeping and humming beside the bed.

"What happens when Derrick Roslyn comes here?" Remi asked.

"We'll be long gone by then."

"And her?" He nodded in my direction.

Levi didn't respond. Another arrow pierced my heart.

"Then fuck you," Remi rasped.

Eli reached for his brother. "You don't mean that, Remi."

"Wanna bet?" Remi jerked away from his brother's hold and shifted his legs as if he would get out of his hospital bed. Midswing, his eyes rolled back in his head and he slumped against the raised back of the bed. All eyes shot to Remi, then Leah.

The woman had been a Valkyrie fighting to get back to her daughter, but right now, standing with the port for Remi's IV in one hand and an empty needle in the other, the fire in her eyes rivaled even that first moment I'd seen her.

"What the hell did you do?" Levi shouted.

Leah placed the needle on a nearby table, then turned to glare at her captor. "What I had to. I said he needed to calm down, but apparently you didn't hear me. Hear me now." She jammed her fists onto her hips. "You can kill whomever you want, but not my patient. Get the fuck out. All of you. Right now."

Chapter Twenty-Two

Levi left. Eli kept telling me not to worry, that his brother was never far away, mostly because he didn't trust anyone but himself when it came to keeping them safe—as if this morning's drama hadn't told me that. I spent the day helping Leah in any way I could.

I was taking in the soup Eli had brought home for lunch when I caught Remi's gravel-rough voice for the first time since Leah had drugged him this morning.

"Who are you, anyway? I know we aren't at the hospital. How did Levi find a nurse?"

"He found me at the hospital, actually, while you were still there. Right before a man tried to attack you. Eli…asked me to come, to help stabilize you."

"You mean he forced you."

Leah didn't answer.

"What's your name again?"

"Leah."

"Leah, I'm going to get you out of here. I promise. No one is going to hurt you."

"Just get better, Remi. If you don't, you won't be able to deliver on that promise."

A smile tugged at my lips. I admired Leah's spunk. I wasn't sure if it came from being a nurse, a mom, or something else in her life, but she had a spark I struggled to find under all the layers of training and attachment and people pleasing that had buried what my personality might have otherwise been, and I knew with sudden clarity that I wanted to be like this woman when I "grew up." When I rediscovered me.

Stepping into the sickroom with my tray drew both occupants' attention. There was something about the way Remi watched me, like I was a bug under a microscope, that made my skin itch. Did he blame me for Levi's actions? Did he think I could change anything in this situation? I was the one with the least amount of power in the warehouse. So why did those amber eyes make me feel guilty?

"I brought lunch."

Obviously. But Leah merely smiled when she took the tray from me. I stood at the foot of Remi's bed just as I had that morning, awkwardly gripping the hem of my T-shirt with nervous hands as I watched her position the tray on Remi's lap, setting her own food aside. Remi's hands shook as he tried to lift his spoon, but Leah was right there, guiding him, making sure he ate. She must be a fantastic nurse, compassionate as well as competent. Would I ever go back to pursuing my degree, or had my dreams of being a nurse died the night I'd been taken?

"Why am I so damn weak?"

It sounded like Remi appreciated compassion as much as his brothers did. If I hadn't been so aware of the man's odd gaze watching me, I might've rolled my eyes.

"Because you've been flat on your back for a week, maybe?" Leah's tone was acerbic. "You were in a coma; you can't expect to just wake up and be ready for a marathon."

"A gunshot wound doesn't put you in a coma unless it's in the head—I've had enough to know. What happened?"

"I guess you wouldn't remember any of it, would you?" Leah lifted the water glass for Remi to drink. "The gunshot missed anything vital, thank your lucky stars…"

Remi carefully wiped his mouth with a napkin. I thought I caught a smirk behind the paper. "Dickhead wasn't as good a shot as he thought."

"Right." Leah shot me an exasperated glance. "Unfortunately it did knock you off a balcony two stories up. You were found on the ground beneath after your brother made a panicked 911 call."

"Levi?"

"No, Eli. Levi didn't stick around."

Remi grunted, then winced. "He would've secured the weapons and cleaned the scene."

"Nice of him."

Remi shook his head, then winced. "More than you'd probably think. Just ensuring we were all covered and I didn't end up in the prison hospital ward."

"What about the other guy?" I dared to ask. "The one who shot you."

Remi's smirk was right out in the open then. "I'm pretty sure you don't want to know."

Probably not. An ache in my fingers had me glancing down. My hands were white, twisted hard enough in my shirt to almost tear it. I'd seen Levi's anger; I really didn't want to imagine being on the receiving end of his full-blown rage.

I deliberately relaxed my grip and smoothed down my tee. When I raised my head, my gaze clashed with Remi's again. Yes, definitely a bug under a microscope. I let my "hostess" mask slip down, surprised it had taken me this long to reach for it. Things were definitely changing inside me. Probably shouldn't be a surprise after all I'd been through, but it left me dangling, without the tried-and-true methods I'd always fallen back on to protect myself. I was caught in the change, stripped bare, vulnerable, and like a doe in the hunter's sites, I had no idea how to protect myself except to run.

"Stop staring and eat, Remi," Leah said, proving her compassion extended beyond her patient. "You won't get better if you don't. I'll need to switch you over to oral meds and get the IV and cath out today."

Remi grimaced, but I noticed he obeyed her. Maybe not all of the assassin brothers were stubborn to a fault.

I also noticed that he didn't look at Leah like he looked at me. Rather than trying to dissect her with his gaze, his look was almost…fascinated? Maybe not that deep, not yet, but something in those amber eyes softened as he watched her, yet became even more intense. Was he attracted; was that it? Remembering Leah's daughter, I hoped not. The last thing Leah needed was to catch the attention of these men. Hopefully with Remi awake, she could go home soon and leave this whole nightmare behind.

I had no doubt I wouldn't be so lucky.

Leah sent me back to the kitchen after they finished their meals. I closed the door behind me, giving nurse and patient privacy to do what needed to be done. A half hour later Leah called Eli in to help Remi walk to the bathroom.

Still Levi didn't return.

Remi continued to improve throughout the day. Late in the afternoon, Eli retreated to his brother's bedside, and the whispered conversations between them told me something was up, but I wasn't sure I wanted to know what was going on. Finally it was Eli who sat me down on the couch.

"What's wrong?" It was the only reason the brother I'd dubbed "the pissy one" would be talking to me. "Is Levi okay?"

What kind of idiot asks if her kidnapper is okay? I mean, really, what was up with this Stockholm syndrome thing?

Eli didn't question it, though. "He's fine. He'll be back soon." The same thing he'd said all day. "There is something else we need to discuss."

There was likely no avoiding whatever the next disaster was, so I didn't bother trying. "Okay."

"There's something being reported on the news sites…"

Eli wouldn't meet my eyes; that's when I knew it was bad. I had the sudden urge to rip the Band-Aid off and get the pain over with already. "Just spit it out, Eli."

"The pictures Levi sent to your father—they were released to a reporter."

The shock hit my chest like a two-by-four. I gaped at Eli, struggling to think of a response, struggling to ignore the sudden blast of mortification inside me. Levi had those images. He was angry. And now he'd shown millions of people the humiliation he'd subjected me to—and started the process all over again.

"That's not all."

A choked-off laugh escaped. Of course it wasn't.

"There is speculation…uh…" Eli shifted in his seat. "There's speculation that you were cheating on your fiancé—"

"He's not my fucking fiancé!"

I don't think I'd ever, in my carefully regulated, regimented life, actually screeched. But I did now.

Eli winced. "Your alleged fiancé—"

I surged off the couch, barely managing to hold myself back before I slapped Eli's face. Oddly enough, he didn't try to stop me, simply sat and waited while I squeezed my fists until they hurt and tried desperately to breathe away the roiling emotions inside me.

After a few minutes, I guess he thought I wasn't going to actually explode. Still, his tone was placating, as if I was a wild animal he didn't know what to do with. "Okay. Okay. They are saying you ran away with your lover to escape that fucker Kyle Pellen, and the photos are proof you were involved with someone else."

Because of course the proper prick, Kyle, would never cuff me or take pictures of me naked. It had to be someone else. Right.

Now that Eli had spit out the words, an uncomfortable silence settled between us. All I could hear was the rush in my ears, the thundering of my heart, the horrible cry of denial locked deep inside where no one could hear it but me. No one needed to know any more about the humiliation of Abby Roslyn than they already did. No one needed to know that the man who had taken my body had also taken my dignity, not once, by sending those pictures to my father, but twice, by sharing them with the world. No one needed to know, and they wouldn't. I didn't even want to know—but I couldn't escape my own brain, could I?

"Abby?"

I could barely hear Eli through the roar in my head.

"Abby, we will find out who did this, I promise, okay? We will—"

Did he really expect me to believe that? "You'll what? Avenge me? Make it right? Get revenge?" I laughed, the sound bitter enough to make me wince. "How are you going to do that? You can't put the genie back in the bottle. Those files are out now, and there's no way to erase them."

"No, but—"

I wasn't done. "You want me to believe you will take up for me, protect my precious reputation? Your brother took those pictures. He's the reason I'm in the news. And he's the only one who had a reason to release those files. Are you going to kill him for me? Because somehow I don't see that happening, Eli!"

"No, he didn't… He wouldn't do that, Abby." Eli had a hand out as if he could calm me with a mere touch, but just the thought made my skin crawl. Skin that no longer felt like my own. It had been exposed—*I* had been exposed—to too many prying, judging eyes. I wanted to tear my skin off with my bare hands, make myself something else, something unrecognizable, something…

I closed my eyes. There wasn't something else, was there? I could never not be me, no matter how much I tried. No matter how much I wished and prayed and cried, I'd always be me. And suddenly that was unbearable.

I whirled around, catching a toe on the edge of the couch, and stumbled away from that hand, from the hated pity in Eli's eyes. In Leah and Remi's eyes as they stared at me from the doorway of the sickroom. Everything inside me screamed to escape, and I let the urge take me, move me, shove me toward the outer door in a last-ditch effort to free myself.

And I almost made it. I'd almost reached the freedom lying behind those thick inches of steel when the door opened from the outside and Levi walked in.

Chapter Twenty-Three

"What—"

That was all he got out before my palm connected with his cheek. Levi caught my hands in a tight grip, flexing his jaw as if to work out the pain. Eyes I'd often thought were cold blazed down at me, delving deep, searching for things I didn't want him to see.

I dropped my chin, hiding—my tears, my anger, the damn need that surged even now. When I jerked my arms, Levi's grip got tighter. "Eli, what happened?"

"You'd know if you'd been here, brother."

"What. Happened?"

I was thankful for the veil of hair curtaining my expression as Eli explained. It gave me time—to hide away my heart, bury my feelings. Wrap myself in a numb blanket of denial, where none of this was happening to me and all I needed to do was wait out the nightmare so I could return to the real world beyond. I wasn't numb enough not to flinch when a string of curses left Levi's lips over my head, though.

"Were you able to hack the reporter, find the source?"

"Not yet. It just hit the radar," Eli said with a wave toward the computers. "We—"

"Do it."

Was Levi really trying to get me to believe he hadn't done this? I wasn't that naive, not anymore.

"Abby…"

I shook with emotions I couldn't control, but kept my feet right where they were. I refused to fight him for the freedom that was rightfully mine. "Let me go."

"Just let me—"

"No." My chest heaved under the strain. "No!"

I don't really know what happened next. One minute I was captured in Levi's simple grip, and the next I was a wild thing, bucking and hitting and kicking. I don't even know if I truly had a target. All I wanted was escape, desperately. To get around him, get through the door. To be anywhere but here, anyone but me. Sounds flooded the room—a female voice that wasn't my own, harsh words and barked orders, a gut-wrenching wail that made my heart hurt for whoever uttered it—and then I was swept into the prison of Levi's arms.

I didn't fight him then. I was too busy crying.

A door banging shut startled me out of the hole I'd dropped into—Levi kicking the bedroom door closed, I realized a few moments later. He carried me to the bed we'd shared for days, and sat on the edge. If I hadn't known he hated cuddling, I would swear that was what he was doing—more likely trying to protect himself from more bruises. But I ignored the knowledge in the back of my mind and held on tight. My only security in the shattered world I now lived in.

Wasn't that thought proof that I'd gone mad? I didn't know anymore.

Long moments later, beneath the shudders and sobs, something else registered, something…odd. I couldn't put my finger on it at first until…God. He was rocking. Levi sat silent, the only sound the pounding of his heart beneath my ear, but his body moved—he was rocking me. Only the slightest bit, but the motion was there all the same. Soothing me. Calming and comforting me. At first I stiffened, afraid to sink into it, afraid of the same reaction I had gotten in bed this morning, but the subtle movement continued, and eventually I melted into it, into the hard body surrounding me.

A relieved breath I hadn't known I was holding escaped when he didn't dump me on my ass.

Levi's chin brushed the top of my head as he tilted down, bringing his mouth to my ear. "I didn't do it, Abby. I would never—"

"You have before."

He didn't reply; how could he? I was right. But the feel of him against me, still tense, said he wanted to argue, wanted to force me to hear him, believe him.

He didn't.

And God help me but I was relieved. I didn't want this moment to end.

It had to, though. The end came with a quiet knock on the door. I buried my face harder against the thick wall of Levi's chest and ignored the door opening, but I couldn't ignore the voice.

"I got it," Eli said quietly.

"Who?"

The word rumbled through my ear, more vibration than sound, but Eli heard it.

"Roslyn."

The blow was almost as hard as thinking Levi had done it. No matter how much of a jerk my only parent was, I still, deep down, wanted to believe he

162

wouldn't hurt me, wouldn't humiliate me. I couldn't resist a denial. "No."

Eli didn't say anything else. Neither did Levi; he simply held me tighter. That was when I knew it was true.

"Why?" I whispered against the soft cotton of Levi's shirt.

I felt a hitch in his chest as he went to speak, then stopped himself. But I needed to know.

"Tell me, Levi."

His sigh felt cool against my tear-wet cheeks. "My bet? It's more alibi building. A plausible reason for your disappearance that isn't criminal. You return home, and it's all a spontaneous, youthful fling."

The current beneath his words told me there was more. "And if I don't return home?"

Levi's pecs pushed against me as he sucked in a breath. "Then he can point the finger at a third party. The jilted fiancé."

I fisted my hand in the material at the base of his spine, forcing back a denial at the word *fiancé*. Levi knew the truth about that by now; I didn't have to point it out. And really, did it matter anymore? Did anything?

"I don't know who I am anymore," I whispered.

"You're Abby. You're strong. You're…"

I wanted to hear that last word, hear what was in his mind, how he truly saw me. This man had been the catalyst that had thrown me out of the only life I'd known, shoved me into circumstances I could never have foreseen. He'd slept with me, fought with me, fed me…forced me. How could he see me as strong? *I* didn't see me as strong. But I wanted to believe he did. I wanted it with everything inside me.

"All those people…" Even if they had blurred out the most private parts of the images, so many people had seen them, surmised what was blocked out, peeked into a part of me they now thought was the truth, whether it was or not. "I can never face them again." Nor could I go back home. Even if my father hadn't done the things I now knew he'd done, nothing would ever be the same. And what good was I as a hostess when all the guests had seen me naked?

Levi didn't answer, and a part of me was grateful. There was no easy answer. My life was in pieces, and superglue wasn't going to put them back together. I was beginning to think nothing could.

And then Levi's hand went from my back to my thigh, scooted me that much closer to him, and desire flashed from his touch to my core. It could be the end of the world, and still, Levi's touch would set me on fire.

Maybe there was one small part of me that didn't need to be put back together.

I gathered my legs beneath me, shifted until I could straddle Levi's lap. His eyes were dark, troubled, his face drawn—for me? I tried hard not to believe it; the Levi who'd held me and rocked me was an anomaly, a glitch in time, though one I didn't want to see disappear. So I closed my eyes and put my mouth on his.

The kiss was hot, deep. It went on and on until finally I had to surface for air. Levi breathed heavily beneath me.

"Abby?"

I didn't want to talk anymore, or think, or worry; I wanted to forget. For just a little while, I wanted it all to go away. Levi was good at that.

"Abb—"

I settled a finger against those full lips. "Levi...don't. Just don't." I stroked over the supple skin, over the rasp of stubble on his chin, down to the throbbing pulse in his throat. "Don't say anything but yes."

Levi shifted his hips, and a solid ridge rubbed against my core. Sparks of desires shot through me. When he grasped the back of my neck and pulled me close, I let him. Warm breath bathed my mouth, and it was hunger that darkened his eyes now. Pure, hot, beautiful hunger.

I ran the tip of my tongue over his bottom lip and met his eyes. Lifted an eyebrow in inquiry.

Levi slid his hand from my nape to my breast, cupping me in his palm. "Yes, little bird."

Chapter Twenty-Four

He couldn't put the pieces of me back together; I'd been right about that. I couldn't even trust that the man who'd seemed to care, to want me and want to comfort me, was the real Levi. Experience said no. What my body and mind had felt in his arms said yes. I decided it didn't really matter in the face of everything going on.

Eli didn't look at me when I came out of the bedroom. Remi was on the couch, half-reclining, a pillow behind his back and blanket over his legs. He reminded me so much of Levi now that he was up and awake, not just the body type and size, but the intensity in his eyes. I bypassed his knowing look and hurried to Leah, to the sickroom—to action, or at the very least, to bask in the woman's calm demeanor. I found her cleaning up the messy room, and peace immediately settled like a blanket over my soul.

She didn't glance up as I moved to her side. "You okay?" she asked, gripping one corner of the sheet that covered Remi's bed.

"Sure."

The word was anything but, something Leah ignored as she continued to strip the bed.

"Eli says they're moving out tonight."

I stilled. "Did he say…"

She bundled the sheets in her arms, then turned to face me. Her blue eyes delved deep, searching, uncovering things I didn't want discovered. Too often lately I felt like an open book for anyone to read—or take advantage of. "He says now that Remi's awake, I'll be going home."

"Oh." Relief loosened my muscles even as a different kind of tension ran through me. What were they planning for me? "That's good. You'll be back with your daughter." And safe.

Leah continued to stare, knowledge darkening her gaze. I reached for the sheets, intent on putting them somewhere out of the way, somewhere that would allow me a few seconds to hide.

"I know what's happening to you," she said softly, continuing to hold her bundle, keeping me close—in her own way, forcing me to be where I wanted to escape. "I may work long shifts, but I've seen the news. And I heard what Eli said earlier."

Hadn't everyone? Even knowing I hadn't done anything wrong, shame heated my cheeks.

"Will they let you go too?"

I glanced up, daring to meet her eyes. "I don't know."

"You don't know if Levi will release you, or you don't know if you want to be released?"

That is the question, isn't it? One I didn't know the answer to.

"Abby—" Leah glanced toward the doorway and lowered her voice even more. "Don't let him fool you."

"I don't know what you're talking about." Of course I did.

One side of Leah's mouth turned up; a smirk. "Right. And you didn't just have sex with the man who kidnapped you."

Every drop of blood in my face disappeared. I let go of the sheets, took a step back. The door was only a few steps away; could I make it?

"I get it," Leah said. "Believe me, I get it probably more than you will ever know." Something haunted and hurting flitted across her expression. "They seem all-powerful, like they can protect you from the hell that is your life. Like they are gods controlling everything, right down to the weather ruining your day, and somehow, over time, you forget that they aren't truly good. You forget that they can hurt you—and they always do. Always."

"No, it's not like that." It wasn't. Was it? I had no illusions that Levi was anything more than a convenience. When this was over, I would walk away, and these feelings would fade.

But you'll never be the same.

Leah's eyes shone with pity. "I wish you were right. But you're not."

I opened my mouth to reply, but snapped it shut when Eli appeared in the doorway.

"Time to go, Leah."

She glanced around at the mess. "I'm not quite finished here."

"Doesn't matter," he said with a shrug. "In a few hours this place will be abandoned anyway."

And where would that leave me? Was I going with them or, like Leah, going home? Was there a home to go back to?

The question rang in my head as I followed Leah into the living area. She went straight to Remi, leaning over the back of the couch to speak, her words too soft to hear, her hands busy checking her patient. The scene was somehow intimate, a moment that deserved protection from prying eyes, and I turned my head away.

My gaze collided with Levi's.

He stood near the outer door, obviously waiting for Leah, but he wasn't watching her; he was watching me. Every time I saw him, I had the same thought: He's beautiful. Tall and built and sexy. He took my breath. But I always looked for one thing. His eyes. They were literally windows, if not to his soul, at least to his mood. They told me where we stood when we came face-to-face.

Right now, the cold expression was back, and I couldn't help comparing this man with the one who'd taken me with such fire mere hours ago. His gray eyes hadn't been cold steel then; they'd been molten silver, blazing with hunger. Which was the true Levi? Growing up with a parent with political ambitions, I was used to people wearing masks. The problem was, I couldn't decide which Levi was the mask—the lover or the killer. Both? Neither?

I didn't know. The only thing I knew with absolute certainty was that when I figured it out, no mask would be able to protect me from the pain.

"Let's go," Eli said, startling me out of the connection that bound me to my kidnapper. Only then did I notice the black material clutched in Eli's hands. Leah noticed it too, her steps hitching as fear flashed in her eyes.

"Leah."

The voice sounded like sandpaper and sleep. Leah turned her head to look at Remi. I did too.

"It's for your protection. That's all. I promised, remember? No one will hurt you. This way"—he nodded toward the cloth—"you can't see anything pertinent, not cars or locations or anything."

And by the time she could help the police trace their way back here, to the warehouse, it would be empty.

"It's okay," Remi was saying, rough voice soothing despite the gravelly tone. "I promise."

"I don't trust promises from men like you," she said. "But I guess I don't really have a choice."

Remi's amber eyes flashed with something I didn't quite understand, then went cold. Just like his brother's. "Not if you want to be with your daughter tonight," he told her.

She gave him a short, sharp nod, then walked the last few steps to Eli. I watched her take a deep breath before the black bag settled over her face. Eli grasped her hand and led her to the door, where Levi took over. Before he walked her out, he glanced at Remi. Something passed between them, something deep. Something serious. And then Levi and Leah were gone and the door closed.

I couldn't help wondering when my turn would come. If it would come. Or, as Leah had said, if I even wanted it to.

I shoved the question away as Eli passed me. Not only had I not noticed the black bag in his hand, but apparently while I'd been with Leah, he'd been packing. A small stack of boxes and cases sat nearby. Eli strode past them to the computer desk, where another box awaited him. He shut down the system, then started disassembling it.

"Anything I can do to help?" I asked. If I wanted to stay somewhere near sane, some of the questions rattling around in my brain had to go, so here was the first one: did helping your kidnappers mean you were crazy?

I would be if I kept worrying about it.

Eli shook his head, completely unaware of the weird psychoanalysis going on in my brain. "You better pack your stuff."

Because you're taking me with you, or because you plan to dump the evidence after you get rid of me? I didn't ask, though. I went to the bedroom. The faint scent of sex rose from the bed, but I ignored it too. Maybe this should become my new modus operandi.

The black duffel Levi had packed my things in still sat next to the dresser, a few sets of clean clothes inside. Stripping off a pillowcase, I proceeded to stuff my dirty laundry into it, then retrieved my toiletries from the bathroom, neatly wrapped in a dry towel. Fifteen minutes, tops. That was all it took to visibly erase my existence from my prison.

Eli was even faster. By the time I reappeared, he had all but the heaviest equipment stowed away. "Let me get these in the van," he was telling Remi. "Then I'll get you settled."

I set my bag next to his stack. "What about me?"

Eli shook his head as he bent to retrieve two boxes from the pile. "You aren't going with us."

"I'm not?" A kick in my gut—fear, shock, maybe anger?—made my breath hitch. "Then —"

"Levi will be back in an hour. You'll go with him."

Right. Of course. To a drop-off point, like he was doing with Leah? Or another location, another prison? Or...

"Abby," Eli said. I glanced up, realizing I was still standing with the strap of my bag in my hand, frozen, every ounce of uncertainty on full display.

I cleared my throat. "Yeah?"

"He's not going to hurt you. I promise."

"There's a lot of promising going on today," I said.

"We mean it."

Since when had the pissy one decided I needed comforting? Maybe around the time that pity had appeared in his eyes. I glanced at Remi. Yeah, it was there too.

"Right. Okay." I gestured towards the pile. "Can I help?"

"Just stay here. Keep Remi company." And he was out the door. The *click* of the lock had a ring of finality about it, and I couldn't help wondering if it was a sign of things to come.

Chapter Twenty-Five

I prowled the warehouse, forward and back, forward and back, trying to work off the nervous energy that buzzed under my skin. Why did I have to stay here? Leah got to leave. Remi and Eli got to leave. They'd promised me Levi would return, but until then I was stuck waiting. Someone else was in control of my life. Again.

That had gotten old several days ago. Now it flat-out pissed me off. If I hadn't been ready to pound something, I might've laughed. I had been raised to glittering prophood—never worry my pretty little head, always look and feel and act perfect without making an actual decision about my life. *Enough*. When I finally made it out of this mess—and I'd suddenly decided I sure as hell was, because I wouldn't let anyone win but me—the prince charming and his king that I'd been raised to let run my life could go take a flying leap. I never, ever wanted to hand control of me over to anyone else. Never.

And that included Levi.

The warehouse seemed eerie with everyone gone. I'd been here alone before, but there was something in the air—or maybe just the knowledge that we weren't coming back here—that made the emptiness heavy, a weight pressing down on me that I couldn't ignore. Pacing didn't help. I switched to lying on the couch, but that only reminded me of Remi, wondering if he was still stable. If Leah had found help yet. If she was holding her daughter in her arms.

Her daughter didn't know how lucky she was.

I was still running the hamster wheel in my head when I returned from the bathroom. At least the toilet paper hadn't been packed. Or the food. I was making a sandwich, plastic knife in hand to spread mayo on a slice of bread, when the hairs on the back of my neck stood straight on end.

What the hell?

Setting the bread on my paper plate, I glanced around the room. There was nothing off that I could see, certainly nothing that had changed in the past couple of minutes. I didn't hear any—

Wait. I did hear something. I focused on the far wall of the warehouse as my mouth went dry. The sound wasn't recognizable at first, just a barely perceptible rumble, more of a vibration that I finally interpreted to be one of those heavy-duty diesel pickup trucks, the kind that took up more than their share of space in a parking lot. All along I'd figured the walls were soundproof given the lack of outside noise that filtered in, but apparently they weren't a hundred percent, because as I crept closer, the vibration grew stronger. And stronger. When I reached the corner closest to the bedroom and placed my hand flat on the wall, I could feel it. Right outside.

Was it Levi?

No, he wouldn't use a vehicle that loud, draw that much attention. Despite the absence of clues, my instincts told me something was wrong, very wrong. The unpleasant tingling running up my spine agreed.

Run. Now!

So I did.

I glanced around wildly, one question on my mind in that instant: Where can I hide? Where can I freaking hide? Everything was too open, the cabinets in the desk and kitchen too small. Still, I had to get away.

I was rounding the kitchen table when the wall exploded behind me.

One moment I was on my feet; the next, pain skidded through my palms and knees as I landed on the concrete floor. Barked words and the pounding of booted feet sent a chill up my spine. *Stand up, get away, Abby!* But no, standing would only reveal where I was. Dust and smoke moved through the cavernous space like fog. Taking advantage of the cover, I crawled toward the back wall of the warehouse and Remi's sickroom. The door hadn't been closed since he arrived, and I didn't have the means to close it, but it was the farthest from whoever had just blasted their way in here. So that's where I hid.

On the opposite side of Remi's hospital bed, crouched behind one of the tables Leah had insisted on, I pressed my spine into the wall and blinked hard against the sting of dust and smoke in my eyes. Tears squeezed out to trace down my cheeks, and the sting got worse. Only when I raised my hand to investigate did I realize I was still gripping the plastic knife, slick with mayonnaise, like a weapon I could use to protect myself. A bubble of laughter rose to my lips, but I clamped them tight. One sound and hysteria would take over, I knew it would. I threw the knife away, watching it skid into the gloom as my tension grew.

"Find the girl!"

Were they here for me? I opened my mouth to call out, but something in the words, the tone, held me back. Something not right. If they were rescuers thinking I was here with my kidnapper, why blow the wall and risk hurting me? Why wouldn't their focus be on finding and securing Levi first?

Unless…

Through the dust and smoke filling the living area, I saw white shots of light, alien probes piercing the darkness. Flashlights. But I couldn't see who held them. All I could do was scramble to push my back as far into the wall as I possibly could, and not let the whimper of fear knotting my throat past my lips.

The lights disappeared.

Minutes passed in silence. Then it came, a soft scrape—boots on concrete. Whoever the man was, he stepped carefully, quietly, hiding his approach, but the dust was beginning to settle, a film on the floor that crunched beneath the rubber of his heels. I sucked in a breath, held it—and almost choked on the dirty air. Stinging tears trailed down my cheeks as I squeezed my eyelids shut. What should I do, surrender or stay hidden? But instinct pressed me closer and closer to the wall, harder and harder, as those booted feet came near.

"There you are."

I forced my eyes open. A man I'd never seen before stood staring down at me, tension in every muscle of his body. He reminded me of Levi that way. Dressed all in black, his head covered in a helmet, he cradled what looked like a machine gun in his arms, bigger than anything I'd ever seen before. That gun was enough to make me hyperventilate. The smile that curved his thin lips made me shudder.

"Axe! Got her!"

Axe? Axe, the guy who sent someone after Remi in the hospital, Axe? Axe, the assassin hired by my father after Levi quit? The shudder became a full-body tremble that rattled my teeth.

"Bring her out."

Rough hands gripped my hair and jerked me out of my hiding place. I stumbled along next to him as he dragged me into the living area. Four men stood there, all big, all in black, all with those machine guns in hand.

A fifth man stepped into the group. Same clothes, same build, but this one had no helmet. Shaggy black hair fell over his brow, and a thick scar bisected his cheek. Axe, I assumed. Now I understood the name. Axe's gun hung from its long strap, resting against his side, a smaller handgun in his grip. He used it to gesture toward the floor. "Let's do it here."

Do what?

Using his grip on my hair, the man holding me forced me toward the group. Onto my knees. I stared up at them, watched as Axe took a step closer, then raised the handgun.

Time slowed to a crawl.

I'd never looked down the barrel of a gun before, and it occurred to me a bit hysterically that Levi hadn't needed one to take me prisoner. All he'd needed was his face and a little acting. I'd been so naive then, but not now. Not anymore.

"Who are you?" I asked, though I already knew. Anything to buy a few more breaths in my lungs. "What are you doing?"

Axe smiled. His scar puckered his cheek, making the expression all the more terrifying. "Eliminating a threat."

A laugh escaped; I couldn't help it. What kind of threat could I be, surrounded by mercenaries with guns as big as my head? I wasn't even wearing shoes, for Christ's sake.

Axe's eyes narrowed in displeasure. He adjusted his grip on the gun, his finger sliding onto the trigger. I watched the move in slow motion, every millimeter seeming to take an eternity as my death crawled closer and closer. The sudden need to pee hit me, and for one agonizing moment I thought I'd wet my pants before he fired the gun.

His fingertip pressed into place—

A shot split the air, loud and echoing and terrifying, and I startled, expecting pain, blood, something. None of it came. The gunshot was followed immediately by a *splat*—a solid object hitting a soft, wet target. Through the dust and darkness, I watched a garish splash of red sprout from Axe's neck, the warm spray of droplets landing across my face, my chest. Axe's startled eyes met mine.

The hand holding me tightened, threatening to tear out my hair. "Axe?"

A gurgle was their leader's only response. Blood bubbled from the wound in his throat. I gagged as his mouth opened, releasing a wash of red before he crumpled to the floor.

Curses bit through the air. Wild glances around the dim room. The man holding me shook himself free of my hair and reached for his weapon.

Another gunshot. Another *splat*.

The man dropped to his knees.

I didn't think, didn't hesitate. Palms flat on the dirty concrete, I pushed myself backward, right under the kitchen table. Away from the shots. Away from the blood. I needed protection. I needed—

More gunshots. Shouting. Booted feet running. The hard *thud* of falling bodies. I crouched under the table through it all, stunned, my eyes locked with the man who'd dragged me by my hair as he bled out in front of me. Only Levi shouting my name broke the gruesome connection.

"Here!"

It was more croak than anything, but he heard me. I knew because he came. His wide shoulders blocked out the sight of blood and death as he crouched beside the table. My eyes glanced over the handgun he gripped before meeting Levi's steel gaze.

He reached for my hand. "Let's go, little bird. Come on."

Chapter Twenty-Six

"Are you hurt?"

I rubbed my hands up and down my goosebumped arms. "I don't—no, I don't think so."

We were driving. Night had fallen, blanketing us in a private cocoon, but I couldn't get past the weirdness of the moment. Calmly talking after staring down the barrel of a gun. Riding in a car in the front seat next to Levi with no bag over my head, like we were a normal couple. Not feeling scared out of my mind being alone with him despite knowing he'd killed six men back there.

Definitely weird. Maybe I'd finally cracked up.

Or maybe seeing Levi kill the man who'd been sent to execute me had cemented everything in my mind. Levi, good. Derrick, bad. Because I had no doubt my father was behind the attack.

"Why did…" I shook my head. Why did I keep asking the same question over and over? The answer didn't change, no matter how much I wanted it to.

I might not have finished the sentence, but Levi knew me too well not to follow my train of thought, apparently. He shot me a glance as he slowed, preparing for a turn. I couldn't read it in what little illumination the dash provided. "For the same reason as everything else, I imagine. Derrick only seems to have one motive: he's cleaning up his mess."

"And I'm part of the mess."

"Not necessarily. I believe this might have been more about framing me for your murder."

"But"—I swallowed hard—"that means having his own daughter murdered." Sure, he'd released those pictures of me, and he didn't seem to be searching too hard for me despite knowing I'd been kidnapped, but ordering someone to murder me?

Levi didn't agree or disagree, and I let the subject drop. If we were right and Derrick's plan had been to have me killed, there was really no understanding that, was there? A father murdering his daughter to protect himself? He'd never been a good dad, but this was beyond my comprehension.

I pushed the thought away and turned in my seat until Levi took up my entire view—tall, tough, sexy even with the dirt on his skin and the grim set to his granite jaw and hooded eyes. His hands on the steering wheel were sure, confident. I focused on the safety those hands provided as we navigated a series of back alleys and cutoffs in a part of town I wasn't familiar with. Heck, at this point we could be out of town altogether and I'm not sure I'd know it. Cabs and limos didn't usually venture this far off the beaten path, and I'd never been allowed to drive. Just another way Derrick had controlled me.

The silence underlying the droning hum of tires on pavement settled my stomach and my thoughts. A wave of fatigue had my eyelids drooping and my head lolling against the headrest by the time Levi pulled behind another nondescript dark building and parked. "Where are we?"

"Someplace off the grid. Let's go."

My brain translated "off the grid" to "minimalist." A lame attempt at a grin tugged at my lips as I opened my door and stepped into the cluttered alley. A couple of dumpsters, boxes, steel barrels looking like they'd spent a hundred years in the rain…the place wasn't inviting, but that was most likely the point. Levi led me around a pile of garbage to a dark passageway. A few feet in, I heard him jostling his keys. How he could see to find the door, much less the keyhole, I had no idea, but after a moment's pause, the sliding of metal on metal, and a faint *crack*, a break in the darkness signaled the opening of a door.

The place was much smaller than the warehouse, and excruciatingly bare. This wasn't minimalist; this was last resort. There was no living room, only a basic kitchen setup and a card table with a couple of folding chairs. I really hoped the hall I saw to one side led to a bathroom, because I was going to need it soon.

Levi shut the outside door but didn't move farther into the room. "There's a bedroom in the back," he said quietly. "A few T-shirts and sweats back there. Toiletries in the bathroom." He eyed my clothes. "Why don't you wash those out as best you can in the sink, change. Get comfortable. I'll be back."

My heart gave a sick thump when he turned as if to leave. "Where are you going?"

Levi stopped. Faced me. A hand came up to stroke my tearstained, scratched cheek. Tension drained out of me, leaving behind a sudden weariness that wobbled my knees. One touch—that's all it took for my fear to settle. I tried to remind myself that relying on this man was dangerous, to my heart if not my body, but neither was listening. I was simply too tired.

"I'm going to make sure Remi and Eli are secure. It won't take long. I'll get food on the way back."

He wasn't abandoning me. And he was right; he had to check on his brothers, wherever they were. They might be fully capable, but he was the big brother, used to keeping everyone safe, used to protecting everyone around him. Even me. He'd protected me tonight in a way I could never have imagined, never have asked for, and still, he hadn't hesitated.

My heart turned over. I stepped closer. Levi's gaze dropped to the key in his hand, the doorknob, anywhere but me.

I didn't care. For once I was going to follow my instincts with him instead of playing it safe. So I eased right up to him, and this time it was my hands cupping his dust-smeared cheeks. I curved my fingers around his jaw to tug his face up. His eyes shot to mine.

"Thank you."

He started to speak—to say what, I don't know; Levi didn't seem like a *you're welcome* kind of guy. But before the words escaped, he abandoned them for a hard, quick kiss.

And was out the door before my eyelids could flutter shut.

Okay, then…

There wasn't much to explore. In the small bedroom, almost completely taken up with a full-size bed and small chest of drawers, I grabbed the smallest pair of sweatpants I could find and an old Atlanta Braves T-shirt that would swallow me whole, and scooted into the bathroom. The sight that met me in the mirror sent a jolt through me. Dust covered my hair, smudged my face, my clothes. Across the front of my shirt, a spray of red droplets caught my attention. Blood. A sudden flash of Axe holding the gun on me, Levi's shot, a spray of red from the man's neck, hit me hard, making my stomach turn over. I snatched the shirt over my head and threw it into the tiny trash can before the turning over became something else altogether.

The sink was too tiny to wash my jeans, so I put them in a corner for later and focused on my underwear. When they'd been washed and wrung out, hanging on the towel rack, I climbed into the tub, turned the water as hot as I could stand it, and flipped the spray on. Thank God for good water pressure.

I didn't hear Levi return, but I felt him. Funny how that worked. It was as if he charged the molecules in the air around him, sending off a signal the hairs on my arms and the back of my neck picked up the minute he walked into a room. My skin became sensitive in an instant, my belly clenched, and that most secret part of me heated. Rivulets of water streamed over my budding nipples, teasing them, mimicking the trace of Levi's tongue.

My reaction was insane—I'd almost been killed, seen someone die for the first time, and here I was, what? Lusting after a killer?

That's exactly what I was doing. And for once, I refused to feel guilty about it.

I cleared my throat as quietly as I could. "Coming in?"

The question hung for a moment in the air; then came the rustle of clothing, the *thunk* of boots—one, two—hitting the floor. I kept my back turned when Levi climbed in behind me, but couldn't resist a peek over my shoulder.

He looked grim. My heart tripped.

"Are your brothers okay?" Please don't let them have been hit too.

Levi's hands landed on my tense shoulders, giving them a squeeze, then shifted down my back to my hips, meandering, almost as if his fingers couldn't resist the feel of my skin. A cool chill followed his sigh as the air hit my spine. "They're fine. Safe."

A little of my tension left me. Levi stepped close to my back, his palms sliding around my hips to settle low on my belly, and a new kind of tension took over. "And Leah?" I'd forgotten to ask about her in the chaos of the past few hours.

"She should be back with her daughter by now."

I covered his hands with mine and pressed them into me. "You're a good man, Levi."

The statement startled us both, but as it settled between us, I realized I truly believed it. Had we met under the best circumstances? No. Had Levi's actions been justified? Oddly enough, I couldn't answer an unequivocal no to that one. If my sibling had been targeted, revenge might've looked like a good option to me too.

What he'd done had hurt, but if it had led me here, to this moment, to this feeling, would I have chosen another path?

No.

"Don't make that mistake, Abby."

I swallowed hard. "What mistake?"

"Thinking I'm good."

A chuckle hiccuped in my throat. "Levi…" How could I explain this to him when I was only beginning to understand it myself? I thought hard for a moment. "My first boyfriend tried to take me to bed. I was sixteen, but I knew something wasn't quite right about him. When I refused, he took great pleasure in telling me how my father had paid him to date me, how the money wasn't enough to put up with a cock tease. Ever since—" My laugh came out this time, but strained. There was nothing I could do about that. "If I'd been someone else, maybe it wouldn't have mattered so much, but I'm not, and I couldn't trust anyone to be genuine. They were all connected to Derrick in some way, you know?"

I threaded my fingers through his against my belly, mimicking the connection I sensed between us every time he came near me.

"So am I."

"You are, aren't you?" I pressed our hands into my stomach until it felt like the imprint would be there forever. "But you're not like them. Like him."

Levi brushed his body against my back, the move at once sensual and threatening. His breath whispered in my ear. "I'm just like Derrick. Just because I took your virginity doesn't mean I won't hurt you to get to him."

Why would I expect anything else? *Because of this,* I wanted to say, clenching his fingers between mine. *The connection of our bodies, deeper than anything I've ever felt before.* But the feeling was the problem, wasn't it?

"No, of course not." I untangled my hands and reached for the soap. "I don't expect you to feel anything, Levi. That's who you are, Mr. Ice. We wouldn't want emotions to bother you in your complicated killer world, right?"

Chapter Twenty-Seven

Levi gripped my waist hard, jerking me around so fast I almost slipped. The soap skidded from my hand to zip around the bathtub, but we both ignored it as Levi used his big body to press me into the wall. His hand spanned my throat, squeezing lightly. I'd accused him of being emotionless, but emotions seeped through his fingers, through the gray eyes boring into mine. "Look at me, Abby. Really look. Not with some rose-colored glasses and Disney princess ideas. I'm not some fairy-tale prince. And your hymen didn't contain any magic that will turn me into one."

I looked; I truly did. But what I saw wasn't the cold assassin who'd shot down six men earlier. No, I saw desperation in his eyes. Who was he trying to convince, him or me?

Levi's grip tightened, his gaze hazing over as he looked at something I couldn't see. "I killed my first man at twelve years old. Twelve. We'd been on the streets a year, me, Remi, and Eli." His thumb raked up my jugular, back down. "The man deserved it, trying to lure Remi off alone. When I stepped in, he didn't like it, but that was okay because he didn't feel that way for long. He didn't feel anything for long, and after that, neither did I."

Pain zinged through my windpipe, and a whimper escaped.

Levi swallowed hard, that distant look still in his eyes. "That's who I am," he whispered hoarsely.

I covered his hand with mine, allowed the hard tips of my nipples to brush across his belly. A tingle swept through my body, but it was the hard push of his erection against my thigh that I wanted. That I got. "That's who life forced you to be. But it's not all that you are."

The planes of his face turned granite hard at my words. With his hand at my throat, Levi lifted me off my feet, sliding me up the wall until our bodies aligned perfectly. My knees went to his hips automatically, seeking purchase, security, and he took advantage, slamming home deep inside me in a single hard thrust. Proving his point. Taking instead of giving. Except...

My body was already wet, soft, hot. Welcoming. The instant he realized it, he groaned. His mouth went to my neck, his hands to my ass, and then he was taking me with abandon, sinking deep, sliding out, over and over to the chorus of our moans and cries and the wet slap of our bodies. The angle slammed his pelvis against my clit with every thrust. Seconds was all it took for my body to seize around his, the powerful contractions pulling him along with me until we both slumped against the shower wall, survivors of a shipwreck we hadn't seen coming and still couldn't quite comprehend. All we could do was hold each other tight in the aftermath.

When Levi softened enough that he slipped out of me, it seemed to wake him up. Hands holding me tight as if worried I would fall, he stepped into the spray of the water and closed his eyes, let the flood cover him for the longest moment. When they opened, the steel had softened to storm clouds and rain.

He pulled me fully under the water. Ran his hands over me. Stared deep into my eyes. "You'll end up getting hurt, little bird."

I stared right back, and knew, in that moment, that I was strong. Right here, right now. Levi might have the muscles and the fighting skills and the weapons, but when it came to emotions, he saw only fear. Or anger. I knew what I was feeling, recognized it—and when it came to him, I savored it. Whatever the future brought, I had this moment, with this man. And I wasn't about to waste it.

"That's nothing new, Levi. But sometimes the hurt is worth it."

I reached for him. Cupping his face earlier had felt odd, tentative, like I was trespassing on sacred ground. This time I stepped out as if I owned that ground—my hands landed on his chest, smoothing down the slick hills and valleys of his body, memorizing the man through my fingertips. His eyes heated again the lower I went and, when I reached the thick swell of his semi-erect penis? Hot, flaming inferno.

Holding his weight in my hands felt surreal. I traced his length, from the wide mushroom tip to the rapidly tightening shaft, long enough to reach deep inside me. I could still feel it, the impact of his body inside mine. He'd carved out a space for himself in a way that had seemed impossible a week ago. The base of his erection was thicker, the soft skin of his sac drawn up as if it could hurry his semen toward its release. When I cradled it, my fingertips pressed just behind, and Levi made a sound deep in his throat that told me exactly what that small pressure did to him.

I couldn't help it; I smiled. Levi traced the curve with a fingertip, his gaze unreadable.

"Think you're pretty smart there, don't you, little bird?"

I shook my head—I didn't have enough ego for that. "No, not smart." With one hand I slid up his length again, then down, fascinated as his eyes lost focus, this time not in a horrible memory of the past, but in the pleasure I could give him. I brought my free hand to his face, traced the rugged stubble along his cheek, the full slope of his bottom lip. So many textures. So much I needed to feel. "This isn't smart, Levi. This is just instinct." And maybe something special. I wouldn't say it aloud, but I could feel it, bringing tears to my eyes and an ache to my heart. Something very special.

Levi nipped my finger as it traveled back the way it had come. "Let me show you my instincts."

There was no time to agree or disagree. The words left his mouth, and he had me out of the shower the next instant. The towel he used was rough, unrefined, but he smoothed it over my skin like butter, a look of fierce concentration on his face as he searched out every droplet, every crease and fold. The anger when he'd first entered the shower had been replaced by determination—to do what? Pleasure me? Maybe find pleasure for himself?

But no, he'd done that against the shower wall, and I didn't think he believed any more than I did that this could be mutually exclusive. Not after the full-body orgasm we'd shared.

The full-size bed wasn't quite long enough for Levi's length, but he stretched me out, from one corner to the opposite, and crawled over me anyway. A growl escaped him as he gathered my arms and locked them above my head, his stare searing me as it took in my bared body. He started at my neck, every lick and scrape of his teeth and gentle suck pooling liquid heat in my core. I pushed up on my heels, needing more, needing him to devour me, consume me until all I knew was him.

Levi didn't waver. He seemed absorbed with the texture of my skin, the rising slopes, the hard, jutting tips, the long slides into the valleys. When his mouth surrounded one straining nipple and he drew on me, a small scream escaped. I couldn't get close enough, press hard enough for the satisfaction I suddenly needed now, immediately. My body craved the peak, and...

"Levi!"

"Shhhh," he whispered against my breastbone, his stubble rasping the mounds on each side. "Anticipation, remember?"

A curse bit through the air as I realized what he really meant: torture. My core cramped with denial. "Damn it, Levi!"

He rubbed his chin along the underside of one breast, up to my aching tip. The scrape of his almost beard shot waves of acute pleasure through me. I arched closer again.

His chuckle held a touch of pure evil.

I tugged on my hands, and surprisingly he let me go. Probably so he could grab my ass, which he promptly did. His massive hands cupped me, kneaded me, his fingertips brushing the sensitive folds between my legs. I speared my fingers through the rich lengths of his dark hair and urged his mouth toward mine, urged him to take me, complete me in a way I'd never discovered with another human being.

Levi levered himself over me. Nudged my legs apart. Aligning our bodies, he wasted no time pushing close, his hips seeming impossibly wide, even after all this time. Cool air tingled along the cream coating my core, and then he was inside me.

His hips weren't the only thing that was still impossibly wide. My body was swollen, tight. I tilted my head back and panted, waiting for the deadlock grip to ease. Levi's mouth at my nipples helped—he moved from one to the other, sucking, biting, rubbing his lips and sandpaper stubble over the sensitive buds. Within minutes I was trying to climb him, crying out, begging for him to move, to give me what I needed, make this torture stop.

One hard push into my body was all it took to detonate the bomb waiting inside me.

Levi didn't stop. Thrust after thrust after thrust drove through my contractions, setting off mini explosions that tied my lower belly into knots. When I could finally open my eyes, that steel-gray determination stared back at me. Levi chased his pleasure as much as mine. Pushed into me until I felt bruised. And when he finally reach the agonizing peak and completion shook him off his knees, I cradled his body close between my legs, against my belly and breasts and neck, convinced that nothing else I would ever experience, in my entire life, could possibly compare to the power of us, joined so tightly together that we became one. I never wanted to let go—of him, of this. So I didn't; I simply drifted to sleep with Levi in my arms.

I hadn't slept that hard or that deeply since the night he drugged me. Sometime in the darkest part of the night, I woke to Levi behind me, inside me, his fingers on my clit, but even the slow roll of orgasm couldn't keep me awake after the long, exhausting day. Tomorrow could take care of itself. Tonight, I had all I needed.

Chapter Twenty-Eight

The silence between us was uneasy the next day. Levi exuded confidence in everything he did—except emotions. I knew that now. Killing someone? No problem. Admitting you cared about someone? Another thing altogether.

The pancakes Levi had run out for earlier—apparently my hit man had an affinity for pancakes—were almost gone when his phone buzzed across the little card table's padded surface. Levi glanced at the screen, set down the plastic spork that came with breakfast, and answered.

"Just a minute, bro." Placing the phone back on the table, he switched the call to speakerphone. One tap on the screen, but the gesture eased something wound too tight in my chest this morning. Levi might not be able to say the words, but he trusted me. Letting me hear his conversation with his brothers proved it.

"Whatcha got?" he asked as he sporked up his last bite.

It was Eli who answered. "Good morning to you too, asshole."

Levi grunted, but I could see a grin pulling at the corners of his lips. "You are such a girl. How's Remi?"

A rough clearing of a throat came across the line, then Remi's gravelly voice. "I'm fine."

I rolled my eyes. The man had been concussed, comatose, shot, and still considered himself fine. Apparently anything else was *being a girl*. Neanderthals. I swallowed the last of my coffee, trying to hide my amusement.

Levi was frowning. "Keep that dressing changed like Leah showed you, Eli. Don't—"

"Yeah, yeah, I got it. Now on to other things."

Levi scrubbed a hand over his face. My grin peeked out whether I wanted it to or not. Levi's laser gaze pinned me as he gripped his jaw. "What's so funny?"

"How alike you are." I didn't bother trying to stifle a laugh.

His eyes dropped to my mouth, heating suddenly. "Keep laughing, little bird. You're just racking up points for later."

Oh really? I raised a brow. "Points for what?"

"Punishment."

My cheeks went hot.

"We've got business to take care of. Can you two play sex games on your own time?" Eli asked, voice rough with impatience and maybe a hint of embarrassment. I guess seeing Levi with a girlfriend wasn't normal.

I choked. *Not a girlfriend. Not a girlfriend. Remember that, Abby.*

Anyway... Eli was the one who'd started the touchy-feely stuff, but I decided not to point that out. Watching Levi choke over his brother saying *sex games* was satisfaction enough.

"Get on with it," Remi told them. Eli followed his brother's lead.

"Fine. While you've been playing—or whatever—I dug up the intel you wanted on Anthony Clark."

I dropped my face into my hand, wondering if I was going to survive the three of them together. Levi by himself was so much easier to deal with.

"A trucker," Eli was saying. "No ties that we could find to Derrick Roslyn. Parents both deceased. Uneventful stint in the army—"

"Get to something we don't know, Eli."

I didn't know any of it, but I doubted they'd meant to include me. At least one lightbulb had lit up in my brain. They were discussing the mark, the man who had been the catalyst for everything that had happened to me. But what did Anthony Clark, a man I'd never heard of, have to do with my life?

"Right." Clicks came through the line—Eli on the computer. If we had any tech capabilities here, Levi had hid them well. There wasn't even a clock radio on the nightstand in the bedroom. "Turns out that while Anthony Clark was deployed overseas during the Gulf War, his only sibling, a sister, went missing. Her name was Caroline Clark. Ran away from home. The police never found any leads, but according to records, Anthony continued to contact the detective assigned to his sister's case for years afterward."

"How does that help us?" Levi asked.

"I contacted Clark's partner in the trucking company they owned. They were partners for fifteen years, so they were pretty close. He told me Anthony said he needed a week off. He was headed here to Georgia, apparently had a lead on his sister. That was a week before the contact."

197

Contacting what? But when I looked at Levi, I knew. A week before he'd been contacted about the hit. The man had been searching for his missing sister right before he was killed.

Coincidence?

"What do we have on the sister?" Levi asked. "Any leads?"

So…not a coincidence.

"I managed to get an address from the boss. Apparently Clark had tracked Caroline to a homeless shelter just south of the city. A worker there remembered the sister and told him this was her first apartment after she managed to get on her feet."

The address wasn't one I knew, but when Eli mentioned the neighborhood, I recognized it as a low-income, somewhat sketchy area of town. Not a place a society girl like me would ever have been allowed to go. I wondered how Anthony's sister had fared actually living there.

"I can check out the location this afternoon," Eli was saying.

"No."

Eli growled. "I can—"

"I don't want you leaving Remi alone," Levi insisted. "I will take care of any legwork."

"I'm fine," Remi complained. "I don't need a babysitter."

"Of course you do. And don't bother arguing," he said over Remi's protests. Levi reached for the phone. "I'm the boss and I said no. Now go take a nap, you big baby."

"I'm not— You dick—"

Levi cut off his brother's sputtering by clicking End. A grin transformed him from grim assassin to gleeful kid in an instant—obviously he enjoyed frustrating his younger brother. I'd never understood the whole sibling-dynamics thing since I've never had any, but watching the brothers interact, I was beginning to see that torture and teasing were a huge part of it. And I knew better than most how good Levi was at the torture part.

A delicious tingle ran through me, alongside memories of last night. That one thought and I was lost.

Levi grabbing the plastic container in front of me jolted me out of the past. I watched as he cleaned up breakfast, staying quiet, giving myself time to think. To screw up my courage. When he turned toward the hall, my decision had been made.

"You're going to check out the address this morning, aren't you?" I asked.

The question brought Levi to a halt. "Yeah. People talk more when they can see your face."

My eyebrows hit my hairline.

"What? It's true."

"Maybe." I was pretty sure that was true, but with Levi? "Are you sure we shouldn't let Eli take this one?"

Levi leaned an elbow on the wall near his head. The act stretched his body out, making him bigger, scarier...sexier. I swallowed hard.

A sexy smirk appeared on that handsome face. "I think I know more than enough tricks to convince someone to talk to me."

And, of course, I knew firsthand how true that was. Fear hadn't even crossed my mind the night I'd met him.

I'd concede the point to him. I had bigger victories to shoot for.

"I think I might go stir-crazy if you leave me all alone here." I cleared my throat. "Would you... I mean..." *Come on, Abby, spit it out.* "Take me with you."

I held my breath, my lungs straining as I waited. Those emotionless eyes examined me like a bug under a microscope, and I couldn't help wondering if Levi thought I was ridiculous. A kidnapped woman wanting to investigate alongside her kidnapper? But I had to take the chance. I needed to understand what had triggered all this, as much—or maybe more—as Levi needed to destroy my father. The question was, could Levi accept me as a partner rather than someone he had complete control over?

I'd taken the risk; now would he?

"I don't like the idea of you out on the street," Levi said, frowning.

The air escaped my lungs in a whoosh. That wasn't a no. "Haven't you heard? I ran away from my abusive fiancé. Who's going to believe otherwise with those...images...all over the TV and Internet?" A fact I still couldn't think about without sweating. "I don't even want to look anyone in the eye, knowing they've seen those. I'll accept any disguise you want to give me." Total honesty. The more we could hide my face so no one knew who I was, the better, in my opinion. "Besides...don't you think I deserve to know the truth?"

Levi stood for a long moment, staring me down, whatever was going on behind those eyes so well hidden that I couldn't even get a hint. When he opened his mouth, I braced myself.

"Get dressed then."

He turned and walked away. Just like that, as if what he'd said wasn't momentous. As if he hadn't just dropped a bomb between us.

And I wasn't going to point it out. Levi was taking me through that steel door into the big, wide, unprotected world for the first time since I'd been taken captive, and I had clothes to put on. I scrambled to do so before he changed his mind.

Chapter Twenty-Nine

I felt a little like a mole climbing out of its hole for the first time in days. Sunlight seared my eyeballs, making me stumble as we left the alleys near the safe house. Levi didn't ask if I was okay, just helped steady me until I could blink away the blindness, then headed for the SUV parked on the other side of the dumpsters.

Neither of us had addressed the fact that he was trusting me not to yell for help or run away as soon as we were among people again. I could only assume that the trust he'd shown this morning, letting me hear his conversation with his brothers, had extended to public appearances. He didn't threaten me or insist I follow his lead. He just…took me outside.

The feeling of the sun on my face—and his trust in my soul—was intoxicating.

But there was still something nagging at me, something I needed to clarify. I strapped myself into the passenger seat, then turned to Levi. "I'm assuming we think Anthony Clark came into town, specifically to go to this address, looking for his sister."

Levi glanced over his shoulder as he backed out of the alley. "Yeah."

Classic noncommittal response.

"And if going there was what tipped Derrick off? Made him set up…" Saying *the hit* sounded too much like we were in *The Godfather*, so I didn't finish the sentence at all.

Levi shook his head, eyes on the road as he navigated the alleys and back roads I hadn't been able to identify in the dark. Still couldn't, for that matter. "Derrick won't have time to get a new team together before we get there."

"Axe's men won't pick up where he left off?"

"There aren't any more of Axe's men. And his was the best team on the East Coast." Levi shot me a cocky grin. "Except for me, of course."

Of course. My father always hired the best, and I'd seen for myself the ease with which Levi had taken down Axe's team. And Axe.

I turned my head to look out the window, and knocked the brim of my ball cap on the glass. Levi had insisted it was all I needed to disguise my face. No one would expect Abigail Roslyn to walk the streets in ratty jeans and a worn sweatshirt two sizes too big, and no way in hell would they expect a ball cap. I had been raised to be the epitome of grace— even if I'd fallen short of those high expectations time and again—and that meant ball caps were out. The thing felt odd on my head, constricting, but the brim hid the top part of my face well.

When I wasn't trying to knock it off, at least.

It didn't take us long to get there, which meant Levi was hiding the two of us in an equally run-down part of the city. The address led us to a neighborhood of small duplexes, almost too small to believe someone could live in them, but the presence of kids running on the cracked sidewalks and dirty toys in the yards said families were sharing the tiny spaces. Levi drove through the neighborhood once, his eagle gaze scanning constantly. I didn't know what he was looking for, so I helped as best I could by keeping quiet. Finally he circled around to a duplex in the middle of the complex and parked.

"Stay behind me," Levi said as I grasped the door handle. I nodded in understanding—though not necessarily in agreement—and got out.

There weren't any toys in this yard, only two clotheslines strung along the outside perimeters, one for each side of the duplex. Levi headed toward the right side, and I followed. I'd always loved his wide shoulders and tall, muscular build, but right now they left me frustrated—I couldn't see anything! Even at five-five, the body in front of me blocked out any possibility of a view. I made do with glancing around the neighborhood, wondering if Levi could be wrong and some hit man had us in his sights right now. I was so busy looking that I bumped into Levi when he stopped at the door.

The sharp sound of his knuckles on wood startled me, loud in the relative quiet of the neighborhood. No answer. Levi rapped again, and I could see his head tilt as if he was listening. To see if someone was home but refusing to come to the door? If I wasn't expecting someone—or if I was expecting trouble—I might not answer either, but I listened as well, and didn't hear a whisper of movement inside.

"If you're looking for the Johnsons, you're too late. They moved out last week."

Levi swung to the left, blocking me from view once again. I fought the urge to growl in frustration.

"I'm sorry," he said to the woman who had spoken. I immediately recognized the tone—pleasant, unassuming, all choir boy meets door-to-door salesman. "The Johnsons?"

"Yes. They were the last tenants. Or maybe you were looking for the Smiths?"

Seemed the residents here tended to come with generic last names.

"No, actually." Levi turned more fully to face the woman. "I'm looking for a tenant from around twenty years ago. You wouldn't happen to know if any of the residents have lived here that long?"

"Well, honey"—I couldn't help but laugh at the idea of someone calling Levi *honey*—"I've been right here in this little corner of the world for nearly thirty years. My memory's not what it used to be, but I can probably help you." The sound of a screen door creaking open reached me. "Why don't y'all come on in?"

I wanted to yell at the nice older lady to not be so trusting, to not invite someone she didn't know into her home, but Levi was already moving forward, charm oozing from his thanks and appreciation for being willing to talk with us.

We walked into the dim interior of the woman's house. The place was almost as small as the hideaway Levi and I were in right now, but much more homey, all aged wood and doilies and green plants in hangers. The older lady, I could now see, was a petite black woman, hair gray with age, a bit of a stoop to her shoulders, but when she turned around, her eyes were sharp as tacks.

"Have a seat," she said, gesturing to the worn plaid sofa near the recliner she occupied. "May I get you some refreshments?"

"No, thank you, ma'am," Levi said. *Ma'am.* A word I'd never thought to hear coming out of his sexy, dangerous mouth. "I apologize, but your name is…?"

"Geneva. Geneva Sanderson. And you?"

I expected some fake name along the line of Johnson and Smith, but he simply smiled. "Levi."

I noticed he didn't give my name.

"Nice to meet you." Geneva smiled up at me. "Well, sit, young lady."

"Th-thank you." I sat. Without thought I reached up, took the cap from my head, and shook out my hair. It wasn't until I heard Geneva's gasp that I realized what I'd done.

Geneva pressed a frail hand over her heart, those intense eyes wide and disbelieving as she studied my face. "Caroline?"

God, what had I done? I darted a glance at Levi, whose narrowed eyes were watching Geneva.

"You knew her, then?" he asked.

Geneva stared at me, and I swore I saw the sheen of tears brighten her eyes. "Oh yes, I knew Caroline very well. Are you…" She raised her hand as if to touch me, to make sure I was real. "Are you her daughter? Little Abby all grown up?"

The words registered in my ears the moment they were said, but it took longer for my brain to puzzle out their meaning. When I finally did, it hit me like a freight train. "Her daughter? Caroline's daughter? I—" A sudden sick twist of my stomach had me swallowing hard. "Levi?"

There was supposed to be a connection between Derrick and Caroline, but not this. It wasn't supposed to involve me. It was… I mean, this was… "I—"

The room started to spin.

Levi's hand slid into mine, gripped me hard. His touch steadied me, helped me catch my breath. But I couldn't look away from Geneva as she soaked in the sight of me, tears trickling down her lined face. I hadn't realized I'd joined her until Levi handed me a tissue.

I looked away.

After mopping myself up, I looked back to Geneva. "You…remember me?"

"Lord, girl. Even if I didn't, you are the spitting image of your mama. But I'm guessing you weren't aware of that." Sorrow settled onto her face like falling snow. "I was afraid of that."

"What?"

But Levi's raised hand forestalled Geneva's answer. "Maybe we should start at the beginning. Mrs. Sanderson, you've already guessed that Abby didn't know her mother." He left out the part about me already having a mother, or at least, thinking I already had one. My mind reeled. "What can you tell us about Caroline Clark? We've only managed to track her here. What happened to her?"

Geneva eased back into the soft cushions of her chair. "She never would tell me where she came from, but her people weren't good to her, from the sounds of it. She worked three jobs to get herself out of a homeless shelter and into her place next door. Wanted to go back to school, but she got pregnant before she could. I do know she was so proud to be here. She worked hard to build a good life for herself—and later, for you too," Geneva said to me.

"But…if she was my mother"—big *if*, right? Had to be…—"then who is my father?"

"She wouldn't tell me, child. I gather he had money; he used to send one of those big black town cars to pick her up sometimes. The last time I saw her, she had you bundled up in the pink blanket I gave her when you were born, and she was getting in that car again. Caroline said her man had gotten her a new place, somewhere her baby could be safe."

Geneva eased her way forward in her chair, preparing to stand. "She wasn't supposed to give a forwarding address, but she did anyway. Worried her brother might come looking for her." She shuffled over to a tall hutch in the corner. "He never did."

Except he had. And now he was dead.

Chapter Thirty

After rummaging for a moment, Geneva pulled a slip of paper from one of the drawers. "Here it is."

"You kept it all this time?" Levi asked. I caught a hint of suspicion in the words, but I didn't care. All I cared about right now was getting that paper in my hands, seeing my mother's handwriting for the first time. A mother who loved me. Wrapped me and carried me instead of handing me over to nannies. I couldn't remember a single picture of me as a child in my mother's arms.

Had Caroline cherished me? Was that even possible?

Geneva placed the paper in my trembling hand.

"Recognize it?" Levi asked.

The address, I assumed he meant. But I hadn't taken it in. I was too busy staring at the graceful loops and elegant lines that made up the words. My mother's handwriting. My mother's—

"Abby."

I jerked my gaze from the paper.

"The address. Do you recognize it?"

I looked again, then slowly shook my head. "No." In town, obviously, given the city and zip code, but I didn't know street names well beyond the major thoroughfares, not being a driver myself. I reluctantly passed the paper to Levi. "Do you?"

"No." He looked up at Geneva. "And she never came back? Not to pick up mail or her things, nothing?"

"Nothing," the older woman confirmed sadly. "I knew when she didn't that something wasn't right, but"—she shrugged—"who would listen to me?"

About a homeless girl who had gotten herself pregnant? Not many people, unfortunately. The story was too common in the big city to care about them all.

I reached for the address. Levi seemed reluctant to part with it, but released it to my care. When I caught myself rubbing my fingertips over the surface as if the paper held some clue beyond the few lines written on it, I slipped it into my pocket.

"Wherever she is, she would be so proud to see you, little Abby," Geneva said.

Would she? I gave Levi a desperate, get-me-out-of-here-now look. He stood immediately.

"Mrs. Sanderson, thank you for your help."

"Anytime, anytime." She reached for me, her wizened hands feeling far too delicate around mine. "You come back to see me sometime, okay, dear? I'll tell you all about your mama. I bet I even have a few pictures here somewhere."

My heart squeezed. I wanted more than anything to come back, but I didn't want to place Geneva in danger. Still... "Of course I will." I leaned in, brushing a kiss on her powdery-soft cheek. "Thank you so much."

Geneva patted my hand one last time, and Levi led me out the door.

The ride back was heavy with silence. Levi insisted on stopping at a drive-through despite my protests that I couldn't eat. Just the thought of food made me feel green. Smelling it wasn't much better, so I cracked my window enough to let fresh air in but not the rain that had begun to fall.

"So Camilla Roslyn wasn't your mother," Levi finally said.

I kept my head turned, biting down on my thumbnail until the cuticle screamed with pain.

"She left to go to your father."

"We don't know that. We don't know the name of the man she was seeing." I clenched my fist. "We don't know that I'm Caroline's either. It could all be a coincidence. My birth certificate—"

"Is easily forged," Levi pointed out. "Especially for someone who has as much money as Derrick does."

True.

"Let's say, just for the sake of argument, that she is your mother." Levi stopped at a four-way, then went straight. "She didn't marry your father, obviously."

"He would already have been married." Derrick and Camilla had been together a couple of years before I made an appearance.

"Right." The light tap of his finger against the leather steering wheel told me he was thinking. "Some women would willingly give up a child, but Geneva's description didn't paint Caroline as one of them."

Also true. Even leaving had been based on the safety of her daughter.

Her daughter. I couldn't say *me*, not yet. I just couldn't.

"What if—"

I held up a hand. Cutting Levi off. "Just…give me a minute, okay?"

I didn't look to him for confirmation, but he fell silent, and that was all the answer I needed. I sat very still, the rain drumming on the hood and windows muffling the world outside, and let the pieces fall into place in my mind.

The man, Anthony Clark, had come here to discover what had happened to his sister, who might very well have been my mother. Caroline had been a young country girl on her first adventure away from a restrictive, possibly abusive home. Anthony was dead—and if this was all true, if Geneva was right, then my uncle, the only family I might've had left, was gone. And my mother had disappeared off the face of the earth.

My father had ordered Anthony killed. I knew that, understood it, but still couldn't truly comprehend it. I tried to examine the fact logically, critically, but I couldn't stop my breath from speeding up, my heart from racing until I worried that I might pass out. Because the mere thought led to one other conclusion—if Derrick had killed Anthony, if he had tried to kill Remi and Levi and even me…then he could very well have killed my mother too.

Why? The answer was simple: politics.

Powerful men had mistresses all the time. My father had married for political and social gain. Like any other child who'd lost a parent, I'd wanted desperately to know about the mother who'd died when I was no more than a toddler, but from what little I could gather from servants and news stories over the years, Camilla and Derrick hadn't seemed to have a particularly passionate relationship. She had been pregnant, though. I'd seen the pictures.

"If I'm not Camilla's child, what happened to her baby?" Even if Derrick's mistress did have a daughter, his wife's child would be the rightful heir, the refined, logical choice to assist Derrick in the life he wanted. Why choose me instead? And where was my half sibling?

"These things can be faked," Levi said thoughtfully.

"But why go to all the trouble?"

"I don't know." Levi reached for me, his firm palm meeting mine, steadying me. "I don't know all the answers yet, but we can find them."

Levi was good at finding the answers, but how long would that take?

I thought about the woman Geneva had described: young, hard-working, loving. A simple country girl would never have made a good politician's wife. But would he justify getting rid of her simply because she was a better mistress for a man like him than a wife? Would Caroline have threatened to come forward, reveal her identity—and possibly stop his career before it had time to truly take off—if he wouldn't care for her and her daughter?

Would Derrick have killed her?

The thought sent grief slicing through me. Surprisingly, the emotion was stronger than any denial that tried to rise. I was actually beginning to believe my father was more than capable of murder. Maybe having a gun held to my face by a man Derrick had sent after me had something to do with that. He had taken everything else in my life—my freedom, my self-esteem, my happiness. Was it really that big of a leap to think he'd stolen my mother too?

Levi threaded his fingers through mine. "I think the most important question we can ask is, where is she? What happened to her?"

I had a terrible feeling in my gut, one I couldn't ignore. "We're not going to find her, are we?"

Levi's sigh sounded as if it came from the depths of his soul. "No."

Just no. He didn't try to sugarcoat it, didn't try to hide the what-ifs. He just held on to me and gave me the truth. I squeezed my eyes shut against the sting of tears.

"Is there any way to prove it?" Prove that my father had killed my mother.

I opened my eyes, needing to see the truth in my lover's face, one way or another. Levi's mouth tightened, his gaze stormy as he glanced my way. "Without a body? Probably not."

How many men knew Derrick had hired a hit man? How many could follow that trail, the same way we had, and uncover the secret origins of Derrick's daughter?

There wasn't anyone else, though, was there? Levi had been approached for the original contract on Anthony Clark, and when he'd refused it… Well, Axe and his team were dead.

"What about a confession?"

Two realizations hit me as I said the words, both so profound that, if I'd been standing, they might've knocked me off my feet. One—I really believed it. I'd gone past the denial, the sense of unreality. It made perfect sense that my father had killed to secure his political future. This whole thing had gone from a hypothetical *maybe* to certainty in my gut.

And two—Derrick's motive for coming after Levi was suddenly very, very clear.

"Covering up."

Levi pulled into a darkened parking lot and put the SUV in park before turning to face me. "What?"

"Derrick is covering up," I said again. "You said the press conferences and leaks were tips to establish his own alibi, throw suspicion on others."

"Yeah."

"That's why he came after you. Not only because you refused his contract, but you also held a valuable piece of information—Anthony Clark's name. Think about it. How many people know, or could figure out, his secret? The most valuable players are all disappeared or dead—Caroline, Camilla, Anthony. Assuming only you and Axe had my uncle's information, only one of you is left. Whoever comes to take you out doesn't even have to know about the previous hit. You are the only person still alive who knows what Derrick did. He's about to make a run for governor, and I assure you, that's only a stepping stone. He's eliminating anyone who could connect him in any way with his—"

His secret past. My mother.

Except there was one connection with his past that didn't have to do with the hit on Anthony, wasn't there?

Me.

And he'd tried to make sure I couldn't talk either, when he'd sent Axe's team to kill me.

I turned my head, glaring fiercely out into the rain in an attempt to stave off the tears threatening to overtake me. Levi didn't push, didn't talk, simply put the car in motion again. It was as if he could sense how close I was to the edge. One step and I might fall, but I couldn't. I had to be strong—for me, for Caroline, wherever she was. Because I was the linchpin connecting all the pieces of the puzzle. And the one with the smallest target on my back if Derrick thought I didn't know.

That made me the only one who could prove what he had done, and take him down once and for all.

Chapter Thirty-One

Levi kept glancing at me as he drove. I caught glimpses from the corner of my eye but ignored them. My mind was racing too fast, too full, for anything else.

"I'm going to stop at Eli and Remi's," he finally said. "We need some supplies."

I made a sound that barely passed for approval—not that he needed any. But informing me of plans was, to me, an affirmation of the trust, still so fragile and new, between us. Things were changing; we were changing. But right now I didn't think I could deal with any more change.

We spent almost an hour driving. My confused mind couldn't keep all the turns and backtracking straight, but I figured Levi was making sure we weren't followed. Imagine my surprise when we turned into a nice, middle-class, older neighborhood with wide-spaced houses on gently rolling hills, with plenty of trees. Nothing like the areas Levi had kept me in, but maybe that was the point. Break the pattern and throw your enemies off the scent.

Levi retrieved a standard garage door opener from his jacket pocket and clicked the button as we neared the last house on a dead-end street. A typical '80s ranch. I guess it was true what they said about never knowing what your neighbors were up to. Surprisingly I felt a grin tug at my lips at the thought of the people who lived here—probably nice, quiet, even staid people—discovering they had an assassin for a neighbor. Levi didn't seem to notice as he pulled into the garage and lowered the door, for which I was grateful. Who wanted to explain how funny they found the fact that their lover was a hit man? Eli might laugh, but Levi?

I shrugged mentally, waiting in the growing gloom as the garage door trundled down and Levi gestured for me to get out.

"I'm going to shower and pack up some of my clothes. Do you need anything, little bird?"

"You got any clothes that would fit me better here?" I desperately missed the bag that had been lost back at the warehouse.

"Afraid not." Levi looked a bit chagrined.

"Then I'm afraid what I need, you can't provide." I gave him a lopsided grin.

One eyebrow cocked in my direction. "We both know that's not the case."

A blush burned my cheeks. Put that way, I guess he wasn't wrong.

He must've seen the answer on my face because he winked. Levi winked. I was still sitting in my seat, openmouthed, staring at the driver's seat, when he opened my door.

Eli met us at the entrance. "How did it go?"

Levi threw a glance at me over his shoulder, his lips tight.

"Go ahead," I told him. Better him than me. If I had to explain what my father had done—and what I suspected he had done—I might completely lose it. Completely.

"Right." He turned to Eli. "Get her a drink."

Eli's raised eyebrows said *that bad?* but he went to the kitchen without commenting. I sat on the couch and ignored Levi giving Remi a hard time about being out of bed until Eli reappeared.

"What is it?" I asked him, eyeing the tall glass he handed me.

"Coke."

I took a large swallow, choked, and whimpered against the burning in my throat. "And rum?"

"Whiskey," Eli said.

"Right." I downed half the glass.

Remi made a sound in his throat, half laugh, half groan of pain. Levi threw him a concerned look.

"What happened?" Eli asked.

"We met one of Caroline's neighbors," Levi began.

I drained my glass, then stood. "I'll be right back.

In the bathroom I splashed ice-cold water on my face for a full minute, the numbness taking over my cheeks and nose and lips sharp enough to stave off the tears that felt like they would drown me if I didn't somehow force them away. All day the plan had been for no one to see me on the street; now, having these three men see me was too much.

Maybe they sensed that. When I came back to the living area, all talking ceased. No one would meet my eyes. I thought about asking Eli for another drink but figured one was bad enough. I needed to think straight, not drown my sorrows. As much as I wanted to stick my head in the sand, let Levi take me back to our little urban hideaway and convince him to take me to bed, I couldn't ignore what I had learned today. I had to do something about it, and right now, while Levi was occupied, might be my only opportunity.

"Okay?" Levi asked, breaking the silence that pressed on me like a fifty-pound wet blanket. I caught the tensing of his hands, the aborted movement toward me, and felt my heart soften. For a man that raised himself to be invulnerable to emotions, to risk, Levi still had good instincts. What kind of man would he have been if his parents had lived?

"I'm okay." I sat next to him on the couch and reached for his hand, closing the distance between us. Levi's fingers immediately tangled with my own. Strong. Steady. Deadly when necessary. Peace flickered inside me.

"We ordered pizzas. Eli's going to help me pack some equipment to take with us." His fingers tightened on mine the slightest bit, then softened. "I don't want to be caught off guard again."

"Of course." I didn't want him to be caught off guard either. Well, by anyone coming after us, anyway. A plan was forming in my head. If I knew anything, it was that Levi would never agree to let me go anywhere alone, unprotected. But the answers I needed were at the one place he couldn't go; I knew it deep in my gut. Derrick was an arrogant, self-righteous bastard—and that was going to be his downfall.

"I'll get a shower, we can eat, then we'll go," Levi said. He hesitated, his fingers coming up to lift my chin until our gazes locked. "Abby—"

I wished he'd call me *little bird*. Birds were fragile, they lived in cages, but in the wild they soared, free and strong, high above all threats. I wanted to be like that right now.

"What?"

Levi didn't answer, just stared into me, delving deep into my soul. What was he looking for?

His fingers tightened on my chin, and he leaned close. "Keep Remi company?" he asked, breath warm on my lips.

What else was I supposed to do? "Sure."

"Good." He held me a moment longer, then settled his lips on mine. I closed my eyes and opened to him—his warmth, his confidence, his tenderness. If someone had asked me if a hit man could be tender, I'd have answered no without hesitation. But Levi had shown tenderness to me from that very first night. He'd taken care of me in my inexperience, in my fear, in my pain. He talked tough, but his actions had revealed the true man, the one he kept locked away so no one could sense that he was vulnerable.

But I'd found the tender underbelly, and I do anything to protect him like he'd protected me.

"He's not going off to war. Just to pack up some AKs. Give it a rest."

Trust Eli to break into the moment. Levi smiled against my lips.

"Right. Let's go," he said, drawing away. Reluctantly, maybe? My heart hoped so; my head said it might be better, when this was all over, if he wasn't as attached as I was. What kind of future did we have, after all, the society girl dethroned and the assassin with a well-protected heart?

I glanced at Remi as his brothers headed down the hall. Those amber eyes were fixed on me, dark, searching.

"May I get you anything?" I asked, the hostess in me rising.

"Yeah, some water?"

Had his voice always been this gruff, or was it lack of use during his injury that had caused it? I hadn't known him before, so… "Sure."

It was in the kitchen, pouring Remi's drink, that the plan snapped together in my mind. I was so focused on the thoughts racing through my brain that I didn't notice the too-full glass until water spilled over my hand and soaked the sleeve of my sweatshirt. "Damn it!"

"Everything all right?" Remi called from the living room.

"Yes, just making a mess." I mopped up the water with a paper towel, but my gaze was locked on the delivery menu sitting on the counter. Pizza was coming. A car… The door…

"Here you go." I passed Remi his water and took a seat on the corner of the couch closest to him.

Remi sipped for a moment. I could feel his scrutiny. I'd gotten used to Levi's intense gaze, but Remi, not so much. When he spoke, I startled.

"I'm sorry about all this. I—" He cleared his throat. "I never meant for anyone to drag you into this…mess."

My life was a mess all right. I shrugged. "If they hadn't, I might never have known about my mother. Maybe getting drugged and kidnapped and used was worth it for that."

Guilt flashed across his face. Exactly what I wanted to see.

"Remi…" I leaned forward, elbows on my knees. I'd never been the manipulative type—only the manipulated type—but I needed him to hear me, needed the truth to somehow convince him to help me. "I want Derrick to pay for what he's done. Do you understand?" This time I stared him down, praying, hoping. "If we are right, he's taken everything from me—my mother, my uncle, my life. He's used me in a way that far surpasses anything Levi ever did. He tried to have me murdered, his own daughter. And I'm going to prove it. I think I know how."

Remi set his glass on the coffee table. "How?"

"If there's anything that ties Derrick to Caroline, anything at all, it will be in his safe at the house."

Remi shook his head. "Levi already checked his office safe. There was nothing out of the ordinary there."

I wasn't surprised that Levi had been inside my father's office, probably the same time he'd spied on all my secrets. "Not that safe. He has another one, in the basement." I wasn't supposed to know about it, but I'd done a little spying of my own, back when I had cared about why my father couldn't seem to love me. I'd thought the answers were hidden in his life, but nothing I had found had given me a clue. Now I had one.

Remi's narrowed eyes made me want to squirm. I held as still as I could, bearing his scrutiny.

"You want us to get into the basement?" he finally asked.

I thought about the numbers on the clock above the stove. "There's no time for that."

"Of course there's time. You make it sound like we have to go today."

"We do." When Remi seemed about to protest, I rushed on. "He was watching the apartment; he had to be. Anthony Clark wasn't targeted until he went there. You think he doesn't know Geneva had visitors today?" He would as soon as he reviewed the surveillance. I was simply betting I could beat him to the punch, so to speak.

"Today is Thursday. He goes to the Patriots Club every Thursday night. It's a ritual he's kept every single week he was in town since I was a baby—everyone who's anyone meets there. It's where his closest contacts have been made. The southern good-ol'-boy system." I clenched my fists together. "If I go tonight, I can get what we need with no one the wiser."

"I?" Remi snorted. "You are not going anywhere. A, what can I do? And B, Levi would kill me—"

"We both know that's not the case. You mean more to him than I ever will."

Remi stopped, mouth hanging open, eyes like saucers. Then he did his own leaning forward, his stare boring into me. "That's where you're wrong. I've known my brother far longer, understand him far better, than you ever will." The truth of his words sent a sharp pain through my heart. "I've never seen him like this. Ever. You've done something to him, Abby, something *good*. He'd never risk you."

"I'd risk me, damn it!" How could I get through to him? "I haven't just done something to him. Don't you get that, Remi? I love him."

Remi's eyes went wide, his choked-off gasp echoing my own. I hadn't known until the words were already out, what I was going to say. Was it even true?

"He's not relationship material."

And I, with my screwed-up life, was? "You don't see yourselves very clearly, do you? I think he's had plenty of experience with relationships. Since you were little, in fact. Loyalty, protection, love—what more could a girl need?"

"Are you saying he loves you?"

Was I? He certainly hadn't said it, might not feel more than lust, but there was something there, between us, that I'd never experienced before.

And really, did it matter if it was love? Whatever it was, I was willing to take a chance on it.

"There's no risk to me going in there. Not with Derrick gone. There's every risk to Levi. I can be in and out before he knows I'm even gone." I hoped, anyway. "But I can't get there without help. I need you to help me. You're the reason I'm here, after all. You owe me."

Chapter Thirty-Two

The pizza guy freaked when I jumped into his car, but the fifty dollars I handed him trumped company policy and got me closer into town. I used the rest of the money Remi had given me to catch a cab.

I hadn't lied to Remi about Derrick being gone. Thursday was also an early night for staff. I had established that habit a long time ago, making that my one night alone—no staff to commiserate with me, no parties to tax my nerves, just me and comfort food and a long soak in a hot tub. I made sure my light was off and the door closed before Derrick came home. A night of peace in a lifetime of demands.

Tonight I'd buy a lifetime of peace with one demand.

The one obstacle I wasn't sure I could overcome was the security system. Derrick might've changed the codes, which meant he would get an alert if I entered the old one. But it was the only choice I had. I chose the back gate, with plenty of trees and bushes to hide me from prying eyes, though not from the security cameras. Derrick would know I betrayed him when he reviewed the tapes. By then I hoped to be long gone.

I entered the six-digit code on the keypad. When a green light flashed and the lock clicked open, I nearly sagged with relief. Taking a deep breath, I pushed open the gate just wide enough to slip through, then closed it behind me. Thanks God we never had guards outside, or guard dogs. I'd known it was coming if Derrick won the governor's race, but that would be at the governor's mansion, not here. Here, Derrick preferred as much privacy as possible, so all the security was electronic.

Jogging through the garden felt...odd. I knew the place like the back of my hand—every flower bed, every hedge, every tree—but now it was the shadows that seemed unfamiliar. Sinister. Hiding Lord knew what. But they hid me too, so I stuck to them until they fell away at the back lawn. Knowing I couldn't avoid the cameras, I walked then, trying to slow my breathing and appear casual for anyone monitoring the security remotely. There was every chance they would contact Derrick at the club. But that still gave me a good half hour to find what I was looking for and get out.

The halls were darkened, as usual. The 5000-square-foot house was far too big for two people, and at night only the occupied rooms were lit. I navigated through the downstairs with the help of the tiny night-lights plugged in every few feet. Each squeak of my shoes and creak of the floor made my nerves jump, but I did my best to ignore them as I rushed through the house. The entry to the basement was through the kitchen—the regular basement, not the wine cellar. One was acceptable for staff use, and one for a man like Derrick, which was why his coming in and out of the staff area when they weren't around had caught my eye.

I had one stop to make first: Derrick's office.

I hated this room. Every reprimand, every punishment, every sigh of disappointment saturated the walls, turning my stomach before I even managed to open the door. I walked to the middle of the room and stood there, in front of my *father's* desk, the same spot I'd stood while he informed me that I'd be marrying Kyle Pellen. "Finally, all the effort I put into you will become useful," he'd said. Useful. I'd known he didn't love me, that I was nothing more than a tool to further his social standing, but to marry me off to one of his staff like I had no right to an opinion on the man I'd spend my life with? Even now that betrayal gutted me.

It had also made me determined to escape. Which I'd done. Not the way I'd expected to, maybe, but…

The key to the safe was on Derrick's ring, alongside the keys to the gates and garages and attic. I'd seen him carrying it each time he'd snuck in or out of the basement. The only problem? I'd never been allowed into Derrick's office without him present, so I had no idea where he kept it. Each second that I searched ticked away to the drumbeat of my racing heart as I scrambled through papers and supplies and files. Finally, in the bottom drawer of the filing cabinet, my fingers closed around them. I heaved a sigh of relief as I hurried out, trying hard not to trip over my own feet in the process.

The kitchen was dark, a single light above the stove lighting my way to the basement. I grasped the doorknob in a sweaty hand, turned, and pulled.

A pitch-black staircase waited for me to descend.

I gripped the rail hard as I felt for each step. "Careful, Abby, careful." The last thing I needed was a sprained or broken ankle keeping me from getting back to Levi. I hadn't realized I was at the bottom until I reached out a toe and hit concrete instead of another step. The shock sent a sickening jolt through me that I breathed away as I stood, trying to orient myself, trying to remember where the light switch was. With the upstairs door closed, a glow from down here would hopefully be faint through the crack underneath. Hopefully.

I felt along the wall, found the switch. Flicked it up.

"Looking for something?"

My heart kicked so hard I nearly fainted.

"Well?" Across the room, Derrick stood from a chair positioned in front of the wall I knew held the safe. "Answer me, Abigail. What were you looking for?"

"I-I—"

"Don't. Stutter!"

The shout shook me. The look in Derrick's eyes, at once full of rage and then, like a flipped coin, cool and emotionless again.

"I didn't spend thousands on making you the perfect hostess for you to stutter."

No, even when faced with his rage, with a gun in his hand, I'd be expected to act with perfect poise. The perfect society hostess. The perfect daughter.

To a killer.

"Fuck you, Dad."

I saw him coming, barreling across the room, rage blazing in his eyes, but I couldn't move. That same old fear, the same instinct that had always kept me statue still as a child, gripped me now, turning me to stone, keeping my hands at my side instead of coming up to protect my face as his fist blasted toward me.

The pain detonated through my cheek like I'd been hit by a truck, not a man. Derrick waited till I hit the ground to kick me in the ribs.

And walked away. As if I was more bother than I was worth.

A trickle of blood hit the corner of my mouth—I reached to wipe it away. The cut on my cheek where the heavy gold fraternity ring he wore had broken the skin was the least of my worries. "Fuck you," I said again.

Derrick laughed. Hands in his pockets like he was wandering his club instead of beating his daughter, he laughed. "I believe you're the one who was fucked, were you not?"

My mind blanked. How could he—

Right, the pictures. I ignored the jab and struggled to my feet.

"I had finally decided the fact that you were frigid would work in my favor. Southern families prefer virgins for their well-bred wives. Pellen was particularly excited at the thought of deflowering you." Derrick turned, his smile smug. "If only I'd known how accommodating you could be, I might've received a higher price."

"You sold me?" I mean, I knew he had, metaphorically. But he'd actually taken money to…

How did you explain that on your taxes?

The thought—and the laugh that followed—came out of nowhere. When Derrick's face darkened, his anger returning, I embraced both. "Guess you lost out, huh?"

He took a step forward, and my gut clenched, but the grin stayed on my face. I'd learned a thing or two under dear old Dad's thumb.

I took a step of my own, then another. "How did you know I'd be here?"

"When else would you arrive? It was only logical." He jangled the change in his pants pocket, a sound I'd heard a million times in my life. A frown curved his lips downward. "If you were going to betray me, it would be now. And I couldn't be certain it was beneath you. The man I hired seemed very...persuasive...on the security videos I saw."

"You seem to have an abnormal interest in your daughter's sex life," I pointed out.

"In human nature, my dear. How do you think I got this far in life? By understanding how people think."

"The man who kidnapped me must've been a surprise, then." I didn't want to give him Levi's name if he didn't already have it, but I did want to rub his failure in his face. "I don't think it was the best insight into human nature that got you this far, though, was it, *Dad*? More like murder."

He was mere feet away when my hand closed around the hammer lying on the shelf next to me. I swung, but not fast enough. Derrick blocked the blow with a forearm as his fingers closed around my neck.

"You really should be careful, Abigail," he snarled. "You don't want to end up like your mother."

"Which one?"

Chapter Thirty-Three

"Where did these brains come from? If I'd known you could actually think for yourself, I might've found you useful for more than just your cunt."

The words registered but without effect. I was too busy trying to breathe, too busy clawing at the tight grip on my throat, on the fabric-covered arm that held me too far out of reach to get at his face. Twisting. Choking. Kicking. Derrick watched it all with a smile on his face.

"No smart-aleck remark?" he asked, raising an eyebrow. "Of course not." Using his hold on my neck, he dragged me toward the chair he'd been sitting in when I turned on the light. Nothing I did stopped him. It was the story of my life in one short journey across the room—no matter how much, how hard I fought, Derrick always won.

Not this time. God, please not this time.

"You are definitely not smart enough to have figured out about Caroline. It was my 'hired help' who solved that puzzle, I presume. I'll have to take care of him soon."

Pain slammed through my butt and hips and spine as Derrick forced me into the chair. With a knee jammed hard between my legs and his hand forcing my head back, away from him, he pinned me down. I made a grab for the gun.

"No," he snapped, shoving the gun into his belt at his back. My hands wouldn't reach there, couldn't seem to do anything that hurt him. The chair rocked as I tried to kick, to bring my knees up and force him off, but Derrick ignored it all as he strapped something around my middle.

My ribs throbbed at the pressure. When he stepped back, I looked down to see a thick leather strap around my body. For a moment, hope flared—I could defeat one belt, surely, if only by sliding down the chair—until Derrick circled behind me to add several more.

Shit.

Derrick observed his handiwork with satisfaction when he moved in front of me again. God, what I wouldn't give to wipe that smug look off his face—preferably with a baseball bat.

"I really did love her, you know."

I scoffed. He could slap me if he wanted to, but no way would I let that statement pass without a fight. "That's the biggest lie I think I've ever heard you tell." And he'd spent a lifetime lying to me.

Derrick stepped back, watching me struggle against my bonds with something disgustingly close to pleasure in his eyes. "Love is fickle, as they say." He shook his head. "Not that you'll ever know that."

"You can't love a woman and kill her."

"I didn't kill her. It was an accident." Derrick paced in front of me, looking thoughtful. "I regretted it, of course, but in the end I got most of what I wanted."

Most of what he wanted? How could I have come from this man's gene pool? "And what was that?"

"An heir." He eyed me with disgust. "Not the one I wanted, and at far too high a price, but I made it work."

"What the hell are you talking about?"

I waited for him to brush me off, to stick his nose in the air and assure us both that he didn't have to explain to anyone. Instead his eyes went distant, his attention on something beyond me. When he crossed the room, I tensed, but Derrick only grasped a dusty chair and pulled it over to join me.

Then he took the handkerchief from his breast pocket and proceeded to wipe away the dust.

I rolled my eyes. Where were we, in a tea parlor, for Christ's sake?

"Caro and Camilla were pregnant at the same time—haven't you figured that out yet?" He tossed the hanky away and sat, one ankle crossed over the opposite knee, leaned back as if he hadn't a care in the world. As if he wasn't discussing murder. "Unfortunately my wife wasn't made of the same stern stuff as my mistress. Her daughter was stillborn." He spread his hands as if he was some helpless victim, not the mastermind of my mother's— and almost my—death. "I had the perfect solution."

"You mean perfect for a heartless, self-serving bastard."

Derrick ground his teeth together. "Caro didn't see things the same way. Her devotion should have been to me—me!—not a child, but she refused to let you go. We were supposed to be a family, she said. She was almost as naive as you." Narrowed eyes seemed to blame me, as if I'd somehow convinced Caroline to choose me over him.

"You wanted to take away her child and give it to another woman, and you expected her to be okay with that?" I shook my head. "You must be insane."

The slap came without warning, doubling the pain in my already bruised cheek. "I'm your father! You will speak to me with respect or live to regret it."

"I don't think so, Councilman."

My heart leaped at the sound of Levi's voice, washing the pain in my body away beneath a tide of relief and, yes, love. How I'd missed it before, I didn't know, but I recognized it now, in this musty basement, my body covered in dirt and bruises and sweat. I searched eagerly but couldn't pinpoint him in the gloom until he stepped closer, his gaze and gun both aimed straight at Derrick.

"Let her go."

Derrick returned to his relaxed position on the chair, resting his hands on his knees as if he sat in the parlor at the club, his cronies around him, brandy and cigars at his elbow. If the sight of the gun fazed him, I couldn't see it. "No."

Levi's free hand reached for his gun, sliding the top back with a sharp *click*. Didn't that chamber a bullet? "Now."

"You don't want to try that on me." One side of Derrick's mouth rose in a smug smile. "I have enough evidence here"—he nodded toward the safe—"to hang you out to dry."

Levi didn't even blink those steely eyes. "You can't give it to anyone if you're dead."

Anxiety that had nothing to do with all the pointing guns in the room fluttered in my chest. "Levi—"

He flicked me a glance. I pleaded with my eyes, the only option I had, praying he would get the message. A slight nod settled some of the churning in my stomach.

His hard focus returned to Derrick. "What happened to Caroline?"

Thank God. He'd gotten it.

Derrick looked thoughtful. "I guess you don't want my secrets to die with me."

No flinching away from Levi's intent, no fear in his eyes. Derrick had spent too many years winning; he didn't believe he would die here tonight.

Levi stalked forward. "I am perfectly fine with you and your secrets going straight to hell." He jerked his chin toward me. "But she deserves the answers. Where is Caroline?"

Derrick raised an eyebrow but stayed silent.

Levi pulled the trigger.

The sound of the shot was far worse than the ones in the warehouse; this was a much more enclosed space, and my ears rang with the echo. I reached to cover them, only to remember I was still tied.

Derrick glared at Levi, but a hint of fear finally showed. Just over his head, I noticed a chunk torn out of a wooden shelf.

"Tell her," Levi said.

Derrick glanced at me, and beneath the anger I swore I saw a flicker of regret. If he'd been anyone else, I'd have believed it.

"I told her I was putting her up in the new apartment. When she arrived…well, she wasn't happy about my plan." His cheeks went ruddy as memories seemed to play in his mind. "When I tried to take you by force, we fought."

I didn't know what I was feeling, didn't have time to process the words. I would do that later, after all of this was over. After I knew everything there was to know. "And?"

Derrick's face went blank. "And she fell. Hit her head."

Hard enough to die? I glanced at Levi, but he was zeroed in on Derrick.

"Where is...she?" I couldn't say *her body*, couldn't think of Caroline decaying without anyone to mourn her or care for her.

Derrick stared at me now, his face hard, unapologetic. If he'd ever loved my mother, there was no sign of it. "Camilla knew how important my career was. I knew we had to do something. I'd started construction on the plaza just before, and they were about to pour the foundation. We took her—"

"Stop."

The word came out strangled, and satisfaction glimmered in Derrick's eyes all over again. "Of course you ended up costing me two women, didn't you? Caro and Camilla. In the end my wife knew too much, had a way to control me. I couldn't allow that." He shrugged. "Her death came at just the right time to win my first political seat. The sympathy vote is a powerful thing."

Tears stung, slithered down my cheeks. "You're a monster."

"Am I?"

The pounding of heavy footsteps over our heads startled us all. Between one breath and the next, Derrick was beside me, his hand coming up to my temple. I caught a glimpse of black metal as the sound of a second gunshot echoed like thunder in the room. Levi advanced, but with Derrick's gun to my head, he didn't fire again.

"I've been planning on making her disappear just like her mother," Derrick said, his breath hot on my face as he knelt behind me. Cool metal stroked my cheek, the contrast sending a shudder through me. "But this works so much better. Two birds, one stone, right? Abigail ran away from her lover, but he wasn't ready to let her go. You followed her home, fought, and she died. Pity."

"It's a scenario you're intimately familiar with, isn't it?" Levi asked. He stepped once, twice to the side, trying to get a better angle, but each move was countered by a shift from Derrick. "Too bad there'd be no proof."

"Proof of a murder is easy to fabricate with the dead body."

My dead body. I stared at Levi, willing him to tell me what to do, show me, help me help him. He didn't even look at me.

"Do you know what the sentence for kidnapping and murder is in the state of Georgia?" Derrick asked.

"Doesn't matter." Levi took another step.

"Why not?" Derrick asked, shifting again. I could see his face now, from the corner of my eye.

"Because you won't be around to see me convicted."

Levi lunged, taking Derrick off guard. I watched as time seemed to stop.

Derrick slid around to my side.

The breath stalled in my lungs.

A gun went off. I braced but…no pain.

Derrick grunted. As he started to fall, I saw one hand rising to clutch at his chest. I couldn't look away. All this time, I'd known the man who fathered me wasn't good. Didn't deserve the accolades and applause he regularly received. But—he was my father.

And a murderer.

I couldn't decide which mattered more as he hit the floor hard, a red blossom of blood taking over the left side of his shirt. I held my breath as the light went out of his eyes, his grip on his chest and his gun going slack. He took one long, slow breath that gurgled near the end, then everything just…stopped.

And all I felt was…nothing.

The straps around my ribs tightened momentarily, then fell into my lap. Levi was in front of me a second later.

"Tell me where it hurts, little bird," he demanded. The hands running over me felt desperate, frantic. They shook. I stared into his panicked gray eyes and tried to find the words to tell him I was fine, but nothing came. Nothing but the desperate need to focus anywhere but on Derrick, slumped on the floor next to my chair, dead and staring.

Levi lifted my shirt.

Instinct had me pushing my top back down. "No." Those eyes. I couldn't think about anything but those dead eyes. Dead. Christ.

"Eli!"

Heavy boots clambered down the steps. Eli rounded the corner, glancing over Derrick's body as if he saw dead people every day.

Levi lifted me out of the chair. "Get rid of those, would you?"

"Sure thing." Levi's brother gathered the straps and walked back to the stairs. They disappeared into a large black trash bag.

A hand ran over my bruised ribs. "Ow!"

My hands came up instinctively to block the painful touch. Levi grabbed my wrists hard and got right in my face, the fierce gleam of his eyes breaking me out of my trance. This time his worry and fear registered. Levi was panicked—over me. "Be still, Abby," he growled. "Let me see." His tone softened the slightest bit. "I need to make sure you're okay."

I took a deep, steadying breath and pulled the hem of my sweatshirt up just under my breast. "I am. I promise. I'm in—"

"I'll be the judge of that."

I held my tongue and let him reassure himself that I was only bruised. Eli was cleaning up, and I wondered how in the hell I could ever explain this to the police without Levi getting arrested. I couldn't live with that, not now. I couldn't face this alone.

"Safe combo?" Eli asked.

It took a moment to realize he was talking to me. I rattled the combination off from memory.

Eli shoved everything from the safe into his handy trash bag. "Bro, gotta go."

I shot a look at Eli, then Levi. "No, you can't. I—"

"E"—Levi jerked his head toward the stairs— "give us a minute."

He started up, throwing a glance over his shoulder that looked suspiciously like pity.

I closed my eyes and breathed deep, trying to calm the rising panic that wanted to choke me. "Levi—"

Warm lips met mine. I opened my eyes to stare straight into Levi's, to see the strength I needed, to drown myself in the knowledge that he wouldn't leave me. Except that's not what I saw.

Levi slid his tongue between my lips, and I surrendered to the rising need, let him delve deep, savored his dark taste on my lips. When he drew back, I couldn't stop a whimper.

Cupping my face in his rough hands, he laid his forehead against mine. "I have to go, little bird."

"No." *Please don't. Don't leave me.*

Levi's brow wrinkled. "I have to. We have to make this look good, keep you safe."

I was safe with him, but my protests didn't change his mind. The gun was placed in my hand. Levi forced me to fire a shot at a wooden shelf near Derrick's body "to get the residue on your hands. You fired once, missed, fired again. Got it?"

I think I nodded; I don't know. It all happened so fast and then he was kissing me again. A sob escaped me as he turned towards the stairs.

"Will I see you again?" I managed to ask.

Levi stopped, glanced over his shoulder, and I swear I saw hell in his eyes. "You don't need me, little bird." He smiled sadly. "It's time to be free."

"Levi—"

But it was too late. He was already gone.

Epilogue

"It's done, Mama."

I stared at the photo in my hand and not the tombstone with Caroline Clark's name etched into it in pretty lettering. I came here to talk to her often. Through Geneva I now had memories and a handful of pictures; I knew my mother, probably better than I had ever known Camilla.

My gaze traced Caroline's pretty strawberry-blonde hair in the image, her beautiful smile. After meeting Anthony's business partner and receiving pictures of him, I knew I shared the family looks. Once DNA proved our relationship, I'd had Anthony moved here, beside his sister. Their matching headstones were etched *In Loving Memory*, Caroline's with the words *Loving Mother, Sister, and Friend* beneath her name.

I missed them, even though we'd never met. I missed a lot of things now.

"I signed the papers for the sale of the mansion this morning," I told her picture. "St. Mary's and the other area shelters will do a lot of good with the money, I think." St. Mary's had cared for Caroline when she couldn't care for herself, and for that I'd be forever grateful. And it wasn't like I needed the money. I was Derrick Roslyn's only living relative too.

"The new place is a little bare yet, but I think it will work out fine. Quiet neighborhood. Close to the university." Now that the details of the investigations were complete, I could go back. Get my degree, although I was considering changing my major. Maybe social work. Wouldn't Derrick roll over in his grave if he knew?

Not that he had a grave. The would-be governor of Georgia had been cremated. I'd considered dumping his ashes in the sewer but settled instead for the Atlantic Ocean. The bottom-feeders out there could feast on him all they wanted.

But it wasn't memories of my father or even the move that weighed me down today. It was memories of someone else.

"I miss him."

The past year had brought so many changes— newfound freedom, Geneva's friendship, breaking ties with anything and everything that had made up the life I used to live. Every time I cut one of those bonds, I felt a little lighter, a little wiser, a little more at peace. And a little more alone, because Levi wasn't there with me. I hadn't seen him since that night, the night Derrick died. I'd had him for such a short time; we'd had each other. I'd give anything to just know where he was, that he was safe. But that was impossible.

Sometimes I imagined I could feel him watching me. It was stupid, I know, a childish mind game I played with myself, but there were moments I swore it was true.

I stood. "Have to go, Mama. Geneva and I will be back Sunday, I promise." I slipped the photo into my pocket, kissed my fingertips, then laid them first on her stone, then Anthony's. "Love you both."

At least I had that. After years of loving no one, that gift was more profound than any other change in my life, even if all but one of my loved ones was gone.

The drive back to the house was about forty minutes, and I took my time. Despite driving lessons, I was still a bit unsure when it came to city traffic, but I'd needed the independence, needed to prove I could do it. And I had, too, just like everything else, one step at a time.

My new place was a little craftsman on a tree-lined street in a neighborhood that saw little traffic. A few houses had children, and the sound of their laughter as they played outside often brightened my afternoon. My house was at the end of a cul-de-sac, a small carport to one side sheltering me anytime it rained. Parking beneath it felt like home, familiar and settled and warm. I'd never felt that way in Derrick's mansion.

It was just so damn quiet. Maybe I should get a cat.

A couple of hours later tears were streaming down my cheeks and curses tripping off my tongue as I cut onions for tacos. When the doorbell rang, my hand jerked, the knife slicing through a couple layers of skin before I could pull it back. "Damn it!"

The doorbell chimed again.

"I'm coming!" A hasty rinse to get rid of the onion juice on my skin—I hoped—and then I was rushing for the door.

Ding-dong.

"I'm coming, I'm coming." But the closer I got to the door, the more I second-guessed the impulse to answer. People had rung the doorbell before, mostly workmen when I'd first bought the place, solicitors, the next-door neighbor with her daughter, selling Girl Scout cookies. It was the reporters that I hated. They'd nearly driven me crazy in the months following Derrick's death. But surely the time for a story on the councilman's sordid past was long gone?

I rounded the corner into the foyer just as the bell rang a fourth time. Through the frosted side panel I could see a tall, dark figure turned slightly away as if staring out into the street. My step hitched, a bump of something I didn't recognize nudging up to choke me as I considered that silhouette mere feet away.

I can't breathe. Why can't I breathe?

As if moving through molasses, I dropped the towel on the foyer table and brought my eye to the peephole.

And my entire world turned upside down for the second time in a year.

"Open the door, little bird."

A laugh snagged in the back of my throat. Demanding as ever. That part I certainly recognized. And the muscular body. The dark hair. The eyes that could command me to do anything and I'd comply without hesitation.

The bouquet in Levi's hands, though? That didn't seem to fit. He gripped them like a weapon, though what he planned to attack with them was beyond me. I found myself reaching for the doorknob, willing him to wait, wanting the gift he'd brought to me almost as much as I wanted him inside my house, branding my space, breathing my air.

I wanted him, period. And yet I hesitated.

"Little bird."

That growl. A shiver ran down my spine. I unlocked the door, drew it back. And stared. It was almost too much to comprehend, Levi here, at my house after all this time, dressed like—

Wow. Like he was going on a date. His clothes were dark, just like every shirt and pants I'd ever seen him in, but the sheen of the material as it reflected the streetlight outside said it wasn't fatigues. More like something intended to impress, maybe? With the way it molded to his muscular chest, his flat abs, his long legs, his...

My eyebrows shot up. Molded wasn't the right word—more like cupped lovingly. And what that fabric cupped was definitely all he needed to impress any woman.

My head spun, reminding me forcefully to *breathe*.

"Do I know you?" I asked through the screen door.

Levi grabbed the handle and tugged, but the lock kept the door closed. "Funny, little bird. Don't make me spank your ass."

"We wouldn't want that, would we?"

The words came out perky and self-assured, but the weight of the past year hung in the silence behind them.

"Abby." Levi stared hard at me, as if he could force me to let him in through sheer will. "Unlock it."

I flicked the latch. And went back to the kitchen. With every step, the spark of resentment that I hadn't known I felt until that very moment flared brighter, burning in my gut like a simmering pot about to reach a boil. After a year of being alone, believing I'd never see him again, wondering if I'd imagined the connection between us. Worrying about where he was and if he was safe. Dreaming of our nights together— and waking hot, achy, and unfulfilled no matter how many times I got myself off. After all that time, he was here?

I walked straight to the stove and turned it off. Knowing my luck, I'd forget about it and burn down my perfectly lovely new house. Levi brushed by me as he reached for the cabinet over the stove.

"What are you doing?"

"Looking for something to put these in."

I didn't help him. Unfortunately, as much as I wanted to keep myself aloof, keep my anger like a shield between us...there was something endearingly awkward about watching him fumble around an unfamiliar kitchen, this man who seemed competent at everything. It shouldn't touch me, but as he filled a vase under the tap and dumped the flowers in without even removing the tissue paper they were wrapped in, I couldn't help it. He was like a little boy trying to please yet resenting the instinct, and the strangeness of it tugged at parts of me I wasn't ready to let unravel.

Instead I went to the poor flowers' rescue.

"What—"

I nudged Levi out of the way with my hip. "You have to cut the stems so they'll have a fresh opening to draw water."

I took my time selecting each stem—a red rose, white lily, purple anemone—cutting off the bottom inch, then placing them in the water. Each one received a silent apology; after all, I knew what getting cut was like. I'd lost everything last year, including Levi. But look at me now.

Maybe I should be thanking Levi for more than just the flowers.

Fuck that.

I slid the last flower into place. Sucked in a deep breath. Turned to face Levi. "Why are you here?"

He narrowed his eyes at me. "To see you."

Well don't sound all happy about it.

"Why now? I've been here awhile. You're good at finding things." Especially things that were a matter of public record. I leaned a hip against the counter. "Why did you finally come?"

Frustration flashed across his expression, like he'd expected this to be easy. Make a little effort and waltz right back into my life like nothing happened. Right. It wasn't going to be that easy, not by a mile.

"Abby."

I shook my head. "Why?"

Levi's hands tightened into fists at his sides, relaxed, tightened again—fighting with himself. Chewing on whatever words he didn't want to spit out. I waited, refusing to help. Whatever it was, he needed to say it. I needed to hear it.

He stepped closer, his gaze fixed on my arms where they crossed over my stomach. "I—"

Silence.

"What?"

Nothing.

"Look, you got yourself here, and I'm sure you can get yourself home." I didn't want him to leave, but I couldn't accept a year of being alone without an explanation. I just couldn't. "Thanks for the flowers."

Levi cursed, squeezed his fists so tight he shook. "I— Fuck!" His head snapped up. Molten steel locked on to me, captured my gaze, just as Levi had always held me captive. "I couldn't wait another fucking minute to see you," he bit out. Moved closer. "I tried, I really did. Told myself you deserved someone far better than me. Told myself you deserved your freedom. But…" He took another step, then another. "I couldn't do it, Abby. I couldn't stay away. I need you."

I need you.

I closed my eyes against the relief sweeping through me. I'd needed him too, far more than I'd allowed myself to think about, because if I had, the hollow space inside me would have swallowed me whole.

This time it was me moving closer. I raised a hand to the stubbled cheek I'd longed to touch for a year now. My fingertips grazed the rough texture, the strong, stubborn line of his jaw, the softness of his lips. A sigh of pleasure escaped me, mingling with Levi's.

"Abby, I…" Another gravelly curse bit through the air. "I have no idea what the fuck I'm doing. I'm not—"

My finger pressed against his lips silenced him. I stared into those eyes I'd missed so much, gathered my courage, and took a chance for the second time in my life. "You know all you need to know."

I kissed him. So carefully I brought my lips to his. Brushed them over, refamiliarizing myself with his texture, his taste. Levi startled, his hand going automatically to my hip.

And then he took over.

There was no escaping—and I didn't want to. His hands were everywhere, gripping my neck, molding my breasts, dragging roughly over the flat plain of my belly as he cursed into my mouth about clothes and need and now, now, now. My body felt like I'd been doused in flames, every touch sending me closer and closer to the pleasure I'd longed for through far too many lonely nights. I needed his skin, needed his mouth, needed him inside me with a desperation I couldn't fathom, much less put into words. But my body could tell him, and did. My tight nipples, my eager tongue, my searching hands.

In moments my shirt and bra were off. Levi lowered his head, his hungry mouth latching on to one hard tip. A keening wail left my mouth.

Levi let go. "Undress me," he barked, then went right back to my breast. As long as he sucked, as long as his mouth was on me, I could obey. Or try, at least. My fingers fumbled the buttons of his shirt until sheer desperation had me grasping both sides and yanking it open. Buttons flew everywhere, but when Levi's gaze met mine, it burned even brighter.

"Come here."

He pulled me to the table, yanked out a chair, and sat. For one crazy moment, all I could think was, here? In the kitchen? Then he had me between his knees and his mouth took my untouched nipple and I couldn't have cared if we were in the middle of the street as long as he kept right on touching me. I slid my fingers through his hair, holding him close, a moment of softness in the sheer brutality of his taking, and gloried in the feel of him, the smell of him, the heat of him in my arms, on my body. He'd come back to me. Every minute of the past year, I'd longed for him, and here he was. Finally. In my arms.

Cool air kissed my lower belly, my legs.

"Step out," Levi commanded. He leaned back from me, watching as I kicked away my pants and panties, his hands busy at his fly. The long length of him pushed out as the zipper lowered, and my mouth watered, but when I would've gotten to my knees, Levi's grip kept me up.

All of me. One minute I was on solid ground, and the next I was in his lap, straddling him, that hard erection I'd wanted to taste pushing without quarter into my body. I gasped, groaned, the sounds mingling with Levi's grunts of pleasure as he forced his way in one thrust at a time until he was seated to the hilt. Only then did he calm.

"I've needed this. Needed you, Abby." He nipped the inside slope of one breast, then the other. Palmed my ass and forced my hips in a circle, pleasuring us both. "God, I needed you so fucking much."

Steely eyes pinned me as surely as his hands did. "Say it, little bird."

Say what? That I loved him? I did; I'd known it for a year.

A brutal grip lifted me along his shaft, then released me. My own weight impaled me on him ruthlessly.

He nuzzled my nipple, bit it lightly. "Say it."

"I need you."

With the words, my body clenched on his, a flood of arousal easing his way. Relief filled the eyes staring into mine. "Again."

"I need you."

"Again."

I kept repeating it, staring down into molten steel as he sucked the nipple he was torturing into his mouth and set up a brutal rhythm with his hips. Over and over, again and again, my core tightening until I thought for sure he wouldn't be able to push back in, but every time he managed to, as if my body knew exactly how to pleasure us both. And it was pleasure—harsh, breathtaking, rough pleasure that exploded in my core and behind my eyes, tearing me apart and remaking me all at once, every spasm putting one more piece back into place until Levi climaxed inside me and finally, finally made me whole once again.

Hours later, Levi stirred beside me in the bed. "I don't know how to do this."

I looked down at our sweaty, naked bodies. "I disagree."

"Not that," Levi growled. "This." He gestured between us.

I had to laugh. "You think I do?" Sex was straightforward, uncomplicated. A relationship? With Levi? I couldn't picture it. I wanted it—God, how I wanted it—but I wasn't even sure what it looked like. Would he live with me? Would I need to leave everything behind and live off the grid with him? Would we marry? Have kids?

A white picket fence appeared in my mind, a sweater-wearing Levi in front of it. I shuddered. That wasn't the man I'd fallen in love with. But how exactly did I live with the man he was?

Levi rolled toward me, gripped my thigh, and dragged it over his, notching our bodies together. We fit. Just like that. Maybe figuring out a relationship was just a matter of finding out where else we fit.

I laid my hand on his heart, felt the strength in each thump, the steel in his muscles. My fingers dug in without conscious thought, holding tight to what I wanted.

"I think we just figure it out one day at a time," I said. "Don't you?"

I'd taken my chances. Now it was time for Levi to take his. I waited, hoping, holding on to him, knowing it had to be his choice, not mine. He had to take the leap.

"One day at a time, huh?"

I held my breath, nodded.

His arms crept around my back, forcing me closer, cocooning me in his warmth. He tucked his face in my neck, and I could hear him breathe me in. "One day at a time it is, little bird."

∞

Did you enjoy ASSASSIN'S MARK? If so, you can leave a review at your favorite retailer to tell other readers about the book. And thank you!

Want exciting extras from the ASSASSINS series? How about free book opportunities and bonus scenes? They're available only through my newsletter. **Sign up at www.ellasheridanauthor.com to get exclusive access!**

Before you go…

Levi and Abby aren't finished yet.

That's right. More ASSASSINS is coming.

ASSASSIN'S PREY
Assassins 2

I killed my first man at the age of twelve. I've been killing ever since. I thought it was all I lived for...until Abby. Until the woman I'd kidnapped became the woman I couldn't walk away from.

She owns a piece of me I wouldn't take back, but the rest? The only way to protect her is to hold back the parts inside me that are too ugly to ever reveal. I'll keep her safe, even from me.

And it works. We have the nights, and I hunt my way through the days. Alone.

Until an attack reveals a threat we didn't see coming. One that could take away the dream I didn't realize I had.

Everything. With her.

I'm on the hunt of my life. My prey might run, but in this fight—for her, for us—they don't stand a chance.

∞

Turn the page for an exclusive excerpt.

ASSASSIN'S PREY

Chapter One

The silken sheets caressed her skin, revealing more than they concealed. Too damn much for my peace of mind. I should be out there, on the hunt, but Abby tethered me to her like a fucking chain, refusing to let go. No matter how much safer she was without me.

A gasp escaped her, and she turned on her side, one hand reaching out, searching—for me. "Levi?"

The room was dark, her eyes glazed with sleep. She couldn't see me in the shadows. It was better that way, but I couldn't leave her searching. Something inside me, something I both hated and hungered for, held as tightly to her as she did to me.

With a curse I couldn't quite hold back, I moved to the bed. And felt it the minute she saw me—my body lit up like I'd touched a live wire. Just like it did when prey appeared, every instinct sparking, every sense zeroed in on the body before me. Only I didn't want to kill this one.

I wanted her life in my hands, not her death.

A smile touched her full lips when my knee settled on the bed. Sheets rustled as she shifted onto her back, tugging me closer with nothing more than her creamy skin and the curve of her mouth. "There you are." The curve slowly flattened. "You're dressed."

Because it's safer this way. Because I can't sleep beside you and not let you all the way inside me.

I grabbed my T-shirt at the back of my neck and pulled. "Not for long."

I stripped as I crawled onto the bed. Crouching over Abby's body, I let the hunger for her take over, felt it in the tensing of my muscles, the lengthening of my cock, the racing of my heartbeat. A visceral reaction I was addicted to. That's all it was. She was my drug, and I'd never get enough. Not till it killed me. I just had to make sure it didn't kill her first.

"You should be asleep, little bird," I growled down at her.

Her eyes left mine, focused somewhere over my shoulder. Telling me all I needed to know. Another nightmare. Less frequent now, but they'd never go away. I knew that from personal experience.

"I never sleep as well when you're not beside me."

Another link clicked onto my chain, choking me with the need to reassure her. *I'll always be here. I need you beside me to sleep at all. I crave your skin against mine until I sometimes think I'll go insane.*

I didn't say any of it. I couldn't. The risk was too high.

So I kissed her.

Abby opened to me, a needy flower, defenseless, so fucking innocent even now. I remembered the first time I'd taken her, the first time she'd let me inside, and a groan escaped into her mouth. Her tight fit, the resistance I'd had to force myself through… Just the memory broke me out in a sweat.

I should hate myself for corrupting her. I did hate myself. But it felt more like she'd corrupted me.

With her sweetness, her fire. It made me weak when I couldn't afford to be. But I couldn't break free either.

Forcing myself back onto my knees, I fisted the sheet and pulled. A slow reveal—nipples, belly, that strip of auburn hair that pointed me straight to the entrance of her body. As if I could ever lose my way. The thought tightened the chain again, choking off my breath.

And then I looked into her eyes. Knowledge glittered there, too much for her own good. Every day it grew; every day she looked at me and that damn knowing was there. She knew my fear, but she never asked for more than I'd already given. Never asked for a commitment. Or if I loved her. As if she knew a yes would damn us both.

For the longest moment I wavered there, on the edge of leaving, fighting the bastard inside me that insisted I stay, the sight of her laid out before me searing my brain. And then Abby shifted, her legs parting, and the scent of her need filled my nose. The balance tipped. An agonized groan rumbled from my brain to my chest and out of my mouth.

I was between her legs before my next heartbeat.

Cream and spice, that was Abby on my tongue. I pressed my mouth to her pussy and pushed deep, seeking out every drop. Filling my senses with her until I knew I was drowning. Her skin was slick velvet against my lips, my tongue, her clit a hard bead against my nose. I licked up, took it into my mouth, and sucked hard, that primal need to nurse, to take my nourishment from her, hitting me like a bullet to the chest. She filled me, sustained me—with her body, her desire, the hungry cries echoing in my ears, the greedy fingers forcing my head closer. Her body and her mouth begged me for more, and I gave it, again and again and again until she exploded beneath my tongue.

I was inside her before the last ripple faded.

"Levi, God, yes!"

My cock was so heavy, so tight inside her hot, wet body. Too much. Not enough. When her seeking hands landed on my chest and slid downward, I knew this would be over before it had a chance to begin, and no way in hell could I allow that.

"No." Her wrists were fragile in my rough hands, but I forced them back anyway, slamming them to the bed as Abby cried out beneath me. "Look at me, little bird. Now."

Frantic, pleading hazel eyes snapped to mine. Abby rolled her pelvis, taking me deeper. "Please."

"Look at me," I demanded. "Don't close your eyes."

I pulled back, the drag of her body around my cock so perfect my eyes threatened to roll back in my head. Leveraging my knees out, I slammed back inside. Abby gasped my name, and I did it again. And again. Those beautiful eyes glazed over, going somewhere deep inside herself where hunger and pleasure roared for satisfaction, taking me with her. Letting me see what no one else had ever seen— Abby, bare, open, completely vulnerable. To me. Alive like no one I'd ever known before, filling and feeding the dead parts of me that I'd long ago given up hope of ever healing.

She could; she did. With her body and her honesty.

I'd never met anyone like her before. And I knew it was only a matter of time before I destroyed her.

Without warning her eyes flared, her legs bending to hook around my hips, pulling me closer. She chanted my name, high and desperate, and I angled my hips up, the head of my cock striking that spot deep inside that made her clench around me, so tight I had to force my way back in. And I did.

My name morphed into a scream on her lips as she climaxed around me. Squeezed me tight and sucked every last drop of semen from my willing body.

The relaxing of her muscles beneath mine drew me out of the fog of pleasure a few minutes later. I raised my head from her neck, glanced down. Abby blinked, her expression smoothing out, but not before I caught a glimpse of the emotions there—longing, desperation, pain. My failure, all in one look. But it was how it had to be.

"I have to go."

Before she could respond, I was up and headed to the bathroom. I cleaned myself up, wiping away the evidence of her pleasure and mine, thankful that with Abby's birth control, condoms were no longer an issue. I could be skin to skin with her, mark her, smear my semen over her body so that no other man would dare to trespass on my territory. I needed it. The animal inside me needed it, demanded it. With her I could soothe the savage hunger.

But no kids. Ever.

I returned to the bed with a warm washcloth. Abby parted her legs willingly. When she was clean, I leaned down until my nose met her pubic hair, and breathed deep. *My Abby. My woman!* the animal inside me roared. But the man restricted me to a brief kiss on her sensitive clit before backing away.

Abby's murmur of disappointment was a knife to the gut.

"I'll lock up before I leave," I told her.

She lay, silent, on the bed, legs bent, body gleaming in the faint light from the crack in the curtains, and watched me return the cloth to the bathroom. With every piece of clothing I added to my body, the silence became sharper, carving me up with its accusing edge.

I moved quickly to check the windows, then walked to the door. I'd melted into the shadows before I heard her voice. "What about a kiss goodbye?"

I couldn't deny her, not when my body screamed for the kiss too. I returned to the bed, let the covers caress her skin once again as I drew them over her. "Sleep, little bird."

Her kiss was the padlock on the chain that held me to her. I welcomed it in that moment—delved deep to tangle with her tongue, nipped her lips, buried my face in the hollow of her neck and the sweet scent of vanilla and flowers.

"Be safe," she murmured as I backed away.

"Always."

And then I was out the door. Every window, every door was checked, secured—I wouldn't risk anything happening when I wasn't here. The shadows in the backyard were deep this time of night, but unmoving. Same on either side of the house. When I walked out the front door and set the security system to on, I did so knowing she was safe inside.

So why did my soul scream at me to go back with every step I took away from her?

Chapter Two

"The fucker will back off if he knows what's good for him," I growled into my earpiece. The words were low enough that the crowds on the sidewalk couldn't hear the specifics, but they didn't need to. They created a wide birth around me from no more than a glance. I preferred it that way.

"He'll back off, bro. No worries." Eli chuckled in my ear. "Your reputation precedes you."

It better. I'd built the fear of reprisal into my business model, and very few risked stepping over the line and triggering it. But this latest contract...

It reminded me too much of Abby's father. And that reminded me too much of Remi being shot, having a gun pointed at Abby's head. The memories could—and did—send me into a rage.

Councilman Roslyn was dead and gone; I tried to remember that. But my body's visceral reaction had me throwing off angry waves the people around me couldn't miss.

My brothers and Abby were the only ones who knew the full story of Roslyn's involvement with, as he would have put it, the unsavory but necessary elements of society. We kept that secret for her safety, not mine. If it had been public, I wouldn't be dealing with the fucking asshat I was now. But I wouldn't risk her by tying her to me. She would never be touched by my life.

I'd made that mistake once. Never again.

My current client, however...he would be touched, all right. And I'd take great satisfaction in doing the touching. And breaking. Two days since I'd seen Abby, *two days*—because this latest contract had been a major fuckup.

"Tell me about this meeting," I barked, still seething as I turned the corner at Holmes and Sanderson and headed farther into downtown.

"Abby's lawyer, Lance Heinz, called," Eli told me. "Seems the forensic accountant was able to uncover some more accounts linked to her father. In order to retrieve the money, they need some signatures and shit. Remi knows the details."

I could hear the shrug in my youngest brother's voice, ratcheting up my tension. Remi was with Abby, not me. I knew he'd protect her with his life, but I didn't want him to. I didn't want any of them in danger. I needed to be at her side, not fucking walking down the sidewalk like I was taking a Sunday stroll. Not that anyone around me could call it *strolling*. More like a bull chasing down a matador.

Which totally worked for me.

Even without the delay, it made sense for Remi to be with her for the meeting at First Bank and Trust. He was a genius when it came to accounting. Not that anyone there would realize it. To the outside world we were her bodyguards. No one knew our true faces—I'd gone to great lengths to keep it that way—so we could safely travel with her, keep her protected, on the rare occasions she had to deal with anything concerning her father.

"Have you got the camera feeds live?" I asked.

Eli's snort drilled into my ear. "Are you really asking me that?"

Yes, because I was a micromanaging bastard. Knowing that didn't stop me from doing it. "Are they?"

"Of course they fucking are. I've got two screens with every traffic camera in a five-block radius. I've tapped into private security feeds, including at the business across the street from the parking garage you demanded Remi use. Nice scowl, by the way. I can also tell you that Remi and Abby are two blocks up on your left, approaching the cross street a block ahead of the light at Sanderson and First Street. Better get a move on, bro."

The intersection where the bank was located was three blocks north of my current location. I broke into a slow jog, my brain automatically scanning, assessing, countering. Traffic, pedestrians, cameras. The crisp fall breeze pushed people along the street, so no one lingered. No hint of a threat arose. Perfect.

The phone in my pocket vibrated against my hip—a text, not a call. I reached for it, glancing at the display. Remi.

Crossing street now.

My nerves went tight. Only two blocks away. I picked up speed as the intersection where Remi would be escorting Abby came into view. There, on the opposite side of the road. The bright red dress coat Abby wore stood out like a beacon, a stark contrast to her auburn hair.

I cursed under my breath. Apparently not low enough, because an older woman passing me skittered to the side at my vicious "fuck." I ignored her recoil and kept going.

Abby and Remi were the only ones at the crosswalk. I knew when the walk light flipped on;

they stepped into the street in front of the rows of stopped cars. My brother's tall, heavy frame dwarfed Abby as he took her arm, staying on the side of oncoming traffic. Everything seemed normal, nothing to worry about. So why did my every instinct scream at me to get them both out of sight?

The loud whine of a motorcycle engine hit my ears.

I glanced back. A sleek black Yamaha shot through the stopped cars, straddling the line as it zoomed forward. I had just enough time to notice the driver—black leather, black helmet, tinted visor that gave nothing away—before he passed me.

Headed straight for the crosswalk. At full speed.

"Abby!"

Remi's head jerked around at my shout. Realization struck, widening his eyes. He grabbed Abby around the waist and ran for the sidewalk—just as the rider drew a gun.

Time stopped. I could see the glint of the sun on the metal barrel. See the leather-gloved finger on the trigger. Remi's eyes went wild, and he launched himself toward the thick, ancient oak waiting next to the street, the only thing that could possibly protect them against a bullet at point-blank range. He and Abby flew through the air as the gun came up.

"Fuck, fuck, fuck!" My hand went to my chest, to the holster beneath my suit jacket, as I sprinted toward them. I'd never make it in time. My heart knew that and roared with impotent rage.

My woman. *Mine.*

Too far.

Between one heartbeat and the next, Remi and Abby hit the ground and rolled, Remi twisting their bodies behind the massive trunk of the tree.

The ping of silenced gunshots—one, two, three—reached my ears a second later. The motorcycle accelerated through the intersection, barely missing a hit from an oncoming semi.

And then it was gone.

I rushed to Abby's side.

"What the fuck?" Remi yelled.

I grasped the lapels of Abby's coat with shaking hands, cursing my own weakness but unable to stop the reaction, and pulled her to sitting. "Late model bike, no plates, no distinguishing marks, driver unknown," I told him, keeping my voice low. Maybe we could get something on the traffic cameras, but I didn't think so. Our man was a professional.

The job I could do. It was handling my woman that was killing me. She was breathing fast and shallow, her eyes dilated with fear. Tremors racked her slender body. "Abby?"

She grabbed on to my coat just as hard as I had her. "I'm okay."

A quick survey showed no visible cuts or bruises, though I knew the latter would show up eventually. She buried her head against me and shook.

A crowd had started to gather. "Let's go."

"But Remi—"

Abby turned to my brother, but he was already up and flanking her. He knew exactly what I did—we had to get her out of here, now. This had been a setup.

"Let's go," I repeated, half carrying and half dragging her through the people circling us. "Now."

She could fall apart later. Right now, safety came before feelings.

Abby knew the tone I used. She was no longer the girl I'd been able to frighten into compliance, but she was smart; she knew when to obey. Her feet stumbled but caught up to my pace, and she held her tongue as Remi and I hurried her down the block, away from the bank.

"Car?" I asked Remi.

"I'll get it." He jerked his chin down the block toward the garage on the other side of the street.

"Eli?" I barked.

My earpiece crackled back to life. "I've got him covered." He'd watch Remi's back from surrounding cameras.

Remi already had his keys out. "Let's go, little brother," he told Eli.

I knew one of them would text me where to meet. In the meantime I wanted Abby out of sight. We hurried down the block, then took a left on the cross street where Remi took a right. A coffee shop waited just ahead. As we stepped inside, I scanned the line, tables, staff. Nothing set my warning buzzers off. I hustled Abby across the room and into a bathroom at the back, making sure to lock the door behind me.

"What are we—"

My mouth on hers ate up the rest of her words. Noise galloped in my ears, drowning out everything but the agony of knowing I'd almost lost her. Lost this. She opened to me just like I needed her to, let me claim her. It wasn't until the taste of salt registered on my tongue that I was able to leash the savage intensity driving me and pull back.

"Shh." I eased away, my fingers automatically wiping at the tears running down her ghost-white cheeks. "You're okay. Everything's okay, little bird."

She laughed, a sickly little sound that ended in a hiccup. "Just reaction. I'll stop soon, I promise."

I hated tears. They were a distraction, a weakness, sometimes a weapon. But I'd learned enough with Abby to know she sometimes had to let it out. She got from tears what I got from sex or a fight—a release.

I hugged her closer, burying her face in my neck, trying hard to ignore the blood pooling in my groin. With Abby in the same room, much less against me, the reaction was a given; with the adrenaline roaring through my system, it was raging-caveman aggressive. I needed to fuck her, reassure us both that we were alive, that she was safe.

Abby didn't need to deal with that shit right now. Later…

Slowly the shudders in her body quieted. I gave her a minute more, then leaned my upper body back so I could look into her eyes. "Okay."

She sucked in a massive breath. "Okay."

I shucked my coat. "Let's get you cleaned up."

Abby removed her coat and blouse at my urging. While she splashed cold water over her face, I took off my button-down. It would be big on her, but what mattered was the color, not the fit. After drying her face, I buttoned her into it.

"I think you might draw more attention than me with that look," she said, eyeing my bare chest, the expanse of tattoos marking my body. And fuck if that look didn't have my cock tighter than a drum. She'd always been fascinated by my ink.

"No doubt." I shrugged back into my sport coat. Buttoned, only a vee of skin at the collar showed. Abby's coat I turned inside out before holding it for her to slide on. "Want the shirt?"

She glanced at her blouse, bunched in my fist. Another shudder shook her. "No."

I tossed it in the trash can just as my phone buzzed in my pocket.

"Remi's ready. Let's go."

Chapter Three

"I'm not going into hiding and that's final!" Abby shouted. "I didn't build a whole new life so some stranger can waltz in and steal it away from me."

"It would just be until we figure out what's going on," Eli said, much more mildly than I could at the moment. All my fury at almost having my woman killed in front of me had found a new target at her refusal to lay low. If my teeth hadn't been clenched so hard I thought a few of them would crack any minute, I'd definitely say something I'd regret later.

Like *I kidnapped you once. Don't make me do it again.*

Yeah, that would go over like a bullet to the gut. A nice, slow, agonizingly painful death.

The stubborn set to Abby's jaw didn't soften. "No."

The need to force her hitched my step as I paced across the room. A warehouse, not unlike the one I'd first brought her to over a year ago. I had a string of safe houses in and around the city, but this was our new base of operations. It was probably good that the floor and walls of this one were cement, or I'd be punching my way through them right about now.

Leaving Abby's refusal for later, I turned my attention to this afternoon's attack. "What have we got so far?" I asked Remi.

He glanced up from the bank of computers where both my brothers sat. "Definitely a professional. I traced the bike through traffic cameras as far as I could, but it disappeared about four miles down the road."

So the driver knew where cameras could track him. Too much knowledge for someone without resources—or a backup team. This had been planned in advance.

"What about the accounts?"

Eli swiveled his computer chair to face me. "Nothing yet. I'm not sure if it's the accountant or the lawyer, but I'll find out."

Someone had set Abby up; it was just a matter of tracking down who. "Or it was neither and they were set up too."

Eli grunted. "Exactly. I'm working on hacking as we speak. If there's anything in their e-mails or bank accounts, I'll uncover it. It'll just take a little time."

Time we didn't have, not if Abby was the target. One second was too long to let that shit stand.

"Remi, see what you can dig up, either online or on the streets. If someone is moving into our territory, they can't do it silently. Someone will know. These guys have to have been brought in from the outside. No one here is organized enough for this, much less has the balls to cross us. Not after—"

Remi's gaze cut to Abby, and I shut my mouth. She didn't need another reminder of her bastard of a father.

"The question is," Eli said, ignoring the byplay, "who brought them in. And why now? Why Abby?"

"We'll find out," Remi said.

Now that both men knew where to concentrate, I turned to my woman. I could see her shoulders tighten, knew she was prepared to fight. The thought excited me as much as it angered me, the sick, volatile mix swirling in my gut. I stalked toward her.

"Levi—"

Not with an audience. Grasping her arm, I kept walking. Abby tried to resist, but we were in the bedroom with the door closed before I let her go.

She glared up at me, the fire in her eyes fanning the flames in my body. "You can't force me to stay here."

One eyebrow went up. Abby swallowed hard, and God help me, but satisfaction made my cock swell even more.

"Look at you." She scoffed despite not being able to meet my eyes. "You act like a peacock, puffing up to intimidate his mate, but I'm not a bird, no matter what you call me. I'm a woman with a life. A life that matters, Levi."

"I never said it didn't."

"No, you just act like it."

Because I had to. There was no use arguing over it.

"I've… I just started classes. I—" She drew her bottom lip in, nibbling on it. "I'm getting somewhere, can't you see that? Don't derail me now."

I wasn't the one responsible. The man, woman, group, whoever it was who'd targeted her—they were the ones to blame. That didn't stop the guilt that rose as I stared into her pleading hazel eyes.

And this was the problem with us, right here. The only consideration should be her safety, not her feelings. Hurting her felt like stabbing myself, but I was used to pain—I hardened my heart and plowed on. "Anywhere you would go, routines, patterns, anything that could be tracked online is a way to find you. To hurt you."

"Then my school, my home, my car—all those records lead right back to me. I can't avoid them and still have a life."

"No, you can't." That's exactly why I lived the way I did. Why my brothers had no life, as she so succinctly put it. Because it was dangerous.

After her father's death last year, I'd left Abby alone, thinking it was better for her to have her freedom. She was just getting started when the hunger became too much, when I couldn't breathe another second without her, and I'd shown up on her doorstep, dragging her right back into my world like the selfish bastard that I was. I'd regretted that for the last three months.

But after today, after seeing her targeted and knowing there was no way for her to protect herself? I'd get down on my knees and thank God for making me a fucking asshole if I believed in him anymore. I hadn't been able to protect my parents, but my brothers and Abby? I'd do it or die trying. Even if she hated my guts for a little while.

"I won't give up everything I've worked so hard for because some dickhead has decided to target me for whatever reason," Abby said.

Frustration turned her creamy skin a pale pink that made me want to run my tongue over it, see if she was as hot as she looked—and tasted as good. I let the need spark in my own eyes, throwing Abby off her game.

Her gaze dropped to my shoulder, but she didn't give up. "Why can't you just protect me at my place?"

"Because I have a job too, and I can't be on top of you twenty-four-seven."

She squirmed, and I knew my words had sent her mind in other directions besides leaving. Good. A solid hour in bed would help work out the frustration coiling me as tight as a drum.

Abby wasn't that easily swayed, though. Stubborn to a fault, she strode for the door. "I'm not staying, Levi. That's final."

I stepped into her path, blocking the door, and folded my arms over my chest.

"Move," she barked.

My blank stare answered for me, and Abby's color heightened even more. She was pissed; I got that. But I wasn't letting her leave. If she needed to take out her frustration, scream, yell, hit me…whatever. I could take it. But I wasn't budging from this spot.

But she didn't strike out. She threw her head back, fists white with tension, her angry growl ripping through the air, but it didn't rock the warehouse. And when she lowered her head and met my eyes again, it wasn't only anger in them. The surface roiled with it, but underneath, there was something else, something that set me on alert. A bomb was coming my way, and I braced for it the only way I knew how.

By tightening down even further.

"I can't…" She squeezed her eyes shut. Blinked them open. "I can't do this anymore, Levi."

My breath caught in my throat, choking me. "What the hell are you talking about?" Because no fucking way did she mean what I thought she meant.

"This." Her anger filtered away as she waved a hand between us. That something under the surface shot to the top—grief. "It hurts too much."

I was giving her everything I had to give. That shouldn't hurt. It should be enough. *I* should be enough.

"I can't keep getting drawn into your world, Levi. The uncertainty. The instability. I can't live without a life, without something that belongs to me."

"I belong to you." As much as I could belong to anyone. I'd given up fighting that after staying away from her for a year and nearly going insane.

She blinked, and a tear rolled down her heated cheek. "Do you?" She gave that little laugh/hiccup sound that had nothing to do with amusement. "You can't even sleep with me. You fuck me and you wait till I'm asleep—if I'm lucky—and then you're gone. You're a ghost that visits when you want sex and hides from me when you don't. I can't live like this anymore. I need all of you."

"All of me isn't available to give, Abby." The words might seem ugly, brutal even, but they were the truth. And that was the only thing I could give her. The only thing I was fully capable of giving.

I didn't believe there was an *all* when it came to me. *All* had been chopped into tiny little pieces by life, scattered and lost, hardened and honed by death, and I couldn't be put back together again. It wasn't possible. If it had been, I'd have done it for Abby a long time ago.

Her fist came up to press hard over her heart. She closed her eyes, and I could see her mentally trying to pull herself together. To re-form the shell that protected her from hurt. From me.

The animal deep inside roared a denial.

"I can't," she finally whispered, the words as broken as she looked. "I can't be with you, Levi."

The animal tore free. "You damn well can," I shouted, stalking toward her.

Abby backed up, her shoulders hitting the concrete wall. "Why? So I can lie there at night and watch you walk out the door? Why is it so easy for you to leave me? And I can't do the same?"

She thought it was easy? When it felt like tearing my guts out every time? But the pain was worth it if it kept her safe. It wasn't easy; it was necessary.

I gripped her arms, my fingers biting into her flesh harder than they should, but I couldn't stop them. Couldn't stop the heartbeat banging in my throat and the blood pooling low in my gut, screaming at me to subdue her, take her, force her to see that she would never walk out of my life. "You're not leaving. You're staying with me until we get this shit figured out. You're going to be safe."

"My body, maybe. You've already destroyed my heart."

The words pierced me, the stabbing pain making me want to curl up and protect my vulnerable underbelly. Too late. She'd already gutted me.

"I won't leave my life behind to skulk in the shadows, waiting around for you to notice me," she was saying.

I barked a laugh through the agony ripping me apart. "You breathe and I notice you. I can't stop noticing you. I take one look and my dick is rock-hard and my entire body hones in on one thing: you. Getting you beneath me." I shook her as if it was her fault, because it was. All her fault. "I can't breathe for wanting you." One step and our bodies came together. Her nipples were hard, poking through the cotton of her bra and my dress shirt. She didn't want to leave any more than I wanted her to.

Abby licked her lips, turned her head away from me. "I'm not talking about sex."

"I am." It was all I knew. The only way to share myself with her. And right now I needed it just as much as I needed my next lungful of air.

The kiss I took then didn't feel like love. It felt like conquering. Overpowering. I pried her lips open with my own, and when my tongue invaded her mouth, she shuddered—not with fear or pain, but with need. I knew because her teeth unclenched and she let me in, a whimper of defeat echoing between our lips. I plundered and invaded, every crack and crevice, until her head was bent back like a broken reed and her eyes were dazed with hunger. Only then did I bury my face in the hollow of her neck. When I bit down on her shoulder, she startled against me.

"You're not leaving," I growled around her flesh.

"Yes, I am."

I nipped the tender line of her shoulder, my fingers tightening on her once more—a threat, a promise. "No, you're not. You're coming with me."

She shook her head as much as she could with my face in the way, my teeth gliding along her skin. "Whether I want to or not? For how long, Levi?"

Forever. "For as long as I say."

That sick little chuckle again. "And what about what I say?"

"Doesn't matter." I could change what she said, whether she chose to acknowledge that fact or not. We both knew it.

I felt her inhale, readying to fight me again. Her chance was cut off by a knock on the door.

I stepped back and stared her down. "Come."

The door opened. The steps hesitated before moving around to where I could see the intruder. Remi.

"Sorry to interrupt, but there's a development you need to know about."

Nothing could be as important as the battle of wills going on right here in this bedroom. The battle for the future. "What?" I barked.

"Lance Heinz is dead."

And God help me, but satisfaction settled low in my gut even as the last bit of light died out of Abby's soulful eyes.

∞

Grab your copy of ASSASSIN'S PREY today!

"Ms. Sheridan writes suspense that grabs you and won't let go."

~ *Tea and Book*

About the Author

Ella Sheridan never fails to take her readers to the dark edges of love and back again. Strong heroines are her signature, and her heroes span the gamut from hot rock stars to alpha bodyguards and everywhere in between. Ella never pulls her punches, and her unique combination of raw emotion, hot sex, and action leave her readers panting for the next release.

Born and raised in the Deep South, Ella writes romantic suspense, erotic romance, and hot BDSM contemporaries. Start anywhere—every book may be read as a standalone, or begin with book one in any series and watch the ties between the characters grow.

Connect with Ella at:

Ella's Website – ellasheridanauthor.com
Facebook – Ella Sheridan: Books and News
Twitter – @AuthorESheridan
Instagram – @AuthorESheridan
Pinterest – @AuthorESheridan
Bookbub – Ella Sheridan
E-mail – ella@ellasheridanauthor.com

∞

For news on Ella's new releases, free book opportunities, and more, sign up for Ella's newsletter at ellasheridanauthor.com .

Made in the USA
San Bernardino, CA
06 July 2020

75069720R00171